Burial of Ghosts

Also by Ann Cleeves

A Bird in the Hand
Come Death and High Water
Murder in Paradise
A Prey to Murder
A Lesson in Dying
Murder in my Backyard
A Day in the Death of Dorothea Cassidy
Another Man's Poison
Killjoy
The Man on the Shore
Sea Fever
The Healers
High Island Blues
The Baby-Snatcher
The Crow Trap
The Sleeping and the Dead

Ann Cleeves

Burial of Ghosts

MACMILLAN

First published 2003 by Macmillan
an imprint of Pan Macmillan Ltd
Pan Macmillan, 20 New Wharf Road, London N1 9RR
Basingstoke and Oxford
Associated companies throughout the world
www.panmacmillan.com

ISBN 1 4050 0113 5

1 3 5 7 9 8 6 4 2

A CIP catalogue record for this book is available from
the British Library.

Typeset by SetSystems Ltd, Saffron Walden, Essex
Printed and bound in Great Britain by
Mackays of Chatham plc, Chatham, Kent

Prologue

My nightmares feature knives and blades and blood. I don't do falling down holes or being chased through deserted streets. And though usually I dream in black and white, the blood is very red, glossy, and it slides out from the rest of the scene, which is flat and dull. The worst thing is that when I wake, I realize it wasn't a dream at all.

I'm in Blyth. It's market day and I'm there to shop for Jess. There's a stall where she buys all her fruit and veg – she knows the bloke who runs it and he always gives her a good deal. It's mid-morning, with lots of people about. It's not long before Christmas and everyone's in the mood when they have to buy, even if the stuff's crap, otherwise they feel they're not prepared. A foggy, drizzly day, and cold with it. There's a raw east wind which cuts into the skin. But it doesn't draw blood. Not like the scissors I buy in Woolworths. I ask the assistant to take them out of the plastic packet to check that they're sharp. I run my thumb across the blade and there's a small red line and then tiny, perfectly round red drops like jewels. I fumble with the money when I pay, not because of the cut, which is already healing, but because my hands are freezing.

1

From Woolworths I wander back into the market square to pick up Jess's vegetables. I stop for a couple of minutes to look at the cassettes and CDs and chat to the ageing punk who sells them, and again to buy a quarter of a pound of coconut ice from the sweetie stall. I have a very sweet tooth. It's all still in pounds and ounces, of course. There are no kilos in Blyth. Then I notice a lad coming towards me with a pile of *Big Issues*. He's wearing combat trousers and big boots, expensive boots, new not second-hand. I walk round him, trying not to catch his eye. Why? Because his thin face reminds me of someone I don't want to think about. A lad called Nicky with a poet's face. Because I don't have a pound and I don't want to wait for change. And anyway he must be working some sort of scam because of the boots.

I'm almost at the vegetable stall. There's a smell of cabbage leaves and oranges. Someone behind me touches my shoulder.

'*Big Issue*, Miss?' Aggressive, sneering, so close I can feel his breath on my neck.

I swing round and stab him in the fleshy part of his upper arm with the scissors. He's a Blyth hard man, only wearing a sweatshirt despite the cold. I get him first go, feel the rip of the skin and the crunch of the bone as the blade hits off it. But when I lift my arm to strike again, someone holds me back. The bloke from the veg stall recognizes me and shouts, and the crowd joins in. They're all screaming. The lad has dropped the pile of papers. The blood soaks through the grey sweatshirt and spatters the news-print in slow motion. Black and white and red all over. Like the joke.

Chapter One

In Morocco I didn't dream at all.

It was midday and hot, only April but there'd been no rain all winter and the river beds were dry. Not that you'd believe that here, where the fields were irrigated and green. Some stream in the mountains had been tamed and channelled through open wooden pipes to a reservoir, then to the tiny fields, the date palms and the hedges of tamarisk, jacaranda and bougainvillaea. The colours of the flowers were exploding in the sunlight. Like it was some sort of trip or mystical experience. Like I was in paradise.

So I was in paradise, riding a donkey led by an eight-year-old beauty with shiny black eyes, a torn skirt and bare feet called Latifa. An Australian backpacker who was staying in my hotel had sent me there. He'd given the directions to the palmery.

'Worth a visit,' he'd said, super-cool. 'If you want to get out of town. Nice views.'

He hadn't mentioned it was on the tripper route and when I got there, bouncing the clapped-out Renault I'd hired for a week over the rocky track, there were two tour coaches from Agadir spewing out German housewives in shorts and vests. After a week on the beach, their skin was the same startling pink as the bougainvillaea petals. I'd almost turned round and gone back. Not my scene. I'm a traveller, not a tourist. I don't do crowds. Then Latifa had come up, dragging the donkey behind her, hustling.

'You like donkey ride, Miss?' Some sixth sense telling her I was British. I looked at her over my shades.

'How much?'

She named a price in dirhams. The equivalent of three pounds, the first bargaining move.

'OK.' She was shocked. Even tourists knew they were supposed to haggle. 'But I don't want to go where they're going.' I nodded towards the Germans, who were being hoisted onto donkeys of their own. 'Somewhere quiet.'

'No problem. They go to hotel. Drink Coca-Cola. Eat big meal. Tagine. Couscous. Bread. Eat, eat, eat.' She puffed out her cheeks. Not a credible imitation of a fat German, but I knew what she was getting at. She clapped her hand over her mouth, thinking her honesty would cost her business, thinking I'd be offended, that we were all members of the same tribe.

'That's OK, then.'

She still looked at me as if I were crazy for not trying to get a better price. I got out of the car. It would be like a sauna when I returned. The coaches had parked in the only shade.

And she took me into paradise. She led me down the sandy paths round the little fields into that light and that colour. It was like swimming into a stained-glass window only there was sound too – everywhere bird-song and the humming of insects. I was as much a part of the jacaranda and the water trickling through the wooden pipes. More than that, it was as if the whole scene had been laid out for my enjoyment. For a moment I lost myself in it. I heard Latifa's voice, as if from a distance, chatting about her family and school, hoping maybe for a few extra dirhams tip for being friendly. Because I'd already proved I was an easy touch.

Driving back to the town I made up my mind it was time to go home. I'd stopped being angry. And after today everything else would be an anticlimax. In Taroudannt I returned my car to the garage and organized a ticket for a bus to Marrakech. The next day I'd begin to make my way back. But slowly, because I'd need to get used to the idea. I'd lost the habit of making plans.

Later I walked through the streets which had already become familiar. My path took me past the bread shop, where the flat loaves were wrapped in a grey blanket, and the shop selling acacia twigs for firewood, past the souk, avoiding the skinny boys chasing goats and the young men with soft, dark eyes who wanted to practise their English or sell me a carpet, or a silver Berber bracelet, to the poshest hotel in town. The one where the German tourists would stay if they had more class. I ate an expensive dinner on the terrace and drank most of a bottle of wine. Then I swam in the pool, which was built into the red stone of the city wall and surrounded by a garden. More jacaranda, more palms and vines. I swam until it was almost dark and I was the only person in the water.

5

I walked back to the place I was staying, a not-so-posh hotel which got its mention in the *Rough Guide* for being central and providing reasonable value for money. I walked slowly, knowing it was the last time. Outside the cafés old men with stern faces drank coffee. Bats dipped in and out of holes in the wall. The muezzins were calling the faithful to prayer from the mosque on the square. The Australian backpacker was waiting for me alone and hopeful by the bar of our hotel. I bought him a beer, then went to bed. Without him. You'd have thought I'd kicked him in the gut.

The bus would take eight hours and cost me less than half the meal I'd bought the night before. It would cross the flat plain of the Souss valley, then head up into the mountains. The other passengers seemed to be local, mostly women and young children going to visit their families. The older women were wrapped up, so all I could see of them were curious eyes and a henna tattoo on the ankle. On the back seat a couple of teenage boys were full of themselves and giggling. At first I thought I would be the only European on it, but then, just as the bus was about to start, a man jumped on. He was middle-aged but lean and fit as a Berber hillsman, not a scrap of flesh on him. He was blond. It was hard to tell from his hair, which was shaved convict short, but his eyebrows and lashes were almost white. There were other seats available, but only next to Moroccan women, who were already looking away from him, willing him to keep his distance. I knew he'd come up to me.

'Do you mind?' He smiled in a shy, self-deprecating way which made him seem half his age.

I *did* mind but I could hardly say so. How could I explain? *Actually I had a near-mystical experience wandering around a bunch of date palms with a girl and a donkey. I want to see if I can re-create it crossing the High Atlas.*

As I nodded for him to sit down, I was thinking too about his voice. Only three words, slightly accented, but I could place him on that. North of the Tyne and south of the Scottish border. He came from the same place as me. Except, of course, I could make no assumptions about my place of birth.

We talked.

'Lizzie Bartholomew,' I said, turning in my seat and holding out my hand, mock formal, a Brit keeping up appearances away from home.

'Philip.' No last name. I wondered fleetingly if he had plans for the encounter. Was he saving himself from embarrassing consequences even then? The impression was confirmed when he took my hand. He was wearing a wedding ring. It was slightly too loose on his finger. 'And where, exactly, do you come from, Lizzie Bartholomew?' My fellow Northerner had placed me too.

'Newbiggin-by-the-Sea.'

Mocking. The full name made the town sound attractive – picture-postcard pretty. You'd imagine a little harbour, children playing on the beach. I was drawn to it. I loved the big church on the headland, the double-fronted stone houses on Front Street. In one sense it was precisely where I'd come from, where I'd been created. But pretty it wasn't. He'd know of Newbiggin by reputation. He'd have heard stories of kids marauding round the council estate,

7

burnt-out cars on the golf course, the black beach caused by washed-up coal dust. I doubted if he'd ever been there.

He raised his eyebrows. 'Upmarket, eh?'

It wasn't said cruelly. He was curious, that was all. We both laughed.

'And you?'

'Newcastle originally. Further up the coast now.' Still giving nothing away.

'You're a long way from home,' I said lightly. 'Holiday?'

'Fulfilling a dream,' he said, deadly serious.

'What dream would that be?'

'Trekking in the Atlas Mountains. When I was a kid there was a picture in a geography textbook. For some reason it caught my imagination. Exotic, I suppose. A bit different from Heaton.'

Heaton was a Newcastle suburb. Not rough like the West End, but hardly smart either. From his voice I'd have said he'd gone up in the world.

'You're on a bus,' I said. 'Hardly trekking.'

He smiled slowly. Everything he did was slow and deliberate. I thought he'd be a good lover. Patient. I wondered what he planned to do when we arrived in Marrakech. Jessie always said I was shameless.

'Today I'm on a bus. I've been walking in the hills for three weeks with local guides. I came back for a few days to rest in a decent hotel.'

That would explain the lean, fit look.

'The Palais Salaam?'

He nodded.

'I was there last night.'

'I know,' he said. 'I saw you swimming.'

'Travelling alone?'

'Ah.' He leaned back in his seat and narrowed his eyes. 'My wife's a saint. She'd deny me nothing.'

I waited for him to continue, but he drifted into sleep. He slept for the first hour, his breathing regular and shallow, not waking even when we stopped in noisy squares to drop off and pick up passengers. I looked out of the window at endless citrus orchards surrounded by vivid orange walls, then at acacia scrub, the trees grazed bare by the goats which scrambled through the branches. When the bus started climbing he woke and continued the conversation as if the nap had never occurred.

'Why are you in Morocco, Lizzie Bartholomew?'

I mumbled something about needing a break. 'Sometimes things are complicated, you know?'

'What sort of complications could you possibly have?'

'It's a long story.'

'It's a very long bus ride.'

So I told him my story. Not all of it. But the stuff I'd spilled out over and over again, trying to impress new acquaintances, to get sympathy, to explain my choice of career. And he was hooked. I could tell.

'I spent most of my childhood in care. Lots of different children's homes.'

'I thought they tried to find foster homes these days.'

'Oh, they tried. Just not very hard. And I wasn't an easy kid . . . Some of the homes were OK. Some were awful. Even in the good ones, the staff were distant. I suppose they had to stay detached or they'd go crazy. But you don't understand when you're a kid.

Occasionally there'd be someone I really liked, but they always moved on in the end or I'd be shunted away. Then there'd be the first day at another school, more kids to laugh, because however hard the staff tried, we always looked different. Clothes that didn't quite fit, no parents to come to open evenings or school plays.'

I was getting absolutely the response I wanted. I should have been on the stage. He was almost in tears.

'Tough,' he said.

'Yeah,' I replied with a bit of a sneer. 'Tough.' What would he know? 'When I was sixteen I left. Or was thrown out. They didn't like me much. Too lippy. Bolshy. Stirring up insurrection among the rest of the kids. And I drank too much. Way too much. They found me a place in a hostel, a sort of B&B for losers, dropouts and druggies, in Newbiggin. A social worker came once a week to check I was OK. I hated her. If I offered her a cup of tea she always said she'd just had one. She was afraid of catching germs. Or something worse.'

'And were you OK?'

'I was brilliant.'

Then I told him about Jess, who owned the place. 'She wasn't paid to be kind to me or worry about my psychological welfare, only to wash my sheets and cook my breakfast. So when she *was* kind it counted.'

Jess had been a dinner lady in the primary school. Her aunt had died and left her the big stone house with its view of the sea. It was too big for her, but she couldn't bear to sell it. So she set up in business.

Perhaps she'd been hoping for respectable guests – the birdwatchers who turned up in the autumn, businessmen, students, reps – but she ended up with us. If she had space she never turned anyone away. We were like the bairns from the infant class she used to treat for grazed knees and elbows. She gave us more sympathy than we deserved.

'Jess persuaded me to go to the tech to take A-levels.'

She was a stubborn woman, as wide almost as she was high, dressed usually in charity-shop jumble, jogging bottoms and a man's checked shirt. That day she'd smartened herself up. She dragged me to the college open day, stood with me at the enrolment desk.

'What do you fancy then, bonny lass?'

I'd taken English because I liked the look of the teacher, a moody guy with hooded eyes, a shaved head and a leather jacket, psychology because Jessie thought it would be interesting and sociology because she said I had to do three. You couldn't get to university without three. None of her lodgers had been to university before. I'd be the first.

'I did it to humour her. Thought she was mad.'

'Of course, you passed,' Philip said. 'Flying colours.' He hadn't spoken while I was describing my time at Jess's, but I could tell he was listening. Properly listening. Not just letting the words wash over him.

'Two As and a B.' I grinned, remembering Jess's face when I waved the flimsy results slip under her nose. 'Only five marks short of an A in sociology.'

ANN CLEEVES

Philip smiled too, as if he was sharing my triumph, but I thought I should probably be more cool. Probably he and all his friends had brilliant A-levels.

'What did you do at university?' he asked.

'A social work diploma.'

'Of course.'

'I thought I could make a difference to kids like me.' I paused. 'Cheesy, huh?'

He didn't deny it, grinned again. 'What did you do when you graduated?'

'I wanted to work in residential care. I took a post in a secure unit.'

'Young offenders?'

'Mostly. Or kids who were very disturbed. Likely to harm themselves or other people.'

I expected another facetious comment, but none came.

'I loved it. Every day was different and challenging. I thought I was getting through to them. I thought I was developing some sort of relationship.'

'But?'

'No buts. It was just tough. I needed a break. Morocco seemed a good idea.'

He could tell there was more to it than that, but he didn't push it, not even when I started shaking. It must have been close to 100 degrees in that bus, but suddenly I was trembling. Philip put his arm around me and pulled me towards him. The woman in the seat in front of us turned and peered out through the slit in her veil. Her eyes were sparkling with interest and amusement.

12

Chapter Two

That morning in the bus Philip got my take on the story, the authorized version of the life and times of Lizzie Bartholomew. I didn't tell him everything. For example, I didn't describe the antics which really got up the noses of the authorities while I was a kid, the court appearances, the thieving. Because, despite his sympathy, he'd be on the same side as them. I could tell the sort of man he was. He'd pay his taxes at the first demand. He'd vote. Write to the papers about crime figures, litter in the street, dog shite. He was decent and respectable.

Lizzie Bartholomew is a fiction, not created by me but for me. I wouldn't exist except for the imagination and prompt action of two middle-aged ladies who stumbled upon me. Stumbled literally. They were walking their dog along the headland at Newbiggin. It was 30 November, six in the evening, already dark. Fog blanked out the buoys in the bay, and they took the path through the churchyard because it was safer.

The dog went ahead of them, so when I said before that they tripped over me, I was fibbing for effect. A bad habit of mine. The story's always more important than the truth. It wasn't the ladies who tripped over me but the mongrel collie bitch.

I was in the church porch, which was open to the elements on the seaward side, wrapped in a plaid blanket. Not newly born, they were told later, but not more than a week old.

There were appeals for my mother to come forward, but no one was surprised when there was no response. I was a very dark baby, with black hair and olive skin made more sallow by jaundice. Not a pretty child. It was assumed immediately that I belonged to the travellers who camped with their scraggy ponies and their clapped-out vans up the coast at Lynemouth. They were a law unto themselves, the gypsies. Local people had no difficulty in believing that they ate babies. Not surprising, then, that they should leave one in the porch of a church. Later apparently, the police went with a district nurse to talk to the group. You can imagine the scene, the animals, the raggle-taggle children, a fire in an oil drum kept alight with driftwood and sea coal. Of course they wouldn't talk to strangers. Why should they? In their position I'd keep quiet too. If there was a young woman among them who had been pregnant, but was no longer, or someone who'd drifted away, no one was telling. The group changed all the time. It wasn't a permanent site.

I'm not sure much else was done to trace my mother. There was an article in the local paper. I've seen that. But the assumption was that I'd been left by the gypsies and that I was better off without a family than belonging to a family of that kind. I'd had a narrow escape. So I was taken off to the hospital in Ashington and became the responsibility of the social services.

14

They had to give me a name. Bartholomew came after St Bartholomew's, the church. I never minded that. It sounded solid and impressive, like the building itself. And Lizzie. Not Elizabeth, even on the birth certificate. I would have liked Elizabeth. Lizzie after the mongrel bitch.

I should have been adopted. That was the plan. A short-term foster placement, then, if my parents couldn't be found, adoption. But it never worked out that way and later, when I asked why, no one could tell me, even when I stormed into the office and demanded to see my file. I suspect it was a mixture of lethargy, prejudice and incompetence. None of the social workers cared enough to make it happen. Prospective parents were put off by my wild looks – I still looked foreign as I grew older – and my history. Perhaps they thought a child with gypsy blood would be uncontrollable. Did they imagine me cursing their cats and selling sprigs of heather at the neighbours' doors?

The children's homes were much as I described them to Philip. They merge in my mind into a blur. There was one dreadful place run by nuns, but on the whole they were comfortable enough, just unimaginably dull. The workers seemed to fall into two camps – either they were earnest young professionals who sat in the office writing reports and waiting to be promoted, or idle middle-aged women who watched hours of television while claiming to be overworked. Perhaps that's unjust and my memory's selective, but I don't recall any of them spending time with us. When I came in from school, for example, there was no one to listen to my petty grievances, and I always

15

had plenty of those. On the television, I saw families eating together, playing board games, laughing. I thought everyone else in the world had that except us. Now, of course, I know better. What I'm trying to say is that there were adults in the building, but they were always doing other things. More important things. They didn't enjoy our company. We were deprived of their attention.

That's my explanation for my behaviour anyway. My excuse. At least it was at the time. They called my aggression attention-seeking. And so it was. Recently everything has seemed much more complicated.

The driver stopped at the top of the Tizn Test pass, at a roadside café, for the driver to eat lunch. We got out to stretch our legs and marvel at the view. It was dizzying. We were looking down at snow and soaring vultures. Philip walked away from the road up a narrow path. He squatted on his heels to look more closely at the scrubby bushes, then called me to join him.

'This is caper,' he said. 'You know, we use the fruit in cooking.'

That is the only identification I remember, but he would have named them all for me, all the plants and the trees, if I'd given him the chance. Shown any interest at all. He could have been engrossed there for hours, but he sensed my attention wandering.

'Are you hungry?' he asked.

'Mmm.' In this mood I was always hungry.

As we walked back to the café, the peace was broken by a car screaming past. It seemed there was a Spanish motor rally taking place. A time trial, I think, not a race. Occasionally a car would flash by and men with stop-watches would wave their arms and yell at each other. I found the speed and the noise exciting, but Philip was furious.

'It's completely ruined. Our last stop in the mountains. How dare they?'

If he'd been alone, I think he would have confronted the loud Spaniards, made a scene. I thought he was used to getting his own way.

'It's no big deal,' I said. 'You'll come back. There are other places.'

'Maybe.'

He wandered inside and came back with a tray. There was a plate with an omelette, a loaf of flat, sweet bread, a bowl of salad and two cans of Coke. He put the plate in front of me on the wooden picnic table, wiping the knife and fork with a paper napkin. Then he opened one of the Cokes and took a swig.

'Aren't you eating?'

He shook his head. 'Too hot.'

He took a pair of binoculars from his bag and looked down the valley at the vultures, wincing occasionally when a car went past. He pointed out a family of wild boars, a mother and four piglets, skittering through the shrub below. As I handed back the binoculars and returned to my food, he said, 'What plans do you have for Marrakech, Lizzie Bartholomew?'

I looked up from the meal, expecting him to be grinning again, but it was almost as if he were holding his breath, waiting for an answer.

'That depends,' I said.

17

'On what?'

'On you.'

He nodded, satisfied. I insisted on giving him the cash for my lunch. It was a matter of pride that I'd never been paid for sex.

Chapter Three

There was other stuff I hadn't told Philip, and that I wasn't so proud of. I didn't talk about the stealing and the court appearance. He would probably have understood. He was a kind man. He'd have made allowances. It might even have made him laugh. I would have liked to make him laugh. But he got the story everyone else got. The expurgated version. We own our own past, don't we? We can do what we like with it. I didn't risk telling him about the time in Blyth. I don't like to think about that tale and certainly there weren't many jokes in it. Nothing to entertain even a kind man like Philip.

I started running away from kids' homes when I was fourteen. I would go to stay with Katie Bell. She'd left care a year before, but she couldn't really cope on her own. She'd never been much of a fighter. She made a bit of a fuss when I turned up on her doorstep, but only because she didn't want trouble with the social. She soon let me in and I slept on her floor.

It was all right in the flat. Katie could have done more with it, but she didn't care about anything except a lad called Danny and the gear he brought with him. Danny didn't like me being there. He said I was crazy, a moody cow. When he was around I kept out of the way, moving to other people's places, from floor to floor. Then he got sent down for dealing and Katie was only too glad to have me back for company.

It was OK. Like we were playing house. When I went thieving, I brought out quilt sets and cushion covers besides the food and the booze. I had no money at that time, but I never did drugs and I never sold myself. There was this dream I'd had since I was small. My mother would come out of the blue to claim me. She'd just knock at the door and she'd be standing there. I'd know her at once. She'd look like me, except her face would be rounder and softer. I didn't want her to find me on the game. Perhaps that was an excuse. Perhaps I was just scared. That's what Katie said, but she'd never been the sharpest tool in the box and I didn't take any notice of her.

I wasn't on the run. Not really. The authorities could have taken me back at any time they wanted. It wouldn't have been difficult to find out where I was sleeping. If they weren't bright enough to guess, any of the kids left in the home would have told them. I even went to school most days. It was somewhere to go when Katie was getting on my nerves and there was a free dinner. I'd never admit it, but I liked school. I liked waking up in the morning knowing there was something to do. I suppose I needed the structure. I thrived on the routine. Of course I'd been institutionalized. I've got A-level psychology and a social work diploma. I know about these things.

They would have let me drift along at Katie's until I was sixteen if I hadn't turned up in court. It was my fault. I'd gone back to an Asda I'd already done before and they must have recognized me and sent someone outside to wait. It was supposed to work like this. You'd put a load of stuff in your trolley but only half the amount you could get rid of. You'd take it through to the till and pay for it, then push it outside. Katie would be waiting for me there. She'd take over the trolley and disappear – in a mini-cab if we were buying booze for other people and they were willing to pay. I'd keep the receipt, go back into the shop and buy exactly the same stuff. Then I'd bypass the till – Asda's good for that, loads of space – and go to the coffee shop for a cup of tea. Dead leisurely and laid back. I'd pack some of the stuff into the spare bags I'd picked up on the first way through, as if I was just rearrranging the load. If anyone stopped me, which they only did once, I'd have a receipt to prove that I'd paid for my trolley load. Of course, all the receipts are date- and time-stamped, but I could explain the difference in time by the tea. That day, though, they got Katie just as she was getting into the cab. The muppet cracked up at once and told them everything. I ended up in court. First offence, so I only got a conditional discharge. I had to eat, didn't I? But social services had to take me back to the home and promise to keep a closer eye on me.

You'd have thought the dreams might have started then. But they didn't. I always slept like a baby at Katie's and in the home. So the dreams can't have been in my blood, can they? I wasn't born with them.

We arrived in Marrakech in the late afternoon. It was busier and noisier than Taroudannt. The sound hit us as we climbed down from the bus, blaring horns and shouting people, everyone on the hustle. We booked a room in a hotel from the *Rough Guide* again. I think Philip had somewhere else planned – I'd guess one of the big American chains, the Hilton or the Sheraton, a halfway house between North Africa and home, somewhere to make the adjustment before flying back to his wife. He didn't say. I suggested this place and he agreed.

Inside it was cool. The lobby was tiled on the walls and the floor, so it was like walking into a swimming pool. There were the same strange shadows and reflections. The air felt as thick as water, moved by a slow fan on the ceiling. We drank black, bitter coffee at a low table, while the man on the desk went to get our room ready.

'Are you sure about this?' I asked. Suddenly I was certain that he'd never been unfaithful to his wife before. I didn't like to think of myself as a corrupter of married men. I still had an idealized view of family life taken from the TV sitcoms I'd watched in the children's homes.

'Absolutely,' he said. 'Another dream fulfilled.'

'What dream would that be?'

'Being seduced by a young and beautiful stranger.' He was quite serious and I loved it. Apart from when he had put his arm around me in the bus, we still hadn't touched, but I felt swept along by the adventure. It seemed an extension of the experience at the palmery: exotic, unreal.

The room was on the ground floor. A door led into a courtyard, surrounded on all sides by high walls covered with vines. There were latticed shutters and more terracotta tiles, a bathroom with a huge old-fashioned tub which had probably been there since the days of the French. A low double bed covered with a cotton quilt stood in the middle of the room.

I bathed and changed into a white dress. It occurred to me for a moment, as I slipped it over my head, that I was being incredibly foolish. I knew nothing about this man. He could be a rapist or a serial killer. If he chose to slit my throat in an anonymous hotel room in Marrakech, he would get away with it without a doubt. Perhaps the dress was white for sacrifice, for innocence and naïvety. But there's no pleasure without risk and anyway I trusted my first instinct about him.

We ate early, in the courtyard, where tables had been set and covered by starched sheets like altar cloths. Brightly coloured birds shouted from the vines. I had thought Philip would be hungry – he'd eaten nothing all day – but he picked at the food, moving it round the plate with his fork like a fussy child. He must be a meat and two-veg sort of man, I thought, disappointed. He hadn't struck me as that type. Afterwards we lingered, ordering more coffee. I think we were both shy then. We wanted to put off the time when we would be alone together in the room, but this deferment of gratification increased the excitement too. It became almost a sexy game. I waited for him to make the first move. For him it was a big deal, not really a game at all. It had to happen at his pace.

At last he pushed back his chair and stood up.

'Shall we go?'

I followed him and saw that he'd left an extravagantly large tip for the waiter. Guilt perhaps. He couldn't pay me, so he left his money to a bald

Moroccan who spoke English with an absurd American accent.

In the room he pulled the shutters closed. Light and the noise of the other diners and the city beyond filtered through the slats, but very faintly. He sat on the bed and carefully took off his shoes and his socks. They had been clean on after the bath – I had seen him take them from the rucksack and they had looked then almost as if they had been ironed. Had his wife done his packing for him? I stood in front of him, so when he looked up he couldn't ignore me. He looked into my face, took my hands and pulled me onto the bed beside him.

He touched me like a blind man whose only understanding comes through the fingertips. A chaste and delicate exploration of my face and neck and arms. But with the heightened sensibility that had stayed with me since the ride in the palmery, I felt every movement over my skin in my gut. It was as if I was tasting it through my pores. Each touch an explosion, like sherbet in the mouth. He lifted me to my feet and pulled the dress over my head. He was patient, as I'd expected him to be, careful, but there was a desperation I'd not expected. He tried to control it but in the end he let rip, like a lad who's been inside for years on his first night out with a woman. In the end it was a glorious, noisy, unsophisticated shag, which left us breathless and close to laughter. I thought his wife must be one of those frigid, overworked, exhausted women who'd do it once a month, and then only if the wind was in the right direction. We lay panting and sweaty, our arms around each other.

'Well?' I asked, fishing for compliments. 'Did it live

up to expectations, being seduced by a strange young woman?'

'Absolutely. Now I can die happy.' He turned so he was lying on his back, looking up at the ceiling. He seemed content, a sleek cat purring on a sunny windowsill. 'What about you? Was it a terrible chore? An errand of mercy for an old man?'

'Dreadful. Couldn't you tell?' I had to joke. I was on the verge of asking if we'd be able to meet again and that would spoil it. Even if he agreed, sneaky lunchtime meetings, evenings when he was supposed to be working, all that would become squalid and shabby. Better to live with this memory.

He rolled lazily onto his side and stroked my hair away from my face.

'What about your dreams, Lizzie Bartholomew? What will you do next?'

'Go back north again I suppose. I can always stay with Jess until I sort myself out. Get a job.'

'With social services?'

'It's what I'm trained for.' But I knew I'd never work with kids again, certainly not in a residential home. After what happened in Blyth I'd be given the boring stuff, if they let me loose on the public at all. I pictured myself in an area office with a caseload a mile long, dipping in and out of people's lives, arranging a home help here, a stair lift there. Sticking-plaster solutions, never having the time or the resources to do anything well. The office would be open plan, with Snoopy posters fading on the walls and plants dying on the desks. The people would be frantic and frazzled and they'd expect me to be grateful for my one last chance . . .

'That's not a dream,' he said. 'Tell me about the dream.'

'I want to work for myself. Doing something I care about. Making a difference. I still want to live on the coast. I want a room in an attic to work in. A sloping roof and a view of the sea.'

'You've thought about it before.'

'No.' It had just come to me. Like a vision. I thought it was time to get back to Jess. I was going loopy and she'd bring me down to earth.

We fell asleep almost immediately, despite the noise of the amplified call to prayer from the mosque on the other side of the square, and the traffic and the people. When I woke, he'd gone. He left a note saying nice things about me, which I'll keep for ever, but no address and not even his full name.

Chapter Four

I was going home. It was mid-afternoon on a grey, sleety day and the train was almost empty. Occasionally I'd conjure up that last night in Marrakech and feel a Cheshire cat grin spread across my face, but none of the other sad travellers noticed. Through the window I looked out for the familiar signs, like marker stones, which would point the way back to Jess. The red sandstone bulk of Durham Cathedral. The Angel of the North, rusted to a darker red, its wings open in an unconditional embrace of welcome. The Tyne with its bridges.

The train slowed to a crawl across the river. The tide was high. On the Quayside there were already lights in the bars and restaurants, reflected in the water. It was rush-hour busy. I saw pasty faces, hunched bodies wrapped against the weather that had nothing of the spring in it. I missed the Moroccan light, the startling colours, and had to persuade myself that I was glad to be back.

The trip from Newcastle to Newbiggin took more than an hour. The talk which eddied around the overheated bus was familiar – Newcastle United's failure to achieve *again*, television soaps, the weather. There was room enough for my rucksack and me to share a double seat and no one spoke to me. Rain and dirt mixed on the windows, so I couldn't see out. I must have dozed, and woke with a start to find the bus empty and the driver leaning out of his seat to yell at me.

'This is it, pet. As far as we go.'

I'd missed my stop, but only by a couple of hundred yards. I stepped out and there was the smell of seaweed and mud, with a faint reek of fish in the background. The pavement was grainy from blown sand. I lifted the rucksack onto my back and walked away from the church. A gang of teenagers, skimpily dressed despite the weather, chased past me to catch the bus back into town. It revved like an old man coughing phlegm and drove off. The town was quiet.

I hadn't told Jess when I was coming home. We weren't family. There wasn't that sort of obligation. I didn't kid myself. She cared for all the dropouts and druggies who were dumped on her doorstep by social services. It was just that I'd stayed there longer, so she was used to me. And I was one of her first. I'd paid a month's rent for my room in advance so she'd hold it for·me. She had to live. I realized that in one sense the connection between us was financial, on her part at least. I liked to think that our friendship meant more to her than that, but it wasn't something I could take for granted.

The stone house where she lived was at the end of an alley off the main street. There was a yard where the dustbins were kept and the washing line was strung, reached through a latched gate in a high wall. This was the back. The front faced the sea and you could only get there on foot along a promenade which the council had created in an attempt to tart up the town. There was a small garden at the front. It had a path of shingle and shells, a few windblown shrubs and a white bench with a view across the small harbour to the church. I'd done most of my reading for university finals there. I went in through the back, past the box of empty wine bottles ready for recycling, the piles of moulding newspapers tied up in string.

There was a light in the kitchen window. I eased the rucksack off my back and looked in. Jess was at the antique gas stove, stirring a pan. Broth, I thought, and felt hungry. She made good broth, with ham shanks and split peas and whatever vegetables she could pick up cheap at Blyth market. She was only supposed to give us a room and breakfast, but if anyone was around in the evenings she fed us, even if it was only bread and cheese or beans on toast. She was a short woman, squat, with most of the weight settled on her hips and bum. Today she was wearing jeans and a long silk tunic which I didn't recognize. She must have been raiding the Oxfam shops again. Over it she wore a green canvas apron which I'd bought her to replace the horrible dinner-lady nylon overalls. She had her back to me but I could picture her face, crinkled now, but only round the eyes, so it looked as if she was laughing, and the biggest smile in Northumberland. Her hair was cropped short. If she was going out, she put on earrings. Today, although she was in, she was wearing long, silver fish. I'd given her those too. I wondered if she'd guessed that I was coming home.

I got closer to the window, intending to knock to surprise her, and then I saw she wasn't alone in the kitchen. There was a man I didn't know. He stood at the table, opening a bottle of wine. A new lodger, I thought. There was a spare room. Just before I'd gone on holiday a smack-head called Stuart had been sent down for thieving from cars. Jess had gone to court to speak up for him, but none of us were sorry. He'd been stealing from us and probably from her too. Jess had said perhaps his conviction was a good thing. It would give him a chance to get clean. Jess is still very innocent. I love that in her. We all do. We try to protect her.

The stranger would have been in his mid-forties, fifty perhaps. His head was almost bald, lumpy as if it had been roughly carved from wood. Usually we got kids to stay, but it wasn't unknown to have someone older, often someone who'd done a long stretch in prison, if there was no vacancy in a probation hostel. I thought it was crazy, but Jess never asked what they'd done. I mean, we could have been sharing broth with a paedophile or a mad axe-man.

'One new start,' she'd say. 'Everyone deserves that.'

I wondered sometimes if she was religious, if that was why she did it, but she never said. So far as I knew she never set foot inside a church. Certainly she never tried to convert us.

As I watched, the new man opened the bottle and put it on the table. He didn't have that drawn, grey look of someone who's been inside for a long time. His face seemed tough and wind-beaten, like those of the old men in the village who'd worked on boats all their lives. And he wasn't frightened. He went up behind Jessie and put his hands on her shoulders, then slid them down past her waist to her hips. Carefully she leaned the wooden spoon against the side of the pan and turned to him, tilting her face to be kissed.

I felt sick. I suppose it must be like if you're a teenager in a real family and you catch your parents making love. I wasn't ready to share her.

I must have moved or made a noise, because she saw me. She spread her arms wide, a gesture as welcoming as the Angel of the North. I opened the door and went in, dragging the rucksack behind me. I stood there in the steamy kitchen, awkward and brittle and defensive as when I'd first arrived.

'Take a seat, hinny, you're blocking out the light.' The same words as she'd used the first time when I'd been pushed through the door by the social worker. She winked to show she remembered that, even after all these years. So what else could I do but sit at the table and take a glass of wine and look pleased to see the new man in her life?

His name was Ray. He was a plumber. He'd come one evening to fix the boiler and they'd got talking and realized they'd been to school together. He'd been married and divorced when he was young and stupid. No kids, thank God. Jess had offered him a bite to eat, because she thought she was some sort of mother to the world. He'd taken her to the folk club in Cramlington, because that was what he was into. Traditional folk and brewing his own beer. Sad bastard. Since then, they'd seen each other every day.

Jess told me all this, her words spilling out so they hardly made sense. Ray didn't say much. He was wearing a thick check shirt and brown corduroy trousers, heavy shoes like walkers wear when they're not on a mountain. It was hard to imagine him young or stupid, anything other than a boring anorak who liked listening to hairy musicians singing with one finger in their ear. Jess could have done better. But why would she listen to me?

The letter came six weeks later.

I had been thinking a lot about Philip. Memories of the night in Marrakech distracted me when I read. Occasionally I believed I saw him in the street, just his back as he disappeared round a corner, the face of a driver as a car went past. But it never *was* him. I liked to think that he would come to find me, but I knew he had too much to lose.

It arrived on the last day of May. We'd had a week of hot, sunny weather. I was sitting on the bench in the front garden reading Virginia Woolf's *To the Lighthouse*. The dreamlike ramblings suited my mood. Jackie, the postman, dropped the envelope into my lap on his way to the house with the rest of the mail. I didn't open it immediately. It was made of thick, cream paper. In embossed lettering on the back flap was printed SMITH AND HOWDON, SOLICITORS.

Oh, Christ, I thought, the lad in Blyth has gone through with his threat of claiming damages. The idea of reliving that experience in front of men in fancy dress made me want to throw up.

When I opened the envelope I was shaking. I pulled out one sheet of laser-printed cream paper.

Dear Miss Bartholomew
I regret to inform you that Philip Samson died on 27 May following a serious illness. His funeral

will be held on 3 June at midday at St Bede's Church, Wintrylaw. As a result of your meeting in Taroudannt, Morocco, he wished me to inform you of his death. There are other matters which I would prefer to discuss in person. If it would be convenient, perhaps we could do that following the funeral.

Yours,

Stuart Howdon

Solicitor

I stared for a moment at the thick cream paper, let my eyes run over the words without taking them in. Then I began to cry. The sun and the breeze from the sea dried the tears on my cheeks, so all that was left was the taste of salt.

Chapter Five

Around that time the dreams returned. Not the pleasant fantasies about bumping into Philip in the street.
I tried to re-create those but couldn't bring him back
to life, however hard I tried. These are different sorts
of images and they have stayed with me ever since.

It doesn't only happen at night. They appear suddenly during the day when I'm wound up or troubled.
Flashbacks, Lisa, my community nurse, calls them,
but that makes you think of memory and these are
more like nightmares; they have that unreal, blurry-
edged feeling. I'm not sure that what I see in these
flashbacks actually happened. I don't trust them.

If there's a knife in the scene I focus in on it
immediately. It's like I'm filming. The knife appears
in close-up. Lovingly, seductively. Sometimes I think
I stabbed the lad in Blyth with a knife, but I know
that's not right. In Blyth it was scissors.

We all have fantasies, don't we? My first fantasies
were about my mother coming to the kids' home to
find me. Then about sex. Now they're about knives.
Lisa asks if I think about cutting myself and I say no.
In my dreams other people do the cutting. Or I cut
them.

So, there's this one flashback. I'm in the secure

unit where I worked when I left college. The kids are fraught and jumpy. It seems as if it's been raining for weeks and they can't get out. So I say suddenly, a brainwave, 'Right, we'll do some cooking.' Because that's a new activity for them, and they're bored out of their brains locked up in that place.

Do I ask permission? No. I'm the senior social worker on duty. Who would I ask?

The kitchen's empty. The cook takes a break after the lunchtime rush. It's early afternoon but outside it's nearly dark and the scene is lit by very white strip-lights. Everything is so clean it gleams. There's a lot of stainless steel, throwing back blurred reflections: a big central table with a shelf underneath for pans. An oven, industrial-sized. And knives. They're kept at the back of a drawer, away from prying eyes, though the kitchen is usually out of bounds to the children.

Zoom in on the knives. There are four of them with yellow plastic handles. All wedge-shaped, but different sizes.

I don't take them from the drawer. Naïve, I might be, but I'm not that daft. I find flour in a stainless-steel drum in the larder and some sachets of dried yeast, and we make bread. Kneading the dough on the table, the kids are calmer than they've been for days. I congratulate myself. I really think I'm good at this job. I imagine that in a few years I could be running the unit, taking decisions, planning policy.

I show the kids how to form the mixture into rolls, by circling it between floured palms like Jess taught me. It's a positive decision to make rolls not loaves. They'll be quicker to cook and these are seriously disturbed children with a low boredom threshold. But

35

it's also because I want the kids to taste their baking. You have to cut a loaf and there's one boy at least I wouldn't trust around a bread knife. So I wasn't thoughtless or reckless. That charge was laid against me, but I tell myself it's not true.

Zoom in on the drawer again. There are only three knives left.

Ray gave me a lift to Wintrylaw. Jess organized it.

'He's got a job towards there anyway,' she said, though I didn't believe her. 'Just give him a call on his mobile when you need to get back.'

He had a creased Ordnance Survey map, but we got lost. The church was next to a big house, a couple of miles out of the village. I could tell that much by the map, but not how to get there. I was supposed to be navigating, but the wiggly lines didn't make much sense. I couldn't tell the footpaths from the unadopted roads. In the end Ray pulled over into the side of a lane.

'You might just as well get out here,' he said. 'I don't think I can get much further. This is it, according to the map, like.'

He was anxious, apologetic, knowing he'd get knacked by Jess for not delivering me all the way. But I was glad to escape.

The ditches were full and the hawthorn hedges grown into crazy shapes and covered with blossom. There were two pillars smeared with lichen, the edges of each stone worn smooth by the wind, like boulders on a beach. No gate. A grass track leading through the trees, the leaves Granny Smith green, shimmering silver occasionally when turned by the breeze. On the floor white, star-shaped flowers and overblown blue-bells, the vivid colours of a Moroccan rug. The sun was behind me and threw my shadow, lengthened slightly, onto the track. I took a breath and stepped between the pillars.

Of course I knew this couldn't be the right way into the Wintrylaw estate. No cars had ever gone down this track. Perhaps once there had been phaetons, strangers on dark horses, children in donkey carts, but no cars. The track turned and below me I saw the house. The crumbling stone gleamed in the morning sunshine. I was looking down on the roof, could see the moss growing in the gutters and the grass between the slates. For a moment I believed I could see into the great chimneys to the hearths and the stoves below. I imagined high ceilings and ornate furniture.

Beyond the house the main drive swept away into the distance, and there was a little grey church. From this perspective all I could see was a squat tower; the nave was hidden by a plantation of Scots pine. Beyond that, a line of light. The sea. Standing on the grass I thought I could smell it and the tang of pine.

I walked on, heading for the church, not shy any more, not worried about meeting strangers or bumping into Philip's family, confident that I could do him proud. I was wearing the white dress from Marrakech. Jess had been put out when I appeared in it: 'Really pet, I don't think that's quite the thing. What about that nice suit we got for court?'

I knew already that a boring business suit wouldn't have done. Not for this place. I had to walk past the house to reach the church, and as I approached it from the back I realized a crowd had gathered. I heard voices first, at least the sound of voices without being able to hear what was said, as you hear the sound of soft foreign sibilants in a market in Africa. Then I turned a corner and saw them, very English in all their eccentricities. Still the tones were muted. They weren't those loud braying voices that I'd heard when I'd gone with Jess to the county show. Voices bred to be heard above the hounds.

There were lots of them, standing around with glasses in their hands, so again I was made to think of the hunt, of the followers waiting outside a pub for the spectacle of the master, all dressed up in his costume of red and black. Here, it is true, there was more black than red. They stood in small groups chatting. I supposed they were neighbours from the village come to say goodbye. Rural Northumberland is very feudal.

I could tell at once which of them was Philip's widow. She was standing apart from the others, surrounded by her family and a couple of friends. She had a striking face. Very thin and gaunt, asymmetrical, with a strangely twisted nose. If that makes her sound ugly then I'm giving the wrong impression. It was a strong face which demanded to be watched. The eyes were thin and long, like a cat's, and very dark. She wore a sleeveless black dress which almost reached to her ankles and over that a tight chiffon jacket. Her shoes were pointed, Victorian in style. It all gave an impression of fancy dress. She didn't wear gloves, though I thought she had probably wanted to. Black, lacy gloves, reaching to her elbows. Someone had told her they wouldn't be quite the thing, just as

Jess had objected to my white frock. Her hair was platinum blonde and waved like a 1930s film star's.

Her daughter was blonde too. *Her* hair lay in a sheet down her back. She had a blue straw hat with a velvet ribbon, held on with thin elastic under her chin, a navy-blue dress with little puffed sleeves and white tights. I didn't notice the shoes because she turned suddenly and noticed me, then pointed to her mother, who stared in my direction too. With hostility I thought. Perhaps Philip had confessed about his fling in Marrakech. Perhaps she needed someone to blame for his death and had brought me here to make a scene. But she frowned as if she had no idea who I was. She asked the small boy who was kicking pebbles on the drive, staring very hard at his feet in an attempt not to cry. He looked up, glad of the distraction, but obviously he didn't recognize me either. I stood, hovering on the edge of the terrace, feeling as insubstantial as a ghost.

I was rescued by a round man in a brocade waistcoat. He gave a few words of explanation to the widow, then walked towards me. His legs were short and he moved with a peculiar bobbing action, like a child's mechanical toy. Something fat. A pig perhaps.

'Elizabeth Bartholomew?' He eyed me from head to toe. 'I'm Stuart Howdon.' He smiled unpleasantly.

'Lizzie,' I said.

'You're not what I was expecting.'

I wanted to know what he *was* expecting, how Philip had described me, but he went on, 'I've told Joanna you work for me and you wanted to pay your respects. It seemed best.'

'Yes,' I said.

39

'Stick with me.' An order. As if left to myself I might cause mayhem. Then he smiled again, an inappropriate grin, the result perhaps of nerves. Maybe he thought it made him appear attractive.

Girls, younger than me, dressed in black frocks and little white aprons, came out through double doors onto the terrace. They carried heavy wooden trays and began collecting glasses. The whole set-up seemed very old-fashioned, like a period drama on the television. I imagined them living in bleak cells in the attic. Mr Howdon saw me look at them.

'A catering firm from Alnwick,' he said. 'It's cost Joanna an arm and a leg, this funeral.'

Again, I wondered if he considered I was to blame.

The crowd spluttered to a silence. The hearse was moving slowly down the drive towards us. There were no flowers on the coffin. The car stopped outside the house and we formed a ragged group behind it, with Joanna and her children in the front. It pulled off at walking pace and we followed.

Once perhaps the church had been for the use of the house and the estate, but now it was clear it belonged to the village. There were notices about Beavers and Rainbows in the porch, a poster left over from last year's harvest festival. I have a fondness for old and neglected churches. Hardly surprising, perhaps. Inside there was a fine stained-glass window. Full sunlight shone through it and I was reminded again of the colours of Morocco, of bougainvillaea and jacaranda. The vibration of the organ music made me feel dizzy. I sat on the polished pew and bowed my head. Not an attempt to pray but to stop myself from fainting.

The vicar was white-haired, rather unsteady on his feet. At first I suspected he might be drunk, but I think he'd suffered from a stroke. He had very long canine teeth, so he reminded me of a vampire. I wondered if the children had seen the likeness, even in their grief. I hoped they had and they'd feel able to share a joke about it. I imagined them looking at each other, pulling monkey faces and rolling their eyes. They were sitting on the front row, so no one would see them except the vicar, and he didn't count. He must be used to small children taking the piss. We stood and sang 'Jerusalem', which seemed a peculiar choice for the occasion. There were very few satanic mills in this part of the country and even the mines and factories further south had all gone.

It was from the white-haired vicar that I heard how Philip had died. Cancer, he said solemnly in his introduction. Of course. That explained the skinhead look, his lack of appetite, his tendency to fall asleep suddenly. I had thought him very fit and a fussy eater and all the time he'd been struggling to stay alive. I learned too that he'd been a magistrate and a church warden. A stalwart member of the community, as I'd predicted. There was no mention of how he'd earned his living. Perhaps he'd been on the sick for so long that no one remembered. As with me.

The next hymn took me back to my first year in secondary school. It had been a favourite of Miss Wallace, who taught us RE. Miss Wallace had taken me under her wing, kept me back after class occasionally to ask how I was. I fell in love with her in a way. Once I'd said to her in a joking, self-protective voice, 'Ever thought of fostering, Miss?' I'd known of course that adoption was too much to hope for. There'd been a look of panic in her eyes and I don't think she answered. Her kindness had been professional, like all the others'.

There's something moving about singing with a big crowd. I joined in. 'Not for ever in green pastures / Would we ask our way to be.' Sometimes Mr Howdon shot me odd looks, as if I was making too much sound or hitting a wrong note, but I took no notice. He was just moving his lips, like someone miming badly on a pop video, so he was in no position to criticize.

When the service was over we went outside. Joanna was standing at the door shaking hands, but I slipped past. The sun seemed very hot. Perhaps the breeze had dropped, or perhaps I felt it more coming out of the cool of the church. The graveyard sloped towards the pine plantation and was reached through a narrow gate. I wondered how the pall-bearers would get the coffin through, but they managed without difficulty. They were six very brawny men with scalped heads. It occurred to me that they might have had treatment for cancer too, that they were there as a symbol of hope, but I overheard someone say that they belonged to a rugby club in Alnwick. Apparently when Philip was fit, he'd been a member too. We filed through the gate after them and past the old headstones to the grave. There seemed to be no recent stones and I thought no one had been buried here in years.

A hole had already been dug and we stood in last year's leaf mould until the ceremony was over. It was completed much more quickly than I'd expected, though when the vicar dismissed us the hole still hadn't been filled in. A mound of earth, as dark as soot, still stood there. I wished they'd use it to cover up the coffin. I'm not sure why the bare planks made me feel so uneasy, but I felt embarrassed, as if an unclothed body was lying there, and as soon as the vicar had stopped speaking I turned away. I expected everyone to wander away then. I hoped at last to discover why I was there. But no one moved. They waited as if they knew something else was about to happen. There was a moment of silence, broken only by the rooks cackling in a deciduous tree near to the church.

Joanna stepped forward. She spoke quietly, so we had to strain to hear her, but that was what she wanted. She had the range to carry her voice right back to the house if she'd put her mind to it.

'This is where Philip wanted to be buried,' she said, smiling sadly. 'He was always something of a pagan. He worshipped in church every Sunday, but I'm not sure *what* he was worshipping. I rather suspect it was all this.' She made a dramatic gesture with her arm which took in the spinney of Scots pine and the sky. 'We've been growing an oak sapling from an acorn. Flora and Dickon watered it while Philip was away on his travels. He wanted us to plant it for him close to his grave. Perhaps you'll allow us time to do that on our own. Please go back to the house. We'll join you there shortly.'

She paused for a moment, like an actor waiting for applause, then gave a quick lopsided smile and took her children's hands. The boy held out his reluctantly. He still looked close to tears. Flora gazed out at us with a clear-eyed stare.

The audience muttered sympathetically and walked slowly back to the church gate. I lingered and looked back once. The spade and the sapling must have been waiting, because Joanna was already digging with great energy. She had hitched up her long, tight skirt and was pressing hard on the blade with her Victorian shoe. In Morocco I'd pictured someone very different for Philip's wife – a repressed and reined-in creature. This woman wasn't the conventional wifey I'd imagined. She pulled out the spade and thrust it in again at a slightly different spot. It cut through the earth like a sword.

Chapter Six

The wide front doors to the terrace were thrown open and tables had been set in the hall inside, long trestles covered in white cloths and piled with food. A central staircase led upstairs. It was a tantalizing invitation to explore, but one of the tables blocked the way. There were elaborate arrangements of white flowers in stands. I thought it was more like a wedding than a funeral, though how would I know? Without relatives you seldom get invited to either.

The lunch was one of those affairs where you have to balance a plate, a glass and a napkin in one hand and continue to make polite conversation at the same time as eating. Not my sort of event, even though the little waitresses were out in force again and it wouldn't have been hard to get seriously pissed. Stuart Howdon seemed to have disappeared. I sat outside on a stone step, looking towards the church, listening to the conversation going on behind me, trying to discover more about Philip. It was what this was about, wasn't it? An opportunity to share our memories. Except mine I would hug to myself.

'Did you see that piece about Philip in the *Sunday Times* magazine?' The voice was educated female, elderly. An aunt of Joanna's, I decided. 'A couple of months ago. He was ill by then, although it wasn't mentioned. Perhaps nobody knew but the family. It was about a garden he'd done in Cornwall. There were pictures. It was very *green*.' A pause. 'I'm not sure I could have lived with it. I do like order in a garden. Some sense of restraint.'

'Is that why Joanna never let him loose here?' Another female speaker, a little younger, jolly.

'This *is* Joanna's house.' The older woman's voice was slightly disapproving. 'And Philip always said he loved it as it is. Who needs a garden in a landscape like this? It would only detract.'

'I rather thought they had landscape in Cornwall.'

The tone was mischievous, but the elderly lady ignored the interruption. 'Besides, I suppose there was the question of money. He might have had to turn down a commission to devote time here, and I'm not sure they could afford to do that.'

'I dare say there'll be insurance,' the jolly woman said.

'I dare say there will.'

I turned round at that point to see who was speaking, but they'd already merged back into the crowd.

The rugby players spilled out onto the terrace behind me. From somewhere they'd obtained cans of Theakston's. Perhaps they'd brought their own supply. I'd only been offered wine. They drank by tipping back their heads and pouring the liquid in a steady stream into their mouths. They seemed to have conquered the need to swallow. Already they looked slightly dishevelled. Ties were loosened, jackets had been discarded.

'Where's Joanna, then?' The can was empty. The

46

speaker crunched it with his fist, resisted the temptation to see how far he could kick it and stared at it morosely. 'She must have finished in the churchyard by now.'

'A nice gesture though, the tree. Loving.' The speaker stopped short, embarrassed by his own sentimentality.

'They were a loving couple, weren't they?' The rugby player holding the crushed beer can had drunk too much to worry about an excess of sentiment. 'I mean, they had the best bloody marriage in the world. Jo's a lovely woman. Philip was a lucky man . . .'

'Until the cancer . . .'

'Of course. Until then.' He yanked back the ring pull on another can and began to drink.

Selfish, I know, but I didn't want to hear any more about Philip's idyllic marriage. I stood up and walked back to the house. I needed another drink too. I was trying to catch the eye of a waitress when Stuart Howdon appeared from a corridor at the back of the hall. The tables were almost empty now, littered with discarded napkins and stale ends of French bread. He seemed flustered. He noticed me standing there and came towards me, the mechanical walk even more awkward than before.

'Miss Bartholomew, I'm sorry to have kept you waiting. There was something rather urgent which needed my immediate attention. Could I ask you to be patient a little longer? I can be with you in about an hour.'

He was almost apologetic, but I'd had enough of this place. He must have sensed my hostility because he added, 'It is important that I speak to you. Rather, it was very important to Philip.' Then came the same insinuating grin.

So I had to agree, as graciously as I could manage. 'An hour, then. I'll go for a walk.' It would be easier to remember Philip alone.

I slipped away from the crowd still gathered on the terrace. No one seemed to notice my going. In my white dress I felt invisible. I took the path towards the church, but instead of turning in through the gate followed a sandy track. It led to the spinney of Scots pine, the trees widely spaced, and on towards the coast. I could hear the sea. Not loud, because it was such a calm day, but there all the same. I couldn't see it until I'd climbed one of the sand hills in the strip of dune which separated the trees from the beach. Then I stood, surrounded by spiky marram grass, looking down on a bay between two low headlands. The tide was out. There was a wreck of bladderwort, driftwood and frayed blue rope on the tide line, then an expanse of ridged wet sand, reflecting the blinding afternoon sun, then the shimmering water. The beach was empty but someone had been there before me. A line of footsteps led towards the sea. I took off my sandals and followed them until they disappeared into the squelchy, shifting sand at the water's edge and my toes were covered by a wave.

The boy stood ahead of me, knee deep in water. His shoes were slung by their tied laces around his neck, socks stuffed inside each one. He had made an attempt to roll up his trousers but the bottoms were already wet. He seemed to be floating on the diamanté light. I caught my skirt of my dress in one hand and waded out to him.

'Hi!' I prefer boys to girls, find them easier to get on with. Little girls like to pose. They care what you think of them. Boys are more straightforward.

'Fuck off.'

I turned round and started back to the beach. He hadn't been expecting that. A shocked response at the language perhaps or an attempt at sympathy, but not an immediate response to his demand.

'Wait. Who are you?'

'Lizzie Bartholomew. Who are you?'

'Dickon Samson.'

'How old are you, Dickon?'

He paused and I thought he was going to tell me it was none of my business. 'Nearly nine.' Then he glared at me. 'What are you doing here?'

'I came to your father's funeral.'

I had let my dress go and the waves sucked the thin cotton of the skirt backwards and forwards round my legs, pushed the sand in piles beside my feet.

'How did you know him?'

'I didn't very well. I met him once, on a bus in Morocco.'

'Yeah? He said that was his best holiday ever. He made me promise to go there one day.'

'I expect you will, then.'

A cormorant dived off a rock. Somewhere above me in the glare of the sun, gulls were calling.

'How far were you meaning to go?' I asked. 'Coquet? The Farnes?' Islands, invisible now in the heat haze.

'I'm not stupid. I wasn't going anywhere. It was hot.'

'A good way to cool down,' I agreed. He sensed

49

the condescension and shut up, turning his back to me. 'Did your dad like the sea?'

'He taught me to swim.'

'Here?'

He faced me again and nodded. Tears started to roll down his cheeks. 'It was April. Fucking cold.'

'I'm going out now,' I said. He wouldn't want me gawping at him. 'I've got a meeting soon. I should try and dry off my dress.'

I turned and plodged out towards the shore. I could hear him following but I didn't look round. I wrung out my dress, then sat on a flat boulder and spread it out to dry. His shadow appeared and I looked up. His hair had a hint of red and there were freckles on his nose.

'I'll be the only person in my class without a dad.'

I could have told him he was lucky, that I'd never even known my father, but I didn't. He deserved his own time of self-pity.

'Bummer,' I said.

'Fucking bummer.' He sat beside me and put his head in his hands. I pretended not to notice and threw pieces of shingle at a target rock a little way off. I was a crap shot. He hit it first time.

'Who's your meeting with?'

'Mr Howdon.'

'What's it about?'

'Work probably.' It could have been true.

'Oh yeah, you work with him, don't you?'

I didn't answer and he didn't seem to find any contradiction between that story and my account of having met his father in Morocco.

'What work did your father do?' I wasn't daft. I'd

worked it out from the eavesdropped conversation, but I wanted to hear the details.

'Don't you know?' He couldn't believe my ignorance.

I shook my head.

'He had his own programme on the television. Only BBC 2, but still . . .'

'I don't watch much telly.'

'He designed gardens for rich people,' Dickon said. 'He didn't do the digging or the weeding. Just the fun bits. That's what he told me. He went all over the world. That's why he wasn't here much until he got ill.' He chucked a piece of shingle with full force onto the rock. 'I was pleased when he was ill. At first. He had more time for me. When he had to stay in bed we played Jenga.'

The tide was coming in quickly now, seeping under the twisted strands of footprints, flattening them from below. I looked at my watch.

'I'd better go. Mr Howdon will be cross if I'm late.'

'I hate Mr Howdon,' Dickon said. Quietly. Not showing off and demanding attention like with the other comments.

'Why?'

'I think he's horrible to my mum.'

I didn't pry. It was none of my business. He'd tell me if he wanted. He didn't.

'Will you show me the quickest way back to the house?'

He didn't answer but he dusted the sand from his feet and put on his socks and shoes. I followed him back up the track. When the house was in sight he gave me a wave and ran on, too fast for me to follow.

Chapter Seven

At the house Stuart Howdon was waiting for me. The crowd had thinned. A stream of people were making their way down the drive towards the village. I looked round for Dickon but didn't see him. The solicitor was clearly impatient. He seemed grumpy and harassed. He didn't bother any more to smile.

'I don't think we should talk here. I'll take you to my office. No need to say goodbye to Joanna. I've explained I have to go back to work.'

He bundled me into his fat, black car as if I were a mad relation causing a scene at a family party. It was obvious that he regretted asking me to the funeral. I thought I might look slightly scruffy with my damp, stained skirt, but hardly mad. He drove very quickly down country lanes, taking bends too fast, braking suddenly at junctions. I wondered if he was quite sober. The road between Wintrylaw and Morpeth was obviously familiar to him.

In Morpeth it was late afternoon and shoppers were making their way home. There was a queue of cars in the main street, waiting to cross the narrow bridge south over the river. I had a sense of returning to the real world which left me depressed. It was like coming back to Newbiggin after my holiday in Morocco.

Howdon's office was in a smart terrace close to the library. There was a highly polished brass plate beside the door and a yard at the back with his name painted on the cobbles to mark his parking place. In reception a bored young woman quickly hid a magazine. She didn't seem pleased to see us. I guessed she'd been planning to finish the article on holiday flings, then to slope off home early.

'Tea please, Penny,' he said. 'Then you can leave us to it. I'll lock up.'

'Yes, Mr Howdon.' She flashed a quick and grateful smile.

The tea arrived very quickly. Howdon was still making himself comfortable. He'd taken off his jacket and hung it on the back of his chair. There were patches of sweat on his shirt which made his back look like a map of the world. A leather-topped desk spread between us. Penny already had her bag over her shoulder and immediately after she left Howdon's room I heard the outside door slam shut. The building was quiet. It seemed we were alone.

'Where's Mr Smith?' I asked.

'He died three years ago. There are a couple of junior partners . . .' He caught himself being civil to me and scowled. 'But that's not really relevant. I've always dealt with Philip and Joanna's business personally.'

'I don't understand what any of this has to do with me.'

'Nor do I!' Perhaps he felt he'd betrayed his feelings too obviously, because he continued in a more measured voice. 'Philip had some strange ideas, especially towards the end. But I've taken advice. I don't think we can contest their legality.'

He poured tea from a tarnished silver pot and lifted my cup and saucer so it was standing on the desk in front of me. As he stretched forward I smelt stale alcohol. It seemed to ooze from his pores. His hands were slender for such a big man, the fingers flexible. He lifted a sugar lump towards his own cup using a pair of old-fashioned tongs, dropped it, then watched the ripples in the liquid, mesmerized for a moment.

'Mr Samson made me his executor,' he went on formally. 'He left instructions concerning you.'

'If it's money I don't want it.' Suddenly I was very angry. Not at Stuart Howdon, but with Philip. Had he thought I'd slept with him for what I might get out of it? 'How did he trace me anyway?'

'He was a magistrate,' Howdon said smoothly. 'Many of his friends were police officers. I imagine it wouldn't have been difficult . . .'

The rugby players, I thought. Some of them looked like cops. And no doubt they'd told him about the court appearances, that time in Blyth . . .

'I don't want his money,' I said again. It upset me terribly that Philip had changed his opinion of me after hearing those stories. He hadn't believed I could make it on my own, so he'd left me a tacky little reward in his will. He'd died thinking I was pathetic. Irrational anger bubbled up in my stomach again and spread to my hands. I wanted to slap Howdon's smug face. I imagined the finger marks slowly fading like footprints in the wet sand at Wintrylaw. Instead I kept my voice reasonable. 'It should all go to his children.'

'It's not quite that simple.' Howdon lifted his cup, wet his lips, set it back on the saucer, then paused. 'Look, perhaps I should just read the instruction left to me by Philip. As I've explained, it's witnessed and it's legal, but you're under no obligation to undertake his commission. As far as I'm concerned it would be better all round if you didn't. Let sleeping dogs lie and all that. It's Joanna and the children I'm concerned about in all this . . .'

I remembered Dickon's words: 'I hate Mr Howdon . . .' It was hard to take the fat solicitor's concern seriously. Why had he made such an impression on the boy? He opened a drawer in his desk, removed an A4 envelope, then shook out a sheet of typescript.

'"To Lizzie Bartholomew of Sea View, Newbiggin, I leave £15,000, £10,000 as a gift to establish and equip an office for her self-employment . . ."'

'No,' I interrupted. 'I told you . . .' But I was moved, despite myself. While Philip was dying, he was remembering our conversation in Marrakech.

Howdon held up a hand to urge my patience, then continued, '"And also a fee of £5,000 for the first commission in that employment, the details of which are to follow. These payments only to be made should Miss Bartholomew attend my funeral of her own free will. The gift is not dependent on her accepting the commission."'

'But he knew I wouldn't accept it without the work,' I said softly. Howdon looked up uncertainly. He hadn't made out what I'd said. 'What is this commission?' I asked more loudly.

He continued to read. ' "To trace Thomas Mariner, lately of 63 Priory Way, North Shields".'

I interrupted. 'What happens when I find him?'

'Philip asks that I give him money. Discreetly. The bequest doesn't appear in the will.'

'Why me? Why can't you trace him?'

'I'm sure I could. But Philip wanted you to do it. Besides, there's more.' He turned back to the paper, though I had the impression he knew the words by heart. ' "Further, I ask that she assists, advises and befriends him. She will understand the importance of this commission to Thomas and to me." '

It was a lot to ask, that. Friends are made, not bought. But it was flattering that Philip had felt I could do something so important.

'Who the hell is Thomas Mariner?'

'I suspect,' Howdon said reluctantly, 'that he's Philip's son. An illegitimate son. This information was left with the letter of instruction.' He passed a second sheet over the desk towards me. 'It's a copy. You can keep it if you decide to accept his commission.'

The details were scrappy. Philip, it seemed, hadn't got very far in his search for his missing son. But then he'd left it for twenty years and waited until he was dying, so it was hardly surprising.

Name: Thomas? Mariner.

God, he wasn't even certain about the first name. After *Mariner* he'd added in brackets *Samson*. Somehow it was very touching, like a young girl practising the signature of her boyfriend's surname.

Date of birth: c. *22 December 1984. Mother: Kay Mariner of 63 Priory Way, North Shields.*

Was that where she was living now? Or where she'd been living twenty years ago?

'There's not much to go on.'

He shrugged. 'Then don't bother. As I said, let sleeping dogs lie. You get the £10,000 anyway.'

'Does Joanna know about Thomas?'

'God, I don't think so.' The thought seemed to horrify him. 'I certainly hope not.'

'Philip and his wife didn't have that sort of relationship, then?'

'What do you mean?'

'They didn't discuss everything?'

'Of course not.' He was scathing. 'Who does?'

'How well do you know them?'

'Well enough.'

He paused, and I thought I'd get nothing more out of him. Despite the late-afternoon sunshine on the tile roofs outside, the room was dark. There was a heavy mahogany cabinet against the wall, the drawers too narrow to contain documents. It held a butterfly collection perhaps. He had the hands of a collector. Or fossils. He would be precise and careful arranging his specimens. The wallpaper was a heavy sludge green, the curtains velvet in a similar but darker shade.

Then Howdon started to talk and I realized he was even more drunk than I'd suspected. Or perhaps it wasn't the drink. Perhaps he was on the edge of a breakdown. The thoughts seemed to fizz in his head and the words couldn't quite keep up with them. Perhaps he was haunted by daydreams too.

'They were a golden couple, Joanna and Philip.' He looked up at me. 'Do you know what I mean?

57

Magic. Like something out of a fairy tale. Too good to be true.' His voice was bitter, as if he meant that literally, as if in his experience no relationship lived up to expectation. 'I brought them together. Old Stu Howdon playing fairy godmother. What do you make of that?' He chuckled. It turned into a splutter and then a cough. 'Philip was a new estate manager at one of the places I look after. He was young, bright, but not the usual public school, county type. He'd been to comprehensive school, taken a degree in agriculture from Newcastle. The only interest he had in gardening then was the plot behind his house. He kept it organic, ferreted about for traditional species, talked about planting an orchard. A hobby, I thought. A good thing. Men need their hobbies to keep them out of mischief.'

Howdon spluttered again. It could have been a laugh.

'Joanna's parents had died and she was an only child, left to cope with the house, inheritance tax. They'd run the place down. I did my best for her, helped her through it. At least I thought that I did.'

He stared at the half-drunk tea, which had gone cold in the cup, and I thought, He fancied her, Philip was a rival.

'The only sensible thing to do was to sell the house and she refused to do that. Too many memories, she said. And she had a responsibility to keep it in the family. She's passionate about the place.'

'Did she work?' I felt weird when I asked the question. Like I'd been in the situation before but now the roles were reversed. This time I was the shrink and he was a patient.

58

'Mm?' He looked up.

'She was young, unattached. I presume she could earn her own living.'

'She was a photographer. Not weddings and kiddies' portraits. She'd probably have made more out of that. It was more arty stuff. Black and white. Landscapes. She had exhibitions. Some of her pictures went into books.' He paused again. 'She talked about developing the house as a country hotel. It might have worked. She had the drive and the spirit, plenty of the right sort of contacts. Then she met Philip and the idea was abandoned. The old place is still falling down.'

'You introduced them?'

'At the county show. You know what that's like. You bump into half the people you've ever met in the world, everyone you went to school with at least. Philip was there on behalf of the estate, Joanna was taking pictures for a glossy magazine. I introduced them, then got caught up with some old bore of a farmer. When I went to find them half an hour later they were sharing a bottle of fizz and a bowl of strawberries, and I didn't like to interrupt. It only took six months for them to marry. She asked me to give her away.'

Poor, sad bastard. I almost felt sorry for him.

'They brought out a book together – traditional gardens in the north of England. She took the pictures, he did the text. When no one would publish it, they brought it out themselves, hawked it round all the local bookshops, took it down to London. One of those daytime television programmes got interested. They were an attractive couple and Philip stirred up a bit of controversy knocking contemporary designers. He said their gardens were too sculptural, too minimalist. He liked a landscape that was extravagant and over-blown, overcrowded even. The programme challenged him to design a place somewhere in East Anglia. He did. Everyone raved about it. After that he never looked back. Like I said, the golden touch.'

Until he got cancer, I thought, remembering the envy of the rugby player back at Wintrylaw.

'You stayed friends?'

'Marjorie and I had them round for dinner occasionally. We went there. To make up the numbers, provide local colour when their London friends were visiting. If I met him at the rugby club, we'd have a few beers. He never mentioned a son, if that's what you mean. We weren't on those terms.'

'Why didn't he look for the boy before?' It came out as a wail, pathetic and desperate.

Howdon looked at me uncertainly. Mad cow, he was thinking. 'Why would he? Lovely wife. Two children. Why would he rock the boat? Later there was guilt, I suppose. He knew he was dying and wanted to get his affairs in order.'

I sat there wondering how Philip could have messed with me like this. How could he be so dumb? Would I like my father to come looking for me? Of course I would. It was what I fantasized about when I lay awake in the early mornings. Someone making the effort to find me. But I didn't need this. Christ, I was screwed up enough already. I didn't care about Thomas. Really, I didn't. But even as I was thinking that, I had the picture of another boy in my head. Not Thomas but Nicky.

BURIAL OF GHOSTS

'I don't think I'm the right person to do this,' I said evenly.

'Philip thought you were absolutely the right person. You read what he said.' He returned the paper to the envelope as if he didn't care one way or the other what I decided.

I intended to turn him down, to tell him where to stick his money. Then I thought what I could do with £15,000. I could kit up the empty room in Sea View with a computer, a phone line and a fax. It would buy me time to decide what to do next. Only rich people have the luxury of not taking cash into consideration. And it wouldn't be like being paid for sex, would it? It would be a legitimate business deal.

We sat for a moment in silence, staring at each other. I was still thinking I could just walk away. Then Howdon reached down, pulled open a drawer in his desk and took out a brown padded envelope. I could tell from the way he lifted it that it was heavy. He pushed it across the desk to me. It hadn't been sealed and it was full of £50 notes.

I reached out my hand towards it. He smiled. He knew he'd won. I was as greedy as he was.

Chapter Eight

There was still a Mariner living at 63 Priory Way. It was in the phone book, right at the top of the list: *A. Mariner*. Some relation? Or had Philip even got the name of his child's mother wrong? I called from Jess's, waiting until she was out before using the phone. When I returned from Philip's funeral I'd just said a friend had left me some money in his will. She didn't pry. It wasn't her style. I hadn't explained what I had to do to get the money. I'm not quite sure why. Because it was between me and Philip, because I wanted some success to report before I told her what was going on.

The phone rang for a long time before it was answered and I was about to give up. Then an elderly woman repeated the number. I crossed my fingers.

'Could I speak to Kay, please?'

'Eh, pet, she's not lived here for years. Who's speaking?'

My brain went into slow motion. I hadn't prepared any sort of cover story. 'Jess,' I said. 'An old school friend.'

'I don't remember any Jess. The high school, was it?'

'That's right. Could you let me know how to get in touch with her?'

She paused, not really suspicious but protective. Perhaps her daughter was strong on privacy. 'Give me your number, pet, and her dad or I will tell her that you called.'

Then I panicked and replaced the phone, glad that I'd dialled 141 before the number to stop the call from being traced.

Priory Way was one of the tidy streets near the Linskill Centre, the old school where Tyneside kids go for their music lessons, close to the overgrown waste of Northumberland Park. North Shields must have a thriving place once, with the ship building and the boats going out to the fishing, but nothing much seems to happen there now. Lots of the shops in the town centre were boarded up. There were posters everywhere for the Fish Quay Festival. The place had come alive for the bank holiday weekend with bands on the Quayside and street theatre and fireworks, then it had slid back into a coma.

I visited the Mariners during the day. If they had a teenage grandchild, I thought they'd have retired and be at home in the afternoon. The woman I'd spoken to on the phone certainly sounded elderly. This time I was better prepared.

Along the street there was a row of trees, all in blossom. Occasional snatches of breeze from the river scattered the petals over the pavement. I'd got the bus into Newcastle, then the metro out towards the coast. I'd looked at the *A–Z* on the train, so I walked down the street now as if I knew precisely where I was going, very purposeful and businesslike in my linen

jacket, carrying the black nylon bag I'd got at a conference on teenage violence and which I'd used as a
briefcase ever since. I could almost believe I was a
competent professional.

The house was part of a terrace halfway down.
More care had been lavished on it than on most of the
kids I grew up with, but it's daft to be jealous of a
house. The windows had been polished and the nets
were so bright that they gave you snow blindness.
The front steps had been swept recently. Only a light
scattering of pink petals covered the path. I stepped
on them and knocked at the door.

After a moment, a woman of about seventy
opened it. She'd left the chain on and I had a glimpse
of a round face and tight white curls.

'Who is it?'

'Miss Bartholomew. Social services.' Hoping she
wouldn't recognize the voice from one brief phone
call, I flashed the pass which had never been taken
from me. She looked at the photo, peered at me and
smiled. It had been issued by Northumberland, not
North Tyneside, but she seemed not to notice. She
unhooked the chain and opened the door wide. She
was leaning heavily on a stick and it took her a while.

'That was quick,' she said. She was delighted to
see me. There'd been no need to fuss that she'd
recognize the voice. 'I only phoned the other day.
Come in.'

That threw me. I'd prepared a story that I was
undertaking a survey of elderly people in the area to
find gaps in local authority services. If she was expecting a real social worker, I'd have to wing it. She led

me into a gleaming living room which smelt of lemon furniture polish and baking.

'Is Mr Mariner in?'

'No.' She smiled fondly. They must have been married for forty years but the sound of his name still made her happy. 'It's his bowls day.' There were awards on the mantelpiece, a photo of a small moley man in specs and whites holding a cup, his arms round the shoulders of a bigger bloke with a red face.

'You sit there, pet.' She patted the arm of the sofa. 'I'll put the kettle on. You'll have to give me a hand when it's made. I'll not be able to carry it through.'

So we sat together in her front room in the sun and she told me the story of her life. Without hesitation. It was scary that she trusted me absolutely on the basis of a bit of plastic and a photo.

'It's the arthritis,' she said. 'I'm down for a new hip but it could take a couple of months and now it's in my hands too. Archie and I manage very well between us. He's turned into a canny housekeeper. But he's anxious if I'm here on my own. I can't use the phone. The buttons are *that* small. He says what if I had a fall . . . Stupid old fool. Nothing's going to happen to me. But he doesn't like to leave me and if he does go out he worries. I don't want that. He loves his bowls and I don't want him rushing back. No reason why he shouldn't have a cup of tea and a bit of a chat with the lads. We thought maybe a panic button, or one of those phones with the big numbers. What do you think?'

'You'd probably be eligible for both.' I'd trained with a lass from North Tyneside who worked with the

65

community care team. She'd put the Mariners on the list for me. It would save one of their staff making a visit. 'Do you have family? Anyone who comes in to keep an eye on you?'

'Would that make a difference?'

'Not to your being approved the gadgets. You don't need someone here twenty-four hours, so you'd still want those. We couldn't expect your family to provide full-time support.'

'That's true enough. Kay's got her own family to look after now. And she works full-time. Pamela lives in Surrey. She married a southerner.' As if it were a different breed.

'Two daughters, then?'

'Aye. I'd have liked a son, but Archie loved his little girls.'

'Any grandchildren?'

'Five.' She hoisted herself to her feet and soon we were poring over photos. The Surrey brood were girls too. There were two of them. Not exactly lookers. They'd inherited their grandfather's prominent teeth and in many of the shots their mouths were full of metal. Mrs Mariner seemed not to notice the beaver features and I heard about their academic success, their brilliance at the piano, the gymnastics classes. Kay had also produced two daughters. Closer in age, they appeared together in school photographs. They were younger too. Even the most recent pictures showed them in primary school sweatshirts, their hair tied up with ribbons.

'Lucy and Claire,' Mrs Mariner said. 'Aren't they bonny?'

They were. Bonnier at least than Abby and Natasha in Godalming.

'Do you see a lot of them?' I didn't want to push for information on Thomas too quickly.

'Not as much as I'd like. They only live in Whitley Bay. I'd have them for Kay after school. Archie wouldn't mind picking them up. But she won't have it. She says it would be too much for me. Maybe she thinks I'd not be able to care for them properly. You can understand her being worried. After Thomas. And Ronnie can afford a childminder. It's not as if they're short of cash.'

'Thomas?' I could have played safe and left it. I already had enough information to trace Kay. But I was curious. There had been a few photos of a young boy among the rest but nothing recent.

'Thomas is Kay's son. The only lad . . .' She shook her head gently. Something about the face and the white curls reminded me of a doll I once had. It moved its head. It was brought by a charity to the kids' home one Christmas. New. Still in its box. All wrapped up. But I couldn't see the point of it, just sitting there, moving its head from side to side. I swapped it for a backboard that made a screeching noise when you chalked on it.

'You don't have to tell me,' I said. 'None of my business.'

'Thomas is Kay's son. Older than the girls.' She looked around guiltily, as though there might be someone to overhear. 'She had him before she got married.'

'Tough.'

'She'd only just left school. We found out she was expecting soon after she finished her A-levels. She had a Saturday job in a big department store in town. That's where she met the father. He was a student, a bit older than her, working his way through university.'

'Did you ever meet him?'

'No. We knew nothing about him. Not even his name. She didn't even want to tell us that much. We tried to help her through it. It was something you thought about in those days: what would I do if one of them fell pregnant? And I knew I couldn't get cross or angry. No point, is there?'

This was all a bit close to home. I was thinking, I wish you were my gran. If my mum had had someone like you, I wouldn't have been dumped outside a church for a collie bitch to sniff out.

'Did she ever think of an abortion?' It was something *I'd* thought about. The dizzying notion that I might never have been born.

Mrs Mariner shook her head. 'By the time we realized what was going on, it was too late for an abortion. And I was glad. I didn't think she'd be able to live with herself afterwards, no matter what she said at the time.'

'What *did* she say?'

Mrs Mariner didn't answer directly. Not because she was becoming suspicious about my questions. Everyone expects a social worker to be nosy. Just because she wanted to explain in her own time.

'Kay was an easy child in a way. She liked everything just so. She always kept her clothes lovely and I never had to nag her to tidy her bedroom. She was organized, you could say. Not like Pam, who was a walking whirlwind. Kay had her life planned. She was going to train to be a teacher. Little ones. She wouldn't have been able to control the older children. And she liked to be in control, our Kay. Then I suppose she met this lad at work and they were careless, unlucky, and she fell pregnant. But it wasn't in her scheme of things. It wasn't supposed to happen. She wouldn't admit it even to herself. Do you understand what I mean, pet?'

I nodded.

'I guessed in the end that she was expecting. You can't live in a house this size and keep secrets. And like I said, with teenage girls it was always something that was a possibility. You'll understand when you've bairns yourself.'

I said nothing.

'It made her ill,' Mrs Mariner continued. 'Not physically ill. She just couldn't accept it, not even when she was the size of a barrage balloon. We couldn't get any sense out of her. She wouldn't talk about the father. We wouldn't have made a fuss. You can't imagine Archie with a shotgun. But we thought the lad had a right to know, to play his part. He'd have parents. Imagine having a grandchild and knowing nothing about it.'

She paused again and I thought it was a story she hadn't told for a long time.

'He was born on Christmas Eve. An east wind that would cut your legs off. Too cold for snow. I went with her to the hospital and helped her through labour and she was as good as gold, breathing and panting just like they'd showed her. Braver than I'd been with mine. I thought it was going to be all right. There's nothing more real than labour, is there? Nothing like holding the babby at the end. She'd have to accept him, then.'

'And did she?'

'She wouldn't look at him. She burst into tears and said she wanted him adopted. *Now* I think that would have been best. I shouldn't have interfered. But I thought she was ill. Depressed even. Not fit to make a decision. I thought she'd regret it when she was better . . .' She was looking out through the window at the snowing pink petals. 'I'd held him, you see. My first grandchild. A boy, like I'd always wanted for myself. I wasn't thinking straight either. Selfish. She'd always done what she was told. Perhaps that was how she got pregnant. She'd go along with what he wanted to please him. And when I said she should keep the baby, she went along with that too.

'I looked after Thomas when she was at college, doing her teacher training. I'd been working in the office at Parsons, not much of a job, not something I minded giving up. He was a lively one, always full of fun and mischief. He kept me young. Kay would be here in the evenings to bath him and put him to bed, and she never took advantage, never stayed out late. But deep down I always felt it was a chore for her. She did it out of duty. Not because she enjoyed it. She'd tuck him in and read him a bedtime story, but he could have been one of her pupils. Do you know what I'm saying, pet?'

I nodded. I knew exactly what she was saying.

'Sometimes I think of the both of them he liked

Pam best. She was a laugh. She took him to the park and didn't mind when he got mucky. When she married and moved south he cried his eyes out.

'Kay was thirty when *she* married. Thomas was eleven. He'd just started the big school and was finding it hard to settle. Nothing serious, but the big lads were rowdy and he could be quite nervy. Then Kay met Ronnie. He owns that big garage on the coast road and she bought a car from him. That's how they met. She was teaching then of course, working in the infants' school in Wallsend, where she's deputy head now. She was doing very well for herself even then, but she and Thomas had never moved into a place of their own. It must have been a shock for the lad. New school, new home, new stepdad . . .'

'And he'd miss you,' I said.

'Aye, I think he did. I think he did miss us. For a while he came for his Sunday dinner but it wasn't the same. And we missed him. Kay didn't tell us what was going on. We'd been like parents to him for all those years, then suddenly we weren't to interfere. She and Ronnie knew best. We found out some. He was bunking off school. Friends of Archie's had seen him in town. He'd been getting into trouble. Kay told us it was none of our business. Not in so many words, like. But that was what she meant.'

'And then she got pregnant again.'

'With the two girls. First Lucy, then Claire. She loves them to bits and I'm pleased at that, but it must have been hard for Thomas to see her with them.'

'How old is he now?'

'Nineteen last Christmas.'

ANN CLEEVES

'Still at home?'

'No.' It came out as sharp as a bullet shot and she clamped her mouth shut after.

'They didn't throw him out?' I was fighting mad on her behalf and Thomas's.

'Not exactly. More like an ultimatum. Behave properly in this house or leave. I can understand in a way. They've got the girls to think of. And I can't blame Ronnie. I don't think it was his idea. It was Kay being stubborn.' She paused. 'We'd have had him here, Archie and me, but Kay didn't tell us what had happened until it was all over. Maybe now it's too late and nobody can get through to him.'

'Where's he living?'

'I don't know.' She was almost in tears. 'I think Kay knows, but she's not telling us. He's not to be spoilt, she says. He's to learn a lesson.'

'Is he working?'

'Yes, and you'd think she'd be proud of that. When he first left school he didn't have anything. Then a friend of Archie's took him on. As a favour to us, like.' She nodded to the photo on the mantelpiece, towards the big man standing beside her husband on the bowling green. 'That's Harry Pool. He took redundancy from Swan's years ago, in the 1970s. He saw the way things were going and set up on his own. He's got a haulage business. He started off with one lorry, now he has a whole fleet and a yard on that little industrial estate where the railway used to go in Shiremoor. A house like a palace in Cullercoats. But they're still best mates, him and Archie. They were at infants' school together. He hasn't changed. Not really.'

'What does Thomas do for him?'

'Not driving. He was too young for that when he started. He works in the office. Sorting out the invoices and such. Arranging the schedules for the drivers. A lot of Harry's business is in Europe. It's a nice clean job. I don't know why Kay took against it. She wanted Thomas to stay on at school and go to university. But you can't force them, can you?'

'At least you know he's safe,' I said. 'If he's working for Archie's friend.'

'Aye, maybe.'

'Can't you find out from Harry where Thomas is living?'

'We don't want to make trouble for him at work. Harry probably thinks he's still living at home. And last time Harry spoke to Archie he wasn't best pleased at the way the lad was carrying on. "If he doesn't mend his ways he'll be on the dole." That's what he said. We can't interfere, can we? We might make things worse.' She turned to me. 'I don't mind if Thomas doesn't want to visit. He's grown up. Why would he want to spend time with us? I just want to know that he's happy and he's well.' Which was what Philip had wanted too.

I couldn't leave her like that. I made her another cup of tea and we chatted about happier things until she saw Archie making his way from the park and her eyes lit up.

Chapter Nine

When I got home from my chat with old Mrs Mariner, Ray was in the kitchen talking to Jess. It was only five o'clock but I had the feeling they'd been there for a while. Everything about him was awkward and clumsy; his hands and feet were enormous and seemed to flap as if he had no control over them. When I looked in from the yard through the window, I saw his legs were poking out from the table. His wide, bony feet were bare. If he'd been sitting there in his boxer shorts I wouldn't have been more shocked. He always took off his mucky work boots when he went into the house but never his socks. They must have been making love. In the big back bedroom, which was Jess's only private place. None of us were allowed in there, not even me. I pushed open the kitchen door and they grinned at each other, smug and sheepish at the same time. I wanted to smack them.

'There's tea in the pot, pet.' Easy, relaxed, as if she had sex with a plumber every afternoon. Perhaps she did. Perhaps that's why I hated the new relationship so intensely – Marrakech had made me realize what I was missing and I was jealous.

She must have sensed my tension. 'Are you all

right, Lizzie?' Then, 'You have taken your tablets today?'

I glared at her. That was none of her business and not something to be discussed in front of lover-boy. All the same, feeling as I did about Ray, still I asked him if he'd give me a lift the next day. I've no pride, you see. Don't see the point in it.

'About time I had my own transport again,' I said in explanation. I'd sold my old car after the incident in Blyth. That was always how I thought of it: 'the incident in Blyth'. I couldn't trust myself with a car after that. Road rage kills.

'Good idea, pet.' Jess beamed. She thought she'd been forgiven after the slip-up with the pills. 'It'll do you good to get out more.' She turned to Ray. 'Can you fit her in, love?'

He nodded obediently. If she'd asked him to take me to the North Pole in his little white van, he'd have said 'no problem' and gone out to look for snow chains in Halfords.

I knew the garage on the coast road. I'd seen the sign, spinning on a pivot in the wind until it was a blur. Ronald Laing, quality motor vehicles. It was close to the 1930s Wills building, which had been converted into expensive flats, and the office behind the forecourt was built in a similar style. Brick. Curvy lines. Probably not original but put up with some care. The cars were a bit special too. The stock wasn't the usual junk – the ageing Micras and rusting Fiestas meant for nervous housewives and first-time buyers. This was second-hand but classy: top of the range BMWs, a Jag, a couple of four-wheel-drive monsters, a Golf convertible only two years old. If Kay Mariner had bought her car from here she must have been saving. Or perhaps Ronnie had gone upmarket since they married.

Why did I go to the garage first and not straight to Thomas or his mother? Nerves perhaps. I wanted a practice run. And I wanted to get this right. How would I feel if some stranger blundered up to me with information about my family? Shocked, sceptical. I'd have to trust the messenger before I accepted the message. So I needed as much information as possible before approaching Philip's son. Already I had fantasies that we might be friends. I know it's soppy, but I dreamt he'd come to see me almost as a sister. I didn't want to cock things up before we'd even met.

Ronnie Laing came out of his office to meet us as soon as we pulled up. I'm not sure what I'd been expecting. Someone big and bullying, perhaps, because he'd stopped Thomas from visiting his grandparents. A blustering, overweight car salesman. He wasn't like that at all. He was slight and small, rather diffident. He was wearing a suit. He helped me out of the clapped-out van as if it were a Bentley. I was glad I'd made an effort to look presentable. There was something about him which made me want to impress. It was warm and I'd put on a sleeveless top and a long, straight skirt, slit at the back so I could walk. I hadn't lost all the Moroccan tan. A *real* tan in early summer always looks expensive. Ray stayed in the van, as he'd been told.

Each time I saw Ronnie Laing I would be surprised by how small he was physically. None of that remained in the memory. What you remembered was the smile, boyish and confiding. It was as if he had none of the normal barriers people put up round themselves for protection. He couldn't pretend. You don't expect that sort of vulnerability in a used-car salesman. And his energy. That first day when he took my hand to help me out from the van, the touch shocked me. I don't know why. I looked at him and he smiled; he knew the effect he'd had and he was almost apologetic.

'Ronnie Laing,' he said. 'Spelled like the art gallery.' His voice surprised me too. It was pleasant, quiet, almost without accent. There was a trace of a stutter. I knew how his name was spelled. There was that big sign by the road. I thought he was trying to tell me something else. That he was cultured, more than a grease monkey. He wasn't showing off, but he wanted me to know something about him. I didn't give him my name. I didn't say anything.

'What sort of thing are you looking for?' he went on.

'Nothing boring. I can't stand boring cars.'

'A woman after my own heart.' In someone else that could have come out as flirty, teasing, but I thought he was quite serious. He gave a little frown as he spoke. With the easy cliché he spoke of a connection between us. That was how it seemed to me then.

He showed me what he had in stock, touching my elbow occasionally to direct my attention. It wasn't hard to appear interested. I really would have to buy a car soon. Thanks to Philip I had some money and I couldn't rely on Ray to ferry me about. But all these were way out of my league and he must have sensed that he wasn't going to make a sale.

'If you have anything special in mind I can look out for it for you.'

'Maybe something a little *less* special.'

He frowned again. 'We don't usually deal with the budget stuff.' There was a moment's hesitation. 'But I'll see what I can do.'

'Oh?' I gave him a quizzical look. I hope that's how it turned out. The effect he was having was so marked that I wasn't in the mood for role playing.

'Nothing illegal,' he said quickly, and the stutter was more marked. 'I don't operate that sort of business. I have contacts, go to auctions. Most of my trade is with repeat customers. I know the sort of thing they want. I might bump into something to suit you.'

'Oh, right.' An embarrassed giggle to show I'd misunderstood. I went with him into his office to pick up a business card. There was a framed photo of a woman and two little girls on his desk. The woman had a hairstyle that could withstand a hurricane and a thin, straight smile. There was nothing of Thomas, but I hadn't expected there to be. Also on the desk was a cardboard dispenser with application forms to join something called the Countryside Consortium. A picture of a bloke carrying a shotgun, wearing green wellies and a Barbour jacket was printed on each one.

'I didn't have you down as the green wellie type,' I said.

'It's a serious issue. You have to do what you can.'

'Oh, right,' I said again. 'Of course.'

'I'll need your name and number.' He paused a beat and I seemed to stop breathing. 'In case I find you a car.'

'Lizzie.' I scribbled the Sea View number on a piece of paper.

'Lizzie what?'

'That'll find me.'

In the car Ray was listening to something plaintive and Irish. Easy listening for him.

'What do you know about the Countryside Consortium?' He'd switched off the tape and pulled out into traffic. Every Sunday he went walking in the hills. I didn't know anyone else who'd have information on the countryside.

'Those buggers.' For Ray the reaction was vituperative. I was surprised. I'd even thought he might be a member.

'What's wrong with them?'

So he told me. They were land-owning bastards who tried to restrict the right to roam on their land. They were townie thugs who thought they should have a free hand to bait badgers and steal raptors from the wild. They were hunters and punt-gunners and they thought democracy didn't apply to them. In Ray's view, they were the scum of the earth. None of that seemed to apply to Ronnie Laing. He was gentle and polite. I supposed his support of the consortium was a ploy to hit the farmers with his fancy four-wheel drives, but even that seemed too calculating for him. I thought Ray must have got the whole thing wrong.

That evening I couldn't put Ronnie Laing out of my mind. I'm an obsessive. It's part of my personality. Occasionally images get stuck in my head and they go round in a loop, like an irritating song. What bugged me most was that I couldn't place him. I couldn't fix his class or his education, even his age. Usually I'm good at that stuff. Ray and Jess invited me to the pub with them, but I stayed at home. I lay on my bed remembering the shock when Ronnie touched me and his quiet voice, the effort it took him to keep the stammer out, the slim, fit body beneath the suit. I was still awake when the clock at St Bartholomew's struck three. I took a sleeping tablet then and eventually fell unconscious.

Chapter Ten

Perhaps because of the pill I felt strange the next day, disconnected. When I woke up Jess was hanging out towels to dry in the yard. The spin on the automatic had gone, so they were very wet. They were heavy and they dripped and she had to struggle to peg them up. I wondered briefly if I should use some of my money to buy a new washing machine, but I didn't go out to help her.

'What's wrong with you?' She turned, the plastic laundry basket in her arms, and saw me watching from the kitchen door. It wasn't cold but I was wrapped up in a big sweater.

'Dunno. A touch of flu.'

She accepted that without question, though she looked at me again more closely. Then she fussed inside to make a hot lemon drink.

'Go to bed,' she said. 'I'll bring it up.'

'I've got to go out. Work, sort of.'

She accepted that too. She didn't like it but she let me go.

The evening before I'd been to the library in the village to look in the Tyne and Wear phone book, hoping to track down an address for Kay and Ronnie, but they must have been ex-directory. I could have put off tracing Thomas's mother for another day, waited until I felt better, but, like I said, I'm an obsessive. I couldn't let it go.

In the photo she'd shown me in North Shields, Mrs Mariner's grandchildren had been wearing bright yellow sweatshirts with St Cuthbert's Primary School in big brown letters on the front. There was only one St Cuthbert's school in Whitley Bay and that *was* in the phone book. I arrived there too early. It was an old-fashioned place built of grey stone, still showing the separate boys' and girls' entrances over the doors. The yard had been marked for hopscotch and it was surrounded by black wrought-iron railings. When a class came out with a basket of skipping ropes and balls for PE I walked on up the street. I didn't want to be noticed staring in at the kids. There was a café near the old bus station and I sat there drinking stewed tea which had been poured from a big iron pot, watching the hands of the clock move round towards three. It only occurred to me when I was leaving that I should have had something to eat.

There was a bunch of mothers waiting by the gate, a couple of grans, a sprinkling of self-conscious dads, an assault course of pushchairs and prams. I stood on the edge of the group, trying to look as if I belonged there. I was starting to panic. Little girls in yellow sweatshirts all look very similar. How would I recognize them?

'I've not seen you here before.' It was a middle-aged woman, comfortably, scruffily dressed, slightly overweight.

'No.' A pause, more panic. 'I've come to collect my sister's kids.' Immediately I thought, That was really dumb. Then, pleading, in my head, Don't ask me the names, don't ask me the names.

'They're always late on a Thursday. Hymn practice. That Mr Cryer, he does go on.'

'Oh.' I felt my breathing become more regular, tried to remember the instructions of the yoga teacher in the hospital. 'Right.'

She turned away to chat to someone else.

In the end when they ran out I knew them straight away. They were in the first group, very tidy in identical pleated skirts and patent leather sandals. They seemed to be heading straight for me, their faces shiny with enthusiasm, their plaits bouncing. I knew they were bursting to tell someone about their day and I almost knelt to listen. They'd have books full of stickers and gold stars and I wanted to see them. But they hurtled past me to the middle-aged woman who'd put me right about Mr Cryer and hymn practice. She finished her conversation with a mother who looked as if she'd just come from the gym, while the girls pulled at her jumper and demanded her attention.

It wasn't Kay Laing. I'd seen a recent photo of Kay in Ronnie's office at the garage and even if she'd suddenly put on weight, the woman with the sculpted hair wouldn't have been seen dead in leggings which were going bald at the knee and a jersey covered in paint. This was the childminder. She gave me a friendly nod, took the girls by the hand and walked off.

I waited until the lollipop lady had seen them across the road and then I followed. The woman didn't look round. Finally she was taking notice of what the children were saying, smiling and murmuring encouragement. They'd arrived at a small rank of shops facing onto a wide pavement. The woman opened the door of a newsagent's and held it for the girls to go in. I looked at the desirable property displayed in an estate agent's window on the other side of the road, then watched their reflection in the glass as they came out carrying ice creams.

'Lizzie Bartholomew. What are you doing here?'

He'd come up on my blind side. There was a jolt of adrenaline in my system which made me want to run, but I turned slowly to face him. For a moment, because I'd been so focused on the woman and the two little girls, I couldn't place him.

'Dan Meech!' So pleased with myself for remembering that it sounded as if he were a long-lost brother. I thumped him on the back because that's what he would have expected. Nothing soppy, though once I'd fancied him like crazy. We'd gone out a couple of times at university but, it seemed he liked his women blonde and willowy. He'd dumped me for a girl on his course because he said we were too like mates. An excuse of course. She was stunning. He'd been doing performing arts. She was passionate about ballet. How could I compete?

I thought I'd carried this encounter off well, but he said, 'Hey, Liz. Are you OK?' And put his hand under my arm as if I needed him to steady me.

Looking past him into the street, I must have sounded absent-minded.

'Yeah, Dan. Course.' The childminder and the little girls had disappeared. 'Look, Dan, I'm in a *real* hurry. I'll have to go. See you around.'

I sprinted down the street. When I turned back

briefly, Dan was still standing there in his baggy trousers, looking as if he'd been set an exercise in his mime class: 'express surprise and confusion'. He always was a drama queen.

Still I couldn't see the childminder and the two kids. I was scared they'd already gone into one of the houses and I'd have to go through the whole charade of playing doting auntie by the school gate again. I wasn't sure I could handle that. This was turning into the smart bit of Whitley Bay. Big Edwardian houses were set back from the pavement. Through painted wooden gates I glimpsed long back gardens with fruit trees and striped lawns. The streets were parallel, running off the main road, where the row of small shops gave the impression of a village. I didn't see it as a place where the childminder would live. The houses round here went for a lifetime's earnings. She was taking the girls to their own home and I didn't even know which street she'd taken from the main road.

I stopped running. I was just drawing attention to myself. People were staring. I must have looked wild. Again I forced myself to breathe more slowly into the pit of my stomach, then began a systematic search. The streets were straight. Although trees had been planted at the edge of the pavements, I could see to the end of each one. There was a group of kids walking down the first I tried, but they were older, loaded down with violin cases and bags of books. There was no adult with them. The second was empty.

That was it. Time to give up. Perhaps I could find Dan again and persuade him to come for a drink. I *really* needed a drink Last time I'd heard, Dan had been working for a community theatre group and he was always broke. I could probably buy half an hour's company for the price of a pint. Or two. Then I heard voices behind me. Children's voices. The minder was carrying a plastic bag with *Alldays Convenience Stores* printed on the side. They'd been in a shop all the time and in my panic I'd run past them.

I was standing on the pavement like a prat, looking crazily around me. There was nowhere to hide. The woman came up to me and stopped.

'That was quick,' she said.

'Sorry?'

'You've got rid of your sister's kids, then?'

'Yes.' She must have thought I was a halfwit. 'Change of plan.'

'Do you live round here?' There was envy in her voice which confirmed that she didn't.

'Nah. I wish. Just meeting a friend.'

We smiled conspiratorially. For a moment it was us against all these rich bastards in their big houses. Then she moved on.

I stood at the corner and watched her go, counting the houses until she went in. She didn't look back. The Laings' house had a storm porch with a blue front door and there was a magnolia tree in the front garden. I wouldn't miss it if I came again. I wasn't sure what to do. I had a choice. A drink with Dan or make an effort to see Kay. A late-afternoon pub, quiet, with only a couple of serious drinkers to compete for the landlady's attention, seemed attractive. Dan would be up for it. We could talk about university, catch up on the news of old friends. He'd probably still be on the main road, expressing confusion and surprise. But I wanted to meet Kay Laing. It was already a quarter to four. Kay was an infant teacher. The kids would be gone by three-thirty at the latest. There'd be clearing up to do, a staff meeting perhaps, but she could be home at any time. Without being conscious of taking a decision, I leaned against the phone box on the corner and waited, watching the traffic grow heavier, my eyes fixed on the blue front door.

She arrived home nearly an hour later. I knew it was an hour because I checked my watch, but it seemed as if I'd only been there for minutes. I couldn't tell you what I was thinking about. She was driving an electric-blue Corsa. It was new. Not something Ronnie would normally stock and not something picked up at an auction. She pulled into the side of the road, so I thought she was going to leave the car there, but she opened the door of the double garage and drove into one side. Five minutes later, the childminder came out through the front porch. One of the children waved to her from a bedroom window, but she didn't notice. She walked down the street in the opposite direction. I waited until she was out of sight before approaching the house.

Chapter Eleven

Kay Laing opened the door as if she expected the caller to be someone dirty and unemployed selling dishcloths. She couldn't have many friends who just dropped in. She'd changed from the skirt and jacket she'd been wearing for work into a grey tracksuit and white trainers. *Very* white trainers.

'Yes?'

This was the woman Philip had made love to more than twenty years ago, the mother of his child. She would have been very different then, of course. A student. And I could tell she would have been pretty in a conventional way. But that was the problem. I wasn't jealous, nothing like that. I was disappointed. I had hoped for more from Philip, that he would have fallen for someone different, more exciting.

'Well?' she demanded. She made to close the door.

I flashed my identity pass. 'Lizzie Bartholomew from the youth justice team.'

I wasn't sure if there was a youth justice team in North Tyneside and at nineteen Thomas Mariner would probably be too old to concern them. But social service provision was labyrinthine, even to the people involved. I didn't think Kay Laing would know the difference.

'He doesn't live here now.'

'I'm aware of that, Mrs Laing. I just want a chat.'

Talking to Kay I felt sharper than I had all day, on top of things for the first time. Philip would have been proud. On the other side of the privet hedge, an elderly neighbour was on his knees weeding. If he hadn't been there Kay wouldn't have been so accommodating. She didn't want him to hear her being rude.

'You'd better come in.'

Ahead of me through an open door I saw the children at a table in the kitchen. They had changed too, one into pink dungarees with matching flowery shirt, the other into blue. I knew their uniforms would be hung up and neatly folded, ready for the next day. They were working with exercise books and pencils. I thought they seemed too young for homework but none of the schools I'd attended had been like St Cuthbert's. And perhaps things had changed.

The living room was yellow and white. Stripped floors. Two big oatmeal sofas with yellow woven throws. A wood-burning stove, cold now. It wasn't what I'd expected. Not Kay's taste, I thought. She'd have gone for something more chintzy and convenient, Dralon and a real-flame gas fire. Ronnie's, then . . . I was impressed.

'What's Thomas done now?' Kay said. 'He's gone eighteen, you know. Responsible for himself.'

'I know that.'

'It's not as if we haven't tried. It's not as if he wanted for anything.' She turned her head, a gesture which encompassed not only the room but the house and all it represented.

'I can see.'

89

She sat on one of the sofas, her back very straight. I took the other. Now I was here, I was feeling good, relaxed, confident I could get the information I wanted. I didn't like Kay Laing and that helped. I didn't mind lying to her. I imagined Ronnie as henpecked and downtrodden. While I was thinking that, my mind was racing, planning the interview: not too many direct questions, I decided. She'd realize then that I knew less than I pretended.

'It can't have been easy for him,' I said. 'Moving here. A new family, new friends.'

'It's easy to make excuses.' Her voice was even. She was trying to sound reasonable. We were two professionals talking together.

'Not excuses. I'm trying to understand.'

'Everyone blames the family,' she said. 'That's what makes me so angry.' She didn't look angry. She looked bitter, embattled.

'I'm not blaming anyone. Really.'

She sniffed, as if you couldn't believe anything a social worker said.

'I'm new to the case. Perhaps you could fill me in on some of the background. I understand that Thomas never knew his father.'

'What has that to do with anything?'

I thought then that she would tell me to leave. I added quickly, 'I'm sorry. I didn't mean to pry.'

She managed to keep her self-control. 'I didn't want to maintain a relationship with Thomas's father. It wouldn't have worked. He had other commitments.'

But Philip wasn't married to Joanna then. That came later, after he'd started work. So what commitments could there have been? Was Stuart Howdon keeping some awkward details from me? A previous marriage? Other children? I was longing to know, but this wasn't the time.

'Thomas was close to his grandparents, though, wasn't he?' I asked.

'He was close enough to them. But they spoiled him. I'm not prepared to buy his affection. He could never accept that.'

I was already wondering what Ronnie had seen in this cow.

There was a shout from the kitchen. One of the girls was asking for a drink. Kay went out wearily to help. I realized she must have been dealing with similar demands all day. Perhaps I was judging her too harshly. I stood up too. I was starting to feel jittery – too much caffeine, not enough food – and couldn't sit still. There was a photograph on one wall of a line of trees in winter, sunlight slanting through bare branches. Next to it on a white shelf stood a row of books. There wasn't much fiction – a few classics left over from Kay's college days and some action thrillers, but most were natural histories, travel, autobiographies of explorers, books on wilderness survival. There was nothing else to hold my interest and I wandered through to the kitchen after Kay.

At first she didn't see me. She stood with a milk bottle in one hand and a plastic beaker in the other, deep in thought. All around her was evidence of her ordered life: calendars, notes, lists. Pinned to the notice board was a reminder that the Methodist Wives outing would be to Hexham Abbey. *Packed lunch required. Fish and chip supper on the way home.*

'When I met Ronnie, when we got together, I

thought it would be good for Thomas. It's not that I hadn't thought it through. He was eleven, just the age when a boy needs a father. And Ronnie didn't mind the fact that I came as a package with the boy. Not at all. He said of course we'd have a family of our own one day, but he'd always wanted a son. And he had this house. So much room . . .'

And wouldn't the other Methodist Wives be jealous? I thought spitefully. How they'd envy Kay moving into the smart house in the most desirable street in Whitley Bay. And wouldn't they be secretly delighted when Thomas got into trouble and things started to go wrong.

'But Thomas wouldn't make any effort to like him. Ronnie tried really hard. He didn't have things easy when he was a lad and he understood. Thomas always had so much energy. Ronnie said it was like having an untrained puppy in the house. He only had to turn round and he'd knock something over. But Ronnie didn't mind that. He took Thomas out walking and climbing with him. I thought he'd enjoy it. The exercise and the fresh air.'

In my experience teenagers hated exercise. They were allergic to fresh air.

'And at first he *did* seem to enjoy it. He talked about training for a job in the countryside. Gamekeeper, something to do with conservation perhaps. But that phase didn't last long. And it didn't stop him doing the things he knew would upset us. Smoking, of course, although we both abhor it. Running away from school. "Attention-seeking behaviour", the teachers called it. As if I couldn't have told them that. He was caught shoplifting in the off-licence at the end of the road. Can you imagine how humiliating that was for me? I teach other people's children but I can't control my own. People look at me as if I'm to blame for the way he's turned out, but I'm not. I won't take responsibility for it. Thomas has to do that.'

'Did you consider discussing Thomas's problems with his father?'

'Never. I'd had no contact with him since before Thomas was born.'

'What was Thomas like at home?'

'Always difficult. Moody and rude. I stopped asking visitors to the house because he embarrassed me.'

And what about him? I thought. Did he ask his friends here? Or did you embarrass him?

She sat there, rigid, unblinking. The sort of woman I'd take an instant dislike to, if I met her at a case conference or if she were sitting on the magistrates' bench. The sort of woman who'd blow-dry her hair every morning and keep a small packet of tissues and a safety pin in her handbag for emergencies, whose life was ruled by timetables and certainties. But I remembered what Mrs Mariner had said about her crying her eyes out when her baby was born and I wanted to get through to her.

'Don't you miss him?'

Her head snapped back so she was looking straight into my face. 'I'll tell you what I don't miss. I don't miss the vomit in the bathroom when he comes in at one o'clock after a drunken party, the loud music in his bedroom and the unsuitable friends. I don't miss the police turning up on the doorstep because the neighbours have complained.'

All that seemed to go with the territory of being a

parent. When you have kids you know they're going to grow up. Did she expect her little girls to stay in every night doing their homework when they were sixteen? They'd be down Whitley on a Friday night showing their knickers in Idols nightclub and throwing up over the sea wall. Of course they would. Then I tried to look at things from Kay's point of view. One moment of freedom and she'd got pregnant. Perhaps she was just being bizarrely overprotective.

'What was the final straw?'

'I don't understand.'

'What made you decide to throw him out?'

'We didn't throw him out. He had a choice. We'd have made him welcome if he'd agreed to abide by our rules.'

'Something must have provoked the ultimatum.'

'I'm sorry. I'm not prepared to discuss it.'

Had she caught him shooting up in the immaculate kitchen? Having sex on her and Ronnie's bed? Whatever it was, she wasn't prepared to face it now.

'Does Thomas have a girlfriend?'

'No one that he was prepared to discuss with me.'

What sort of answer was that?

'Did he pass any exams in the end?'

'Only GCSEs. He dropped out before A-levels. And nothing spectacular. Cs and Ds. B in English. He did manage an A in music. But music's his obsession.'

I couldn't understand why she was so dismissive. The grades weren't bad, especially if he'd been bunking off school. But perhaps it was a good sign that she remembered them at all.

'What did he do when he left school?'

'He stayed in bed. For days on end.'

'No job?'

'How could he have a proper job? He was going to be a rock star. So he told us.' The sarcasm was scathing and well practised.

'Was he in a band?'

'Apparently.'

I didn't know how she could be so stupid. Music was his passion but she'd made no effort to understand what he was into. I couldn't push it though. Soon she'd remember I hadn't told her what I was doing there.

'Were they any good?'

She looked at me as if I were mad. 'How would I know?'

'You never went to see them play?'

'I'd be the last person he'd want there. And no, they never came here to rehearse. The neighbours are elderly. They wouldn't have stood for it. The band practised in a garage belonging to another parent. Someone more tolerant than us, according to Thomas. Occasionally they were booked to play in a pub. It hardly counts as a career.'

'Doesn't Thomas work at all?'

She paused. I wondered why she was so reluctant to admit to the job with Harry Pool. Would she have preferred Thomas to be unemployed to justify her action in throwing him out? Or was she so snobby that she couldn't bear him to be working as an invoice clerk for a friend of her dad's?

'He works for a haulage firm. There's no future in it.' She looked at me. 'He's not a stupid boy. With a bit of work and effort he could have gone to university. It's the waste which makes me so angry.' And this time she did look angry. Her hands were clasped together and the knuckles were white. 'I don't like the people he mixes with there. They're a rough crowd.'

'Did he enjoy the work?'

'He got out of bed to get there on time, so I suppose he did. He was never prepared to do anything he didn't want to. He's not badly paid for what he does. I suppose he enjoys the money.'

'When did he leave home, Mrs Laing?'

'About four months ago.'

'And you haven't seen him to talk to since then?'

'No.'

'How did he get on with your daughters?'

It wasn't a question she was expecting. 'He spoiled them. They adored him.'

'So they were upset when he left?'

'Children adjust easily at that age.'

'Has he been back to visit them?'

'He wasn't invited.' I said nothing, but she continued as if I'd accused her directly of being callous. 'We couldn't take the risk of upsetting them again. They're settled now. Why disrupt them? My son is unreliable, Ms Bartholomew. He could promise to visit but not turn up. Or he could arrive drunk. The girls have seen enough unpleasantness. I'm not prepared to put them through more.'

'Did he ever turn up out of the blue? Uninvited?'

'I wasn't here. Cath, the childminder, let him in.'

'And?'

'The girls were pleased to see him. Naturally. He bought a bag full of sweets. But he left them overexcited. They couldn't sleep. It wasn't good for them. I told Cath she wasn't to encourage him.'

'So he's not been back?'

'He tried once or twice. Not in the last few weeks.'

'Thomas hasn't reported to the office either,' I said, 'though I've sent him a couple of letters. He is at the same address?'

She looked at me, anxious for the first time. 'Well, you'd know more about that than me. You found him the place. Absalom House. That hostel in Bennet Street.'

'Of course. It's just that he seems to be a bit elusive at the moment.'

I stood up. Despite my fascination with Ronnie Laing, I didn't want him arriving now and recognizing me. But although she'd been so reluctant to talk to me, now Kay didn't want to let me go.

'Are you saying you've lost him?'

'Of course not. Nothing like that.'

'He *is* all right, isn't he?' she asked.

'I'm sure he is.'

'Can you call me when you've talked to him? Just to let me know. This is my work number.'

She wrote it carefully on a piece of paper. Why didn't she want me calling her at home? It wasn't as if she could be scared of Ronnie. I thought she liked to keep her life compartmentalized and Thomas didn't have a place here any more.

I was letting myself out of the front door when she called after me.

'I thought I was doing the right thing. Tough love. Isn't that what they call it?'

I supposed she'd read about tough love in a women's magazine. Or perhaps the Methodist Wives had been given a talk on it. To me, it seemed like an excuse.

Chapter Twelve

Absalom House was double-fronted, part of a terrace in a shabby street running up from the sea front. When family seaside holidays were popular and the workers of industrial lowland Scotland thought Whitley Bay would be a glamorous place to spend a couple of weeks in August, it had probably been a hotel. Now it was a place to dump homeless young people.

'It's not a hostel,' said the woman who answered the phone when I rang. She sounded indignant. 'I mean it's not the sort of place where they're pushed out of the door after breakfast and not let in until suppertime. We're a real community.'

Maybe so, but from her voice – middle-class prim – I doubted that she lived there. More likely she went home every night to a nice home in a nice area. She could have been a neighbour of the Laings. I doubted too that she had much contact with the residents. I imagined her as one of the social workers of my childhood, locked in her office writing reports while we played fretfully outside, desperate for adult company and support.

This time I'd planned a different cover. I told the woman I was a journalist researching a feature on young runaways. She was sniffy until I implied that

the publicity would be good for fund-raising and promised faithfully not to use individual residents' details
without their consent. If I'd said I was a social worker
she'd probably have let me in more easily, but I knew
I'd get nothing out of Thomas and his mates that way.

I conned a lift out of Ray again. It wasn't much
out of his way, he said, though I knew fine well his
next job was in Berwick, in completely the opposite
direction. He didn't speak all the way down the Spine
Road. He just sat with his eyes on the road and a daft,
dreamy grin on his face.

'What *is* going on with you and Jess?' I asked
suddenly. I wanted to know how things stood. I must
have sounded like an angry father asking the intentions of a daughter's suitor, because he blushed.

'I think I want to marry her,' he said.

'What do you mean, you *think*?'

'I mean I do.'

'What does she say?'

'I've not found the courage to ask yet.'

But he would. I could tell by the self-absorbed
smile. He couldn't stop thinking about her. She was
there, with him, at every sooty boiler and leaking
radiator. I wanted to ask what would become of me
then. Would they sell the house in Newbiggin? Would
they keep it for themselves? In the end I didn't say
anything. I left him to his marshmallow fantasies. But
the thought of Jess as a married woman added to my
edginess and uncertainty. If she settled down with
Ray, where would I go? Somewhere like this?

There was another jolt when the door was opened
to me by Dan Meech. We stared at each other on
the doorstep. Inside there was the sound of music.

Through an open door I saw a couple of lads bickering over a pool table, but they took no notice of us. I was embarrassed. It occurred to me that Dan was living there. He'd never made much money at work. Like most actors, he seemed to be without a job for most of the time. Perhaps Acting Out, his community theatre group, had finally disbanded through lack of interest. I suspect he felt equally awkward. I'd behaved very oddly when we met the day before, lurking outside an estate agent's. Perhaps he'd heard rumours of the incident in Blyth – these things are hard to keep quiet – imagined I'd had a breakdown, been kicked out onto the streets.

The silence was broken by the prim voice from the phone. It sailed over the upstairs banister, followed by an eccentric woman in a long velvet skirt, trailing scarves and big boots. She had dyed ginger hair backcombed into a bush, and very bright lipstick which strayed wildly from the outline of her lips. She was more elderly than the voice suggested and quite different from the social work clone I'd pictured.

'You must be Ms Bartholomew,' she said. 'Come in, my dear. Dan, this is the journalist who's promised us some publicity. Dan Meech, one of my part-time staff. He and I are the only ones who live in.' More shattered preconceptions.

'Lizzie and I are old friends,' Dan said. 'We were at university together. Journalism is it now, Lizzie?' Not giving me away, but making it clear to me that he didn't believe a word.

'Can you do the tour of honour?' the woman said. 'I've just had Charlie's social worker on the phone.

His mother wants him home. *Apparently*. I don't believe a word. We need to talk.' She drifted away towards the arguing voices, leaving a cloud of patchouli behind her. We watched her go.

'That's Ellen,' Dan said. 'She runs the place.'

'A character.'

'That's the impression she likes to give. She's not as dotty as she makes out.'

'And she's your boss?'

'That's right. I'll show you upstairs first, shall I?' Sarcastic, as if he knew I had no interest in the fittings and furnishings.

'What happened to Acting Out?'

'I still work there. It was never exactly a full-time commitment.'

I followed him along the top floor, peering round doors, interested despite myself. Ellen had been right. This wasn't an institution. It was a big, shabby home. The ceilings were high and the rooms were airy. Most had their own bathrooms. If Jess did decide to sell up Sea View, I could do a lot worse.

He was leading me back to the main staircase when a door opened and I had a glimpse of two faces. Girls with dark eyes wearing soft white headscarves. The door shut again quickly, although they must have been on their way out before we appeared.

'Who are they?'

'No personal details, Ellen said.' He was still hostile.

'I'm not asking for names. I'm interested, that's all.'

'Looking for a story?' He was sneering again.

'That's right.'

'They're sisters,' he said. 'Eastern European originally. They've been through a bad time.'

I would have liked to know more, but that wasn't why I was here and I didn't want to antagonize him with more unnecessary questions.

We went back downstairs and sat in the kitchen. It had that grubby untidiness which you always seem to get when young people live together. Biscuit crumbs on the floor and unwashed mugs piled up in the sink, a fruit bowl of shrivelled oranges and overripe bananas. But it was a pleasant room. An open door led into a glass lean-to and then an overgrown garden. Dan put on the kettle before he turned on me. Perhaps being in charge of all these people had gone to his head.

'What exactly are you doing here, Lizzie? And don't give me the crap you gave Ellen. Journalists make notes. I bet you haven't even got a pen on you.'

So I told him. Not about Philip. Just that I was on the sick and that I'd been asked to trace a lad. He made a pot of tea and rinsed out a couple of the mugs. He didn't ask about my illness, but I gave him something to be going on with. 'Depression,' I said. 'Stress-related.' I almost felt I had him eating out of my hand. Almost but not quite. Dan Meech was never a soft touch, except when it came to blonde dance students.

'Thomas Mariner,' I said, staring at him, hoping for a flash of recognition. None came. Perhaps I'd underestimated his skill as an actor.

'I can't tell you anything. I work here. It's confidential.'

'Look, all I've got to do is wait for one of those lads

playing pool. They won't stay in all day and I can be very patient. If Thomas is living here they'll tell me. If I give them a tenner I'll know the colour of his underpants and when he last had sex. But it's delicate, isn't it? He wouldn't want them all knowing someone's looking for him. Besides, if Thomas is here you'll know him better than anyone. If you were involved from the beginning you'd be able to help.'

'He isn't living here.' As if that was the end of the matter. Either he'd never known me very well or he'd forgotten how stubborn I could be.

'But he did once. And you'll know where he is now.'

'He doesn't want anyone to find out. I promised I'd not say. And how come you're involved anyway?'

'This is personal, Dan. Almost family.' And really, that was what it felt like.

I was expecting more of a fight, but suddenly Dan gave in. Perhaps he could tell how much this would mean to me. He held up his hands, a gesture of surrender. 'All right. You win.'

'An address, then?'

'Look,' he said wearily, putting off the inevitable, 'do you fancy a pint?'

There was a pub a couple of streets away. It was very small, one bar not much bigger than Jess's kitchen. The landlord was a big-jowled man, flabby and loose-skinned. He nodded at Dan as soon as we walked through the door and had his pint pulled before we reached the bar. He seemed offended when I said I'd have the same. If ladies drank beer at all, it was clear he preferred them to have halves, which he'd serve in glasses with stems.

ANN CLEEVES

'How did you get involved in Absalom House?' I asked.

'Acting Out did a workshop there for the residents. Ellen and I got talking. She offered me a job.'

'Who funds it? Social services?'

'They fund a few of the residents. Kids who've been in care and need a bit of support. But it's a charity. Ellen set it up thirty years ago in memory of her son. He was sleeping rough in London, got mugged and died two days later in hospital.'

'Is there a Mr Ellen?'

'I suppose there must have been once. She never mentions him. She probably wore him out. She's tireless. There are other trustees, but she does most of the work. She's provided a home for hundreds of kids over the years. I don't know how long she'll be able to keep going. I don't dare ask her age but she must be at least seventy. She was an actress in rep before she started up in this. Perhaps that's why she took to me. In my darker moments I think she might be expecting me to take the place over when she can't manage any more.'

'Grooming you for stardom?'

He grinned. 'Something like that.'

'Thomas Mariner was one of your residents?'

'Aye, for a couple of months. He had the room next to the lasses you saw. The sisters in the headscarves. But he's working. It wasn't hard for him to find his own place. Absalom House was always going to be temporary for him. Perhaps his mother thought it would bring him to his senses, send him home promising to be a good boy.'

'What's he like?'

'He'll do all right.'

'Come on, Dan. You can give me more than that.'

'He'd had a row with his family. Uptight middle-class bitch and a stepfather I never met.'

'But you did meet the mother?'

'She helped him move in, brought round some of his gear in the car. There was something heavy going on between them. Not just him moving out. I mean, he was old enough to be independent anyway. With a bit of time he'd have been able to find a flat. But she wouldn't give him the time. There was something else. They'd fallen out big style.'

'Did he ever tell you what it was all about?'

'No. I was just starting to know him when he moved out. There was a student, a lad Thomas had been friendly with when he was at school, who needed a body to share a house in Seaton Delaval. The lad's father had bought this place and done it up. The mortgage worked out cheaper than hall of residence fees apparently and I suppose he saw it as some kind of investment. Anyway, Thomas could afford the rent and he moved on.'

'Did he talk about his work?'

'Not much. He likes to impress, does Thomas, and moving paper around in the haulage firm didn't give the impression he wanted to create. Not in front of the other lads. He'd rather be talking about the band he's in, the gigs he plays.'

'Is it paper?'

'What do you mean?'

'It'd be computers now, wouldn't it? Any invoice and booking system?'

'Well, he'd be all right, then.' Dan was starting to

105

get impatient. 'He knows all about IT. Ellen's system went on the blink and he got it going again. Bragged about it for weeks, but he certainly knows his stuff.'

'You don't sound as if you liked him.'

'Like I say, he'll do all right.' He must have realized that wasn't enough for me. 'Look, he's young, a bit cocky, a bit arrogant. Or maybe he's just not very sure of himself and needs to put on a show. Whatever. None of them are angels.'

'Why's he still working for the haulage company if he's so good with computers? He could get a job programming. It'd pay more.'

'Perhaps he likes being a big fish in a little pond. The confidence thing again.'

Some mystical or telepathic signal must have passed between Dan and the landlord, because two more pints appeared on the bar. This time I paid.

'Anything else you can tell me?'

'He'd started doing voluntary work, fund-raising for some conservation charity. It was probably Nell's influence.'

'Nell?'

'His girlfriend. The love of his life. At least she was while he lived at the hostel. They've split up recently.'

'Does she live at Absalom House?'

Dan shook his head. 'She's still at school. Sixth form of Whitley High. Lives at home with Mummy and Daddy. Staid and respectable in an arty, theatrical sort of way. Mummy and Daddy are arty too. Very liberal.' He paused, gave the sheepish grin which made me remember why I'd fancied the pants off him at university. 'She did her work experience at Acting Out.'

BURIAL OF GHOSTS

I was relieved. That explained Dan's ambiguous attitude to Thomas. There was nothing sinister and I hadn't been imagining things. They were rivals for the affections of a pretty girl. Dan was still speaking. 'Her real name's Helen. Helen Ravendale. But known to all her friends as Nell.' Suddenly he stopped short. A question he should have asked upfront had just occurred to him. 'If his mother wanted to find Thomas, why didn't she come and ask?'

'Because you wouldn't have told her where he was.'

'It *is* his mother, then, who asked you to trace him?'

I tapped the side of my nose and told him that I had client confidentiality to respect too. 'Let's have that address in Seaton Delaval.'

'Look, he really didn't want anyone to know. He made a point when he left. If he asks, you didn't get it from me.'

'OK.'

'It's 16 Isabella Street.' He stopped pretending to resist. 'I remember because I was preparing to forward some mail to him this afternoon. If you come back to the hostel you can pick it up. You might as well take it with you. Save me a trip to the post box.'

Chapter Thirteen

That night I had the Blyth dream again and woke up shaking.

In the morning I went to Delaval. I hadn't slept well, but I couldn't put off seeing Thomas. I'd woken to the same obsession, the same drive, to carry out Philip's instruction. Perhaps I had become so caught up with his commission because it was a way of burying my own demons. I didn't think the flashbacks would end when I found Thomas. Not consciously. But I felt it was a way of taking control again. Of my own life and my own mind.

It wasn't until I was sitting on the bus that I realized I didn't know what I was going to say to the boy. Philip hadn't given me any clues. We pulled up a bank past a row of grey, terraced cottages. A colliery wheel fixed in concrete surrounded by bedding plants marked the end of a village and an Alsatian dog was cocking its leg against it. What will I tell him, I thought. *I'm a friend of your father's. But by the way, he's dead.*

In the seat across from me sat a very fat woman, so fat that she was ageless. She had huge chins and sagging bosoms and she took up the whole double seat. She was muttering to herself about buying a pair of shoes, telling the whole story of what would happen when she went into the Co-op to choose them. No one took any notice of her. When you see mad people, usually you ignore them, put them out of your mind. But that day in the bus that woman really bugged me. I wanted to yell at her to shut up. I had plans of my own to make which were more important than buying shoes. I didn't shout, of course, but that's what I wanted to do.

I still hadn't decided how I was going to play my meeting with Thomas when I got out of the bus. It was possible that he was well and contented – that, having escaped from his mother and stepfather, these new friends had provided a surrogate family. Perhaps he wouldn't need my advice or my friendship. I could take him out occasionally for a drink or a meal, like a distant godparent. Stuart Howdon could deal with the rest. But somehow I didn't believe in the fairy-tale ending, and anyway, wasn't friendship what I was hoping for? I was confused and miserable. Perhaps my low mood had to do with the weather. A sea fret had come in from the coast, bringing a persistent drizzle. I felt paler, greyer, as if it had washed away my Moroccan tan. In the street everyone walked with their heads bent. It was so dark that I expected street-lights and their absence threw me.

There was something else. Something more worrying. For the last few days I'd thought I was being followed. It'd happened before. It happened just before I lost my temper that time in Blyth. However much I knew really that no one was following me, I couldn't get the sensation out of my head

Seaton Delaval was once a pit village. The streets

are straight and grey; little Tyneside houses or flats with two front doors side by side, one leading upstairs and one down, face onto the narrow pavements. In fine weather young mothers sit on the steps, smoking and chatting. Today Isabella Street was empty except for one figure in a long black coat hurrying to get into a car and out of the rain. Number 16 was a house. The upstairs and downstairs flats had been knocked together. Where the second door had been was now a sheet of plate glass, so I could see inside to a hall and staircase. There was a brown cord carpet on the floor, which was covered in so much muck and dust that it looked as if it hadn't seen a hoover since it went down. A bike was propped against the wall and there was a mountain of random boots and shoes. I rang the bell. There was no reply. I didn't try it again. The feeling that I was being watched was making me really jumpy and I fled back down the street the way I'd come. This needed more preparation and I was glad of the delay.

On the roundabout there was a shop run by an Italian family. The place was famous for its ice cream. Jess and I had queued there on Sunday afternoons after a ritual visit to the gardens of a local stately home. Jess had an immense curiosity about the aris-tocracy. Ray would have disapproved, I'm sure, if he'd known – he was something of a revolutionary on the sly – but I don't think she'd ever let on. Inside the shop a few tables and chairs had been set out as a café. It was all dark-panelled wood and dusty shelves with jars of boiled sweets, brightly coloured sherbet and liquorice sticks. I sat over a milky coffee and tried to make sense of my position.

110

Suddenly it occurred to me that Thomas was unlikely to be at home at this time anyway. Wouldn't he be working at Harry Pool's? Perhaps Thomas's student friend would be in on his own. If he could confirm that Thomas was living there, I could report back to Stuart Howdon and leave the friendship thing until I felt better prepared.

This time someone was in. From upstairs came the thud of a bass line, music I didn't recognize. I pushed the bell and heard it ring faintly above the sound. Still there was no response.

The door of the next house opened and a girl looked out. She was fourteen or fifteen, dressed in black trousers and a white shirt which I took to be school uniform. Beneath the white shirt was the neat dome of a pregnancy. Otherwise she had the figure of a child – very slight and boyish. Her feet were bare and she stood in her own hall and peered round the door at me.

'They won't hear,' she said. 'They never do.'

'Are they both in?'

'Who are you?'

'Lizzie Bartholomew.' This time I didn't show my pass.

'From the social?'

'No. Nothing like that.'

'What, then?'

I only hesitated for a second. 'Housing officer from the university. I have to check it's a reasonable place for students to live.'

I know. Unlikely. But the girl bought it anyway. Or she was looking for an excuse not to go straight back to school. 'Course it is. They've done it all out.

111

It's better than the other houses in the street. Better than in here.' Her voice was wistful.

'All the same . . .'

'I don't know who's in,' she said. 'I've just come back from the doctor's. I got caught short on the way back to school. You never stop pissing, do you, when you're pregnant?'

I banged on the door again to show I was serious about getting in.

'Look,' she said. 'There's a key. I'll show you.' She slipped her feet into black boat-like shoes with big square heels and joined me on the pavement. On the front sill of number 16 was a wooden window-box. There were three clay pots inside. The plants were dead; the student obviously wasn't into gardening. The girl took one of the pots, knocked out the plant and inside there was a key. She tipped it into her hand, wiped the earth from it on her trousers and gave it to me. I expected her to go home then, or to make her way back to school, but she stood beside me, curious, proprietorial.

'Go on, then,' she said.

But when I put in the key it wouldn't turn. I pressed the handle and the door opened. It was already unlocked.

'They're daft, those two,' the girl said. 'I've told them they should be careful. They'll get burgled. They've got no idea what it's like round here.'

She pushed ahead of me and charged up the stairs. I shut the door behind me. The music was louder inside. Much, much louder. And weirder, pierced by a sudden shrill high tone. Then the music stopped and the piercing screech continued. It was the girl wailing.

The noise came from somewhere in the back of her throat. That was what made it so high-pitched. It must really have hurt her to make it. And even when I was standing right behind her she wouldn't stop.

She stood in the doorway of a bedroom. I pushed her out of the way and suddenly I'd walked into my own nightmare. It was like reality and flashback had collided with the violence of a nuclear explosion. The result was blood. It was everywhere. Glossy and very red against the monochrome decoration, spreading out from the grey figure curled on the floor.

But where was the knife? In my dream there was always a knife. I scanned the scene but I couldn't see it. It certainly wasn't centre-stage, where I'd expected. Then the girl's screaming got to me. I took her by the shoulders and shook her, forgetting about the baby she was carrying, just wanting the noise to stop. It was like a drill inside my head. It was hurting me, like all that red was hurting my eyes. There was silence. She turned and stared at me, her mouth still open. I touched her shoulders again, this time an apology, a clumsy attempt to comfort.

'Is there a phone in your house?' I demanded.

She nodded, still unable to speak.

'Phone the police. Not from here. From your house. Can you do that?'

She nodded again.

She was halfway down the stairs when I called after her. 'Who is it? Which one is it?'

Her voice was a croaky whisper, as if she'd regained her powers of speech at last after a lifetime's silence. 'Tommy Mariner.'

Of course, I'd known all along that it was Thomas.

113

It was as if I'd been expecting it. As if I'd seen it before in a vision. Since I'd stabbed that boy in Blyth, I'd been waiting for it to happen again.

I began to sob. 'I'm so sorry,' I said. 'So, so sorry.' I wasn't talking to Thomas but to Philip.

Chapter Fourteen

So, I was back in the same room. High walls painted
that thick cream gloss that you only ever find in
institutions. A high window, slit horizontally like a
post box in a door. A graffiti-covered table bolted to
the floor, and on the table a fluted foil container which
they used as an ashtray but which might once have
held a mince pie. It looked as if it had been there
since Christmas. Since the last time. Four chairs,
moulded plastic. The same policeman asking the
questions, and he made the connection too.

'Another stabbing, Miss Bartholomew.'

He spoke sadly. It was as if I'd let him down. A
woman sat beside him. She was only a bit older than
me, thin-lipped with blotchy skin. She didn't speak,
didn't even move. The fourth chair was empty.

The man's name was Farrier. He was large, a
middle-aged schoolboy with a beer belly, curly hair
and round specs. Away from work I could imagine he'd
be jolly, the life and soul of any party. He wasn't fit
and he wasn't hungry. He was decent. I'd realized that
the first time. The woman was a sergeant called Miles.

'I didn't stab Thomas Mariner,' I said quickly.

He paused. 'But would you know if you had?
Really? That's what we have to decide.'

There was a moment of panic when I wondered if he was right. I dredged back through my memory for a snapshot picture of Lizzie Bartholomew with her arm raised, a knife in her hand. There was nothing. And I hadn't seen Thomas before I found his body. I was certain I hadn't killed him. Almost.

'There was no knife,' I said quickly.

'Not by the time we got there, certainly.'

'I remembered stabbing the lad in Blyth.'

'You did,' he agreed. 'But it would have been hard not to. All those people pulling you off, the noise, the fuss. Do you remember it now? Properly? Everything that led up to it?'

I shut my eyes and lived through it again.

'Oh, yes,' I said as I opened my eyes. 'I do remember it properly. Everything. Not just stabbing him, but everything that led up to it. And I remember perfectly everything that happened today.'

I hoped he'd take me through it then, so I could get it over with. I could make a statement and get back to Jess. If they'd told her I was here, she'd be waiting outside. As she would if I was one of her junkies being bailed to her care. But Farrier seemed in no hurry to come to that.

'Remind me what happened in court that time. After you stuck the scissors in that lad from Blyth,' he said. He would know already, of course. Even if he couldn't remember, he'd have looked it up.

'Six months' probation,' I told him, playing the game.

'Ah, yes,' he said. 'After all, there were extenuating circumstances.'

He was talking about Nicky. My solicitor had made

a lot of that. I'd hated it. Not just reliving the experience in court, but hearing myself portrayed as victim.

Farrier looked at me, prompting me to continue.

'The probation order contained a condition that I
receive medical treatment.' I forced out the words.

He looked at me seriously. 'Did you? Receive
treatment?'

'Yes.'

'And it was helpful?' He leaned forward towards
me across the table, frowning slightly. I could almost
believe he was concerned, that it was my feelings he
was considering, not the paperwork involved in getting my medical records released before he charged
me.

'I suppose so.' I hesitated, teasing him, making
him wait for the information he really wanted, then
continued, unemotional, as if I were presenting a
report to a case conference at the unit. 'I saw a
consultant psychiatrist as an outpatient. I still see him
every month. I attended some classes – relaxation,
yoga. The doctor thought it might help if I went away
from the area for a while. I followed his advice and
took a holiday. Occasionally a community psychiatric
nurse comes to the house. We talk about how best to
manage my condition.'

'Which is?' His voice tailed off delicately, but I
knew he wouldn't let it go.

'I have a bipolar disorder.'

He continued to look at me and still the question
hung between us.

'Mood swings.' I paused again. 'Manic depressive
tendencies.' I knew there were only words, but they
hurt. I carried them round with me like a wound.

Manic depression is what real crazies have, like the mad woman on the bus.

'But treatable, surely?'

'With medication,' I said. 'Really it's almost miraculous.'

I held my breath and waited for a question which didn't come.

'Do they know what causes it?' As if he were genuinely and objectively interested.

'There's probably a genetic factor.' Bad blood, I thought. I expect my mother was mad too. That would explain a lot. I added, 'In my case it seems to have been triggered by stress.' I breathed regularly as Lisa, the community nurse, had taught me. 'Breathe through the fear,' she'd said. Then I looked straight at him. 'The incident at the secure unit, where I was working. It took longer than I'd expected to get over it.' I was proud that my voice stayed strong, though Nicky was in my head, smiling.

'I know,' he said kindly. 'A bad business.'

We looked at each other for a moment in silence.

'This medication . . . You have been taking it regularly?'

Sod it, I thought. He's been talking to Jess.

'Sure,' I said. 'I mean, why wouldn't I? Some days I forget, but mostly yeah, of course I take it.'

I had stopped in Morocco. The prescription had run out and I couldn't face the hassle of finding an English-speaking doctor to renew it. Then there'd been the experience at the palmery and I'd thought, If this is madness, give me more of it. I'd felt alive. I'd thought, I don't want a bland, twilight world. I can put up with the lows if I can get these highs. I'd thought I was cured. I'd survived for more than twenty years without drugs. I didn't need them.

'We can check,' he said mildly.

The thin-lipped woman was looking at me as if I were an unpredictable dog who should be wearing a muzzle. I had an almost overwhelming urge to live up to her prejudice and smack her. I ignored Farrier's comment and leaned back in my chair. My hands were clasped together on the table. They were blood-less and white.

'I could use some coffee.' Farrier nodded towards the sergeant.

She got up reluctantly and left the room.

'Tell me about Thomas Mariner,' he said later, when the DS had returned with a tray and the tape machine was listening again.

The coffee came in polystyrene cups and, although it wasn't as nasty as I'd expected, it had an aftertaste of plastic. Miles had brought biscuits. I dipped a digestive into the hot liquid and nibbled it. It was delicious, sweet and nutty, and for that moment it was more important to enjoy it than to answer the question. Farrier seemed to understand that, because he waited patiently.

'Why were you visiting Thomas Mariner?' he prompted at last.

I didn't really want to tell him. It wasn't anything to do with confidentiality. It wasn't as if I had a professional reputation to think of. I'd lost that when I stuck a pair of scissors in a homeless lad's arm. It's just that in my experience it's usually safer to keep the police in the dark. The more you tell them, the more ammunition you give them for later. Information which might seem harmless at the time comes back to haunt you. Then I looked up at Farrier and suddenly I'd had enough of being there. I just wanted to get out. I wanted to be home, sitting on the sofa in Jess's front room, drinking cocoa and watching a crappy soap on the television.

'It was work, sort of,' I said.

'Social work?'

'Not really.'

And then I told him. I didn't go into details about my relationship with Philip, but I gave him the rest – the letter from Stuart Howdon, the funeral at Wintry-law, the commission to trace Philip's illegitimate son. He wrote it all down. Occasionally he interrupted to ask for details, gently, so at the time I didn't realize he wanted to test the consistency of my story.

'Where was the solicitor's office?'

'Morpeth, that street opposite the library.'

'And the date of the funeral?'

'It was 3 June. A Thursday.'

He seemed satisfied, jotted down a scribbled note, then looked up at me again.

'How did you find the boy?'

By that time I felt light-headed through having talked so much. I don't like being the centre of attention. Showing off has never really been my thing. Sitting there with both of them staring at me made me feel strange. I wanted to put my hands over my eyes and pretend I was on my own.

'Go on,' Farrier said kindly. 'Take your time.'

So I explained about talking to Thomas's grandmother, and Kay Laing, and going to the hostel in Whitley Bay. I didn't tell him the lies I'd told to get through the doors. Like I said, that sort of thing can come back to get you. And I didn't mention Ronnie Laing. I'm not sure why.

'Dan Meech, one of the residential workers in the hostel, gave me Thomas's new address.' I looked up at Farrier bleakly. 'I thought I'd been really clever. A brilliant piece of investigation.'

'You should consider a career with the police.' Of course he didn't mean it.

'Do you think I could have caused his death. Indirectly, I mean? I didn't set out to. But could I have stirred something up with my poking around?'

He smiled again. He had a lovely smile. I wondered if he was a father, if his kids knew how lucky they were. 'Nah,' he said. 'Shouldn't think so for a minute.'

'Do you believe me, then?'

'Well, it's a helluva story to make up.' He stood up and beckoned for Miles to follow him. 'Wait there for a tick.' At the door he gave a bit of a wink. 'We won't be long.'

The uniformed policewoman who came in to sit with me brought more coffee and a plateful of biscuits. I think they were probably Farrier's idea too. He was longer than I expected and I was starting to feel twitchy again when he came back in. I half stood in my seat, thinking they'd let me go immediately, but he returned to his chair on the other side of the table. He looked troubled, slightly puzzled. It could have been an act, but I didn't think so. Miles wasn't with him and he asked the policewoman to stay. She must have given her name for the machine but I don't remember.

121

ANN CLEEVES

'Is there anything about that story you'd like to change?' he asked.

'No.' I didn't get any sense of danger. I was tired. My concentration had gone.

'I've just spoken to Mr Howdon. That letter he sent, asking you to meet him after the funeral, did you keep it?'

I'd had it with me when I went to Wintrylaw. I'd shown it to Howdon in his office, as a proof of identification, before he started explaining about Philip, but afterwards he had held on to it. I felt exhausted, too tired to explain all that, so I just shook my head.

'No matter.' Farrier still sounded cheerful to me. 'The bank will have the details of the cheque you paid into your account.'

'It wasn't a cheque. It was cash. There'll be a record of that.'

'Not quite the same though, is it? It could have come from anywhere. And it seems a bit odd. A respectable solicitor carrying round a bundle of used tenners.'

'Twenties,' I said. 'And fifties.' At last his scepticism cut through my apathy. 'What's going on?'

'Mr Howdon . . .' He paused, and I could hear the quotation marks. '. . . doesn't recollect meeting you after Mr Samson's funeral. He doesn't think you were there even.'

Chapter Fifteen

They decided to let me go in the end, though I could tell Miles didn't like it. Even walking to get bailed by the custody sergeant, I was still trying to persuade Farrier that I'd been telling the truth.

'There was a receptionist at Howdon's office. Show her my photo. She'll know me.'

'Perhaps.'

But I could tell he didn't hold out much hope. Nor did I. She worked for Howdon, didn't she? She'd do as she was told.

He felt sorry for me. Like the bystanders that day in Blyth, he thought I was a nutter. He felt a bit foolish because he'd been taken in by my story, but, as I've said, he was a kind man. He suggested I make an urgent appointment to see my psychiatrist. 'No trekking in the Atlas Mountains this time, though, pet, whatever he says. You mustn't leave the country.'

I nearly told him about the feeling I'd had in Delaval that I was being followed. It was possible that there was someone else in Isabella Street that morning. But I couldn't. All I'd had was a sense of being watched. Glimpses of shadows. He couldn't take that seriously and nor could I.

Jess was waiting for me by the front desk. I'd been

bailed to stay at her house. She didn't see me immediately. She was sitting on a padded bench which ran along one wall, staring ahead of her. Not reading or knitting, just sitting, as if sitting was an active pastime in its own right. She was making a statement and she wasn't going anywhere. Then she saw me and she opened her arms wide.

'Eh, bonny lass,' she said. 'Fancy stumbling on something dreadful like that.' To show me and the officers with me that she didn't believe for a minute I was capable of hurting a fly. She never believed any of her lodgers were guilty of the crimes they were charged with, but it was still comforting. She pulled me onto the seat beside her and gave me a hug. I wanted to cry, but I'd save that for later. We stood up together and walked out to the car park, where Ray was waiting patiently in the van.

As we joined the Spine Road a big brown cloud covered the setting sun and the light seeped out from behind.

'I've asked Lisa to pop in,' Jess said casually. So she intended to treat me as an invalid, not a murderer.

'Jess, man, it's eight in the evening. She'll want to be out.'

Lisa was a party animal. Her idea of business wear was a short leather skirt and fishnet tights, a skimpy cardie which left nothing to the imagination, and a jacket on top to make her look professional. Often she turned up on a visit with a hangover. She'd done a stint attached to the drug and alcohol abuse clinic. 'I know,' she said, when I'd pointed out there might be a tad of hypocrisy in her position. 'I met a couple of patients in the Bigg Market the other weekend and I was in a worse state than they were.' She'd been brought up in Ashington, had one of those accents which pinpoint where you were born to a couple of streets. During our first session she'd invited me to talk about my family. 'After all,' she'd said, 'our parents are always with us.' When I'd explained that mine very certainly weren't, she choked with laughter over one of Jess's milky coffees and apologized for not having read my notes properly. After that we'd got on fine.

'She was on call anyway,' Jess said. The three of us were squashed in the front of the van, with Jess in the middle, and I felt her tense. 'Humour me, eh, pet? I feel the responsibility, you know. I'd rather have a professional give you the once-over.'

Ray dropped us in the back lane. He wouldn't come in. He muttered something about his neighbour's ballcock, but I suspect all the talk of madness was making him feel uncomfortable.

A couple of lodgers were sprawled in front of the telly in the front room. You could tell their minds weren't on the programme. They'd stayed in especially to find out what had happened with the police. Murder was well outside their league and I sensed a new respect. They were probably disappointed that I was there at all. It would have been much more dramatic if I'd been arrested. Jess got rid of them, bribed them probably with a couple of quid each to spend in the club. Then we sat looking at each other.

'I spoke to that Mr Farrier,' she said. 'He doesn't think you did it.'

'No? You could have fooled me.'

She ignored the interruption. 'Not possible, he said. Time-wise. The boy wasn't long dead when you found him. Mrs Russo remembered you in the ice-cream shop. You were sitting there like a wet week-end, she said. Apparently. Then there was that lassie that let you into the house and went up with you. She went in first, didn't she? She swears you couldn't have killed him then. So when could you have done it? And what did you do with the knife?'

'I was at the house earlier. No one was in, but I could have done it then and got rid of the knife.'

'No,' she said. 'You were too long in the ice-cream shop. And why would you go back to the house if you'd killed the lad?'

She stared at me. A challenge to be rational. I wondered how she'd got all that out of Farrier. Why had he given away the information? She went on, 'What *were* you doing there, anyway?' So that was it. He'd asked her to find out.

I gave her exactly the same story as I'd given the police. 'But Farrier doesn't believe I'd been asked to trace Thomas. He won't accept that's why I was there. He thinks I'm crazy. Or lying.' I paused. 'Did I show you the letter from the solicitor, Jess? The one telling me about the funeral at Wintrylaw?'

She shook her head slowly. 'Sorry, pet. I never did see it. You were outside, do you remember, when the postie came. But of course there was a funeral. Why else would you get Ray to take you all that way up the coast? You'd never heard of the place before, had you?'

That was true. Philip had never mentioned it.

Outside in the lane there was the sound of a car

being driven too quickly, the painful squeal of brakes. Lisa had arrived.

'That lass'll kill herself one day,' Jess said automatically. It was what she always said. She caught my eye and gave an awkward grin to show she realized she was repeating herself, then stood up to let Lisa into the house.

Tonight Lisa was in casual mode: jeans which seemed moulded to her backside, a sleeveless top and nothing else apparently except short shiny boots with big heels. Jess very obviously left us alone. She said I must be starving – she knew she was – and she'd sort out some food. Lisa seemed to have skipped that part of her training which emphasized the need for a non-judgemental approach, for tact and discretion.

'What's been going on, then?' she demanded. 'Jess says you've not been taking your pills.' Thanks Jess, I thought. Who else have you told? Perhaps you put a note in the Newbiggin parish magazine?

I explained how good I'd felt in Morocco, how I hadn't thought I needed them.

'You'll need them now.' No argument, no discussion.

'Maybe.'

'No maybe. It'll be a stressful time. Don't you think anyone walking into a room and finding what you did would be shocked? For Christ's sake, Lizzie, accept that you're human.'

'Could I have dreamt up my whole reason for being there?' I asked suddenly. 'I mean, could it be a symptom of the illness? Like the dreams and the flashbacks.'

'You've not been hearing voices too?' Jokey, but

she really wanted to know. 'Instructions down the telephone wire? Over the radio?'

I shook my head impatiently.

'Nah,' she said. 'You've a perfectly sound grasp on reality. You've enough on your plate without going down that road. Trust your own judgement, Lizzie. I believe you.' Then her pager bleeped and she said she was off to see someone more ill and less stubborn than me.

So I wasn't mad. Lisa said it, so it must be true. But if I wasn't mad, Stuart Howdon must be lying. Why would he do that? Did it mean he had killed Thomas? And that idea, that someone as fat and respectable as Stuart Howdon might have stabbed a teenage lad to death, was the craziest thought I'd had all day.

We ate in the kitchen. Soup cooked the day before and heated through. One of Jess's specials, made from neck of lamb and pearl barley, so thick a spoon would stand upright in it. Jess wanted to ask what Lisa had said and thought she was being tactful for not asking. In fact the silence was as dense as the broth, suffocating, so at last I said, 'Lisa doesn't think I'm mad.'

'Of course she doesn't, pet.'

It sounded as if she was humouring me. Like I was a kid. Maybe she wasn't. Maybe she meant it. But I lost my temper. All the tension of that day in the police station came streaming out of my mouth, all the crap of the last six months. I shouted as loud as I could, filth, words that I hadn't used since the kids' home because I knew Jess hated them, because I'd wanted to be different from the dumb-arse morons who couldn't speak without swearing. She sat there and took it, a gesture as active as her sitting and waiting in the police station. She didn't move. She just waited for me to stop. It took a long time, minutes that seemed like days, but at last the screams turned to sobs and she gathered me up in her arms and stroked my hair, pushing it behind my ear, away from my forehead.

'I'll be good,' I said. So who was the kid, then? 'I'll do what Lisa says.'

Then we opened a bottle of wine and sat together on the sofa, watching a soppy film, just as I'd imagined in the police station.

It must have been midnight when I went up to bed. It was comfortable on the sofa, dozing in front of the story with its impossible happy ending, and I couldn't quite face being on my own. Jess would have stayed up all night with me, but I knew she'd be tired. One of the lodgers had a New Deal job and she got up every morning to make sure he left the house in time for the bus.

In my room I'd gone beyond the need for sleep. I opened the window wide and looked out over the sea. There was a moon, not quite full, not quite perfectly round. I thought of Philip. Listening to the water stirring up the shingle, I allowed myself a self-indulgent rerun of the last night in Marrakech. At least he would never know how his son had died. I didn't believe in God and couldn't imagine them meeting up for a cosy chat in heaven.

I went over the events of the day, trying to make sense of them. Had Philip asked me to trace Thomas because he knew his son was in danger? Had he expected me to protect him? If so, I'd failed him big time.

Come on, Lizzie, dump the guilt. It was something Lisa would say in the sessions when we talked through the mistakes I'd made in the past. I could hear her voice now, persuasive, in my head.

But today I had more to be guilty about, another death on my conscience.

You can't take responsibility for all the crimes in the world. Another of Lisa's sayings. If I wasn't responsible for Thomas's death, who was? Who had stabbed and cut at him, then slipped into the street just before I'd arrived? Did it really matter? Why should I care?

I did care. I'd let Philip down. I couldn't let it go.

On the window-sill was a pile of papers, my unofficial in-tray: a tax return form still to be completed, bank statements, something complicated about the local authority pension, the latest sick note. And the letters Dan Meech had given me to deliver to Thomas. I'd forgotten to put them in my bag when I set out that morning. There were three of them. I lay them on the bed and tried to divine from the envelopes what they might contain.

The first was easy. It was a bank statement. I used the same bank and recognized the long white envelope and the return address on the back. The second was postmarked in Whitley Bay. The address was handwritten in spiky italics using a real fountain pen. The third had been typed, but it didn't look like a circular or junk mail. The address wasn't printed on one of those labels which spew out of a computer. Then I turned it over and saw a portcullis and a House of Commons stamp on the back. A letter from an MP. Most likely a response to an enquiry Thomas had raised. About what? Homelessness? Dysfunctional families?

I knew exactly what I should do with those letters. I should put them back on the window-sill and in the morning I should phone Mr Farrier and tell him about them. But I left them on the bed and stared at them, as if with enough concentration and willpower I could develop X-ray vision and see what they contained. I found myself calculating the chances that Dan Meech would tell Farrier he'd given them to me. Practically nil. Farrier would talk to Dan, of course. If I hadn't killed Thomas, the most likely suspect would be one of the kids from the hostel. They're unstable, the homeless. According to the cops. Capable of anything. But Dan has a memory like a sieve. He's famous for it. I'm surprised he recognized me that day in the street.

Then I thought, Well, I can give Farrier the bank statement. How interesting can that be? If Dan *does* remember giving me letters to deliver he won't remember how many. And at the same time I was thinking again, Why am I doing this? Why interfere? I promised Jess I'd be sensible. The only answer I could come up with was that I wanted to take some control. I hated the sensation of things happening to me.

I opened the handwritten note first. The envelope wasn't very firmly stuck. I slid my thumb under the flap and separated the gummed paper carefully, managing not to rip the envelope at all. If need be I could restick it and no one would ever know. Inside was a square of red card. Written on it in the same italics were a couple of lines:

I'm really sorry to have given you that grief. Can't we still be friends? I hope they forward this. Please forgive me.

No name at the top and no signature, but I thought it must be Nell, Thomas's girlfriend. There was no address for her, which was a bummer, but Dan Meech had mentioned her surname: Ravendale. The family might be in the phone book and it wasn't a common name. I scribbled *Ravendale* on the back of the card so I wouldn't forget it, then realized what I'd done. It would be impossible to hand the thing back to Farrier now without explaining that I'd opened it. Stupid. And why would I want to trace the girl anyway?

I opened the letter from the House of Commons without any attempt to keep the envelope intact. It was from our MP, a woman called Shona Murray, newly elected in a by-election. She had a reputation for being radical and honest, but then she was very new. I'd seen her once on *Question Time*. I remembered a lot of hair, wild in an untidy, untamed way, not as if some designer had spent hours with a comb and the mousse. I'm not sure what she'd said – pretty much the party line, I think – but she'd impressed me with her humour. She, or more probably her secretary, had written:

Dear Thomas
Thanks so much for the information. I do need of course to be certain of its accuracy before I can

use it. I'm sure you understand the responsibility of an MP in a situation like this.

The letter was laser-printed, but Shona Murray had signed it. The use of Thomas's first name seemed significant. Had there been a regular correspondence? Had they met?

I felt suddenly exhausted. It was too much to take in. I returned the letters and the unopened bank statement to the window-sill. A container ship was moving slowly towards Blyth docks. I didn't expect to sleep but lost consciousness immediately.

Chapter Sixteen

It's evening. I'm pacing a long corridor. There are pools of shadow where the security lights don't reach. No sound. The children are asleep.

Then, ahead of me, I see a boy. He seems to have appeared from nowhere. It's Nicky, a fifteen-year-old with a fine, drawn face and the pallor of a pensioner. I think of him as one of my successes and approach him without any sense of danger.

'Miss!' His voice is urgent. His eyes burn as if he's just woken up from a nightmare.

'Back to bed, Nicky. It's all right. We'll talk in the morning.'

I'm close enough to touch him. Nicky killed his grandmother. Recently I've persuaded him to speak about it. Everyone here has to confront their offending behaviour. The necessity of doing that is a fundamental belief, as essential as the belief in God in a monastery.

'Just a few words, Miss.'

That's when I see the knife. Was he holding it all the time? Behind his back perhaps? Through the white fingers I see the yellow handle.

'Nicky . . .'

But his arm is round my neck, choking me to silence, and the knife is pointed at my stomach.

He kicks open the door into his room and pulls me inside. We fall onto his bed like lovers, our legs tangled, his arm still around me.

He squirms free and sits over me. The point of the knife is held at my throat. He makes a sound, a bubble of excitement. In my head I scream to the mother I have never met to save me.

I woke with a start to a knock on the bedroom door. I knew immediately it wasn't going to be a good day, but it took a moment to remember why. Jess was standing in the doorway with a mug of tea in one hand. She'd never done that before, not even when I was ill. I'm not much of a tea drinker but it was a kind thought. She was looking harassed. She'd woken me up to talk. I hope she didn't notice the opened letters on the window-sill.

'The phone hasn't stopped ringing.'

'Farrier?' I knew he'd want to talk again.

'The press. Not just the *Journal*. Some from London.'

'Put on the answerphone.'

'But that'd make things worse, pet, wouldn't it? They'd just come round, camp out on the doorstep.'

'They'll do that anyway.'

'I don't think they will. Not now.'

She waited for me to sit up and handed me the mug. I took a sip. The tea was strong. I thought I could taste the enamel dissolving from my teeth.

'I lied,' she said. 'I told them you'd been trouble ever since you'd got here and I'd thrown you out. This was the last straw.' She paused so I could tell her how clever she'd been.

I obliged. 'You didn't!'

'Do you know, everyone believed me. Every single one.' She was indignant. 'As if I'd do a thing like that.'

I didn't tell her she was different from most land-ladies. I was miserable, ungracious and not in the mood for giving compliments. 'What else did you tell them?'

'That I thought you'd gone to stay in Heaton with an old friend from college.'

Heaton. Where Philip had grown up. Did his family still live there? Was there another set of grand-parents for Thomas?

Jess must have said something, but I was so wrapped up in my thoughts that I didn't hear her. When I came round she was looking at me, concerned. She's not a daydreamer, doesn't understand it. I made a show of reaching over to the bedside table, shaking a couple of pills from a little brown bottle and taking them with the last of the tea. She didn't say anything but she left the room beaming.

I started phoning Stuart Howdon's office at nine o'clock. The woman who answered wasn't the recep-tionist I'd met there after Philip's funeral. This person was older and she had a Scottish accent.

'Oh, he isn't in the office yet,' she said, as if I was mad to expect it.

He must have arrived by the time I rang at ten, because the response was different, if just as chilly.

'Who should I say is calling?'

I gave my name without thinking. A mistake. 'I'm sorry, Ms Bartholomew, he'll be in a meeting all day.'

I wanted to go to Morpeth and drag him out of his meeting, but Jess persuaded me not to.

'Leave it to Mr Farrier, pet. It's his job. He knows what he's doing.'

I wished I could believe her, but Farrier was convinced I was guilty. He just didn't have enough evidence to keep me in custody.

At lunchtime Dan Meech turned up on the doorstep. He'd tried to phone, but Jess had given him the same story. He hadn't been taken in by it. He was carrying a bunch of flowers, as if I was an invalid or the one who had died. As if there'd been an accident and he wanted to mark the spot.

'The press have been to Absalom House too,' he said. 'Daft bastards. They've been handing out money to the residents in return for a story about Thomas. Of course they'll get a story that way. It'll probably be a fairy tale, but what do they care? I shouldn't stay long. Ellen's on her own there, fighting them off.'

I waited for him to mention the mail he'd asked me to deliver to Thomas, but he didn't bring it up. Not then or later. Unless the police specifically asked him, I didn't think he would.

'It was kind of you to come,' I said.

It *was* kind, but it was weird too. We'd been close at one time but not recently, and he'd never much cared about my feelings. I wondered if a ghoulish curiosity had brought him. Like the readers of the journalists who were pestering us both, perhaps he wanted the details. To know just *how* much blood there'd been. A description of the scene in close up and Technicolor. He looked awkward and embarrassed when I repeated 'very kind', so I thought I was right.

But he added quickly, 'It's Nell.'

'What about her?'

'She wants to speak to you.'

'Why?'

'She's got it into her head that you spoke to Thomas before he died.'

I couldn't take it in. It was as if he were accusing me of murder. I felt I had to defend myself. 'He was dead when I arrived at the house. There was someone with me who can confirm . . .'

'No.' He almost shouted the interruption, realizing too late how I'd taken the words. 'Not like that. Of course not. She thinks you might have phoned him to make an appointment to visit. Or met him on a previous occasion.'

'Well, I didn't.'

'Could you tell her that?'

'What?' The question was pitched louder than his interruption.

'She's out of her mind. She won't take it from me.'

'She's a bit young for you, Dan, isn't she?' It was a snide remark, intended only to hurt, but he coloured, twisted the flowers in his hands, scattering petals. I took them from him, set them on the kitchen bench and invited him in.

'Is that what the row between Nell and Thomas was about?' I asked carefully. 'You?'

'He didn't know it was me. Nell told him she'd met another man. Someone older. He didn't take it very well.'

'I wonder why.' I was amazed that Dan could be so crass. Thomas had been dumped by everyone he'd ever cared about. 'Is that why he moved up to Delaval?'

'One of the reasons. If he'd still been going out with Nell he'd probably have hung around.'

He looked up and saw my face, gave a melodramatic shrug, a gesture to slide off any trace of responsibility. 'I thought he'd get over it. People do. How was I to know that he'd die when he was still angry, before Nell had a chance to make things up with him?'

It was very similar to the tone he'd used with me when we were still in college. *Hey Lizzie, I didn't know you felt like that. How could I realize you'd take it seriously? We're mates, right. It was a bit of fun.*

As an actor, I thought again, he had a limited range. No wonder he'd had to find a day job.

There was a pause. In the distance I could hear Jess hoovering the upstairs rooms. I sat, refusing to break the silence.

'I could take you now,' he said. 'Nell hasn't gone into school today. I've borrowed Ellen's car.' Suddenly his voice went flat and bleak. 'Please, Lizzie. You don't know the state she's in. I can't go back without you.'

I considered him suspiciously. Was he better, after all, than I'd realized? A bit hammy but with more emotional tone than I'd given him credit for? Then I thought none of that mattered. If I went it wouldn't be for Dan. It would be for the girl. She'd be blaming herself and me and Dan and her parents. Everyone except the person with the knife. And what else did I have to do? I stuck the flowers in a milk jug and left a note for Jess on the table. She'd only have tried to stop me. I closed the kitchen door quietly behind me, but I didn't think she'd hear anyway, above the hoover. Dan drove to Whitley Bay in silence, which meant either that he really cared for this girl or that he had more sense than to be triumphalist.

Nell's family had a house in one of the streets parallel to that where the Laings lived. Presumably Dan had been on his way there when we'd met the week before. It was on a corner, detached, mellow brick with ivy growing up the side, a more modern extension built on the back. At the gate I stopped, blocking the path, so Dan had to listen to me.

'How did you know I'd found the body?'

'Radio Newcastle.'

'I was named?'

He nodded. 'A twenty-five-year-old social worker.'

Oh, well, I thought, it could have been worse. Farrier could have added, 'Who's currently on sick leave following a mental breakdown.' I'd always thought he was decent.

I stepped aside and let Dan past. He led me round the back of the house and opened a door in the flat-roofed extension. I expected to step into a kitchen, but this was Nell's room, a cross between an artist's garret and the *Blue Peter* studio. Everywhere was colour. One wall was orange, with Pollock-like splashes in red and brown, another was washed deep blue fading into lilac. On that body parts had been printed in black gloss – not just the handprints you see in nursery schools, but feet, arms, buttocks and some smudgy marks which were probably tits. There was a big window looking out over the garden. A long trestle table had been built beneath it. Below the trestle were sets of drawers on castors, baskets with brushes and tubes of paint; beside it, a couple of high stools. Everything was messy and chaotic. The tubes of oil paint had tops missing. On the opposite wall was a sink. More brushes stood in jars of white spirit on the draining board. On the floor were piles of paper. I saw some pencil drawings which made me think for the first time that Nell was more than a spoilt brat who didn't look after her things. In one corner a construction was under way, involving chicken wire and plaster. Perhaps it was finished and making a statement about impermanence, but I don't think so. There were splashes of plaster on the floor and they still looked wet.

Nell could have been another installation. She was curled on a huge purple cushion on the floor. There was more plaster on her hair and her jersey. When she heard us come in she sat up.

'This is Lizzie,' Dan said.

We stared at each other.

'Look, coffee, yeah?'

He ran away through an internal door. He seemed very at home in the house. I presumed Nell's parents were at work. Left alone, we continued to stare at each other.

She was very small and dark. Black hair, which I don't think had been dyed, chopped in a jagged cut around her ears. A little face. Dark eyes made even bigger by the panda shadows which surrounded them. Even as she was sitting, cross-legged, I could tell she had that dancer's grace which Dan always went for.

'You found him,' she said.

I nodded. There were no chairs, and no way would I sit on the floor with all the crap. I was wearing a decent pair of trousers you could only dry-clean. I pulled out one of the stools, dusted it with my sleeve while my back was to her and sat on that.

'I'm not sure why you want to see me,' I said. 'He was dead when I got there. There's nothing I can tell you.'

'You must have spoken to him to arrange the visit. I want to know how he was. If he was OK, perhaps I won't feel so bad. Now I just remember how I betrayed him.'

I know all adolescents are intense. I'd been intense myself in my search for justice, my mother and the great Newbiggin dream, but no one had ever looked at me before with such haunted and piercing eyes.

'No.'

'What did you want to see him for?'

I could have lied, but I didn't see the point any more. The only people I'd have any qualms about hurting or offending were already dead. I told her the whole story. 'My problem now is that the solicitor claims never to have heard of me. It makes my position a little . . .' I hesitated '. . . uncomfortable.'

'The police think you might have killed Thomas?'

I nodded again.

'That's ridiculous.' She was scathing. 'Why would you?'

I shrugged. 'I don't think they need to prove a motive.'

'At least I wrote to him,' she said. 'To apologize.

We'd had a dreadful row. At least he still knew I cared about him.'

I didn't say anything. No point in stirring that up either. I moved the conversation on quickly, thinking that Dan might come back any minute and the last thing I wanted was talk of letters.

'Did Thomas ever mention his father?'

'Not his real dad. He talked about Ronnie. His mum always wanted Thomas to call *him* Dad, but he never would.'

'What did he say about Ronnie?' I tried to keep my voice casual, but I knew it was important. The relationship between Ronnie and Thomas mattered in all this. It could explain why Kay had kicked him out of the house.

'Thomas *said* he despised Ronnie. He said Ronnie let Kay walk all over him.'

'But?'

'I'm not sure. He was pretty screwed up about the whole parent thing, you know.'

I knew.

'I mean, I think deep down he wanted Ronnie to like him.'

'Is that why Thomas started volunteering for a conservation charity? Ronnie's into the countryside too, isn't he?'

She looked at me. One of the nuns in the kids' home I'd been in when I was seven had looked at me like that. Appraising, judging. I'd thought she'd been able to tell exactly what I'd been thinking. It had scared me rigid.

'What do you know about that?' she asked.

'Only what Dan told me. That Thomas volunteered as a fund-raiser.'

'I didn't approve,' she said.

'Oh, Dan thought you'd introduced him to the charity.'

'I don't think of it as a charity. More a lobby group. Field sports. Hunting. Political, really. I was surprised when he went for it. He said I didn't understand. If I understood properly what was going on there, I'd approve.'

I remembered what Ray had said after my meeting with Ronnie Laing. 'Are you saying Thomas worked for the Countryside Consortium?'

'Only as a volunteer. Marcus organized it.'

When she spoke she opened her mouth wide. The words were very defined. An actor doing a voice exercise. Another drama queen. I thought she'd suit Dan fine.

'Marcus?'

'He worked for the Consortium in his gap year. We both knew him, though he wasn't at our school. I was surprised when Thomas got involved. He'd made fun of the whole thing at first. Ronnie was a supporter. That was enough to turn Thomas off. And he knew my feelings on the subject. But he seemed to get sucked in. When he started with them he didn't talk about it much. Like it could have been some secret society. Like it was some big deal and he was saving the world. He liked being mysterious.'

'Do you have an address for Marcus?'

'His father owned the house in Seaton Delaval. Thomas was living with him. I didn't realize until he died and the address was in the paper.'

144

She turned away, so I couldn't tell what she thought of that.

'What about his paid work at Harry Pool's? Did Thomas have any friends there?'

'Drinking mates,' she said. 'People to go to the pub with when they all finished on Friday nights. I never met any of them. Not my thing.'

'Did he enjoy work?'

'I think it embarrassed him. It was ordinary. Thomas always thought he would be famous. He talked about what he'd do if he got the chance – journalism, television, music.' She paused sadly. 'And now he's made the front page, he's not around to appreciate it.'

Dan came in then, clutching three mugs by the handles, spilling coffee on the way. He handed the first to Nell, carefully, and set mine on the trestle. He sat beside her on the dusty purple cushion, put his arm around her and held her close. She looked at me over his arm and she smiled, not a horrid smile but gentle, pitying, as if she was able to sense my jealousy and didn't want to hurt me.

'I should go,' I said. 'Jess will be worrying.'

He didn't move. That made me cross. I was only there because of him.

'You don't mind taking me, Dan, do you? Only I don't really want to wait for a bus.'

'Right.' He got reluctantly to his feet. What else could he do? 'If there's nothing else . . .'

He looked at Nell. I thought there was something else *I* wanted to ask. About Shona Murray, the MP, and what Thomas might have been writing to her about. But mention of an MP might trigger a memory of a House of Commons stamp on the back of a letter, so it would have to wait.

On the way back to Newbiggin he asked me what I thought of Nell.

'Bonny,' I said. 'She's really bonny.' It was true.

Chapter Seventeen

When I arrived back at Sea View, Jess was in the kitchen ironing. She always stood up to iron, her feet planted firmly apart, and she attacked the washing with the same sort of energy as if she'd been doing aerobics at the gym. I stood for a moment watching her, thinking about her and Ray and whether they'd get married, and Dan and Nell, and wondering if I'd ever have sex again with someone I cared about. Then Sally, the pensioner who lives on the estate round the corner, turned up with her shopping trolley of *News Post Leader*s. She's seventy-five if she's a day and our paper girl. Jess always makes her tea because we're about halfway through her round, and anyway she knows the old girl's lonely and it's an excuse for her to chat. Sally's a spinster and I wondered if she'd ever had sex at all.

I sat with them at the kitchen table, drinking tea and flicking through the paper while they gossiped about people I'd never met. The *Leader*'s a free sheet but there's usually plenty of local news in it. It's not all advertising features and car sales. Today there was a full page on Shona Murray, headlined 'A Day in the Life of Our MP'. A reporter had followed her round the constituency until she took the night train from

Newcastle to get to the House in time to vote on an education bill. According to the article she was specially interested in education because she'd been a lecturer in a sixth-form college before she joined Parliament. A lot of her shadowed day had been spent visiting schools.

I stood up and slipped out of the room, taking the newspaper with me. Jess and Sally seemed not to notice. They were talking about Jerry, the community policeman, and Sally's hairdresser, Trish. According to Sally, they were having an affair. There'd even been a passionate weekend away in a hotel in Scarborough. Sal might never have had sex, but she loved to talk about it.

I'd hidden Shona's letter to Thomas in my knicker drawer. Jess never came into my room without asking, but I hadn't wanted to take any risks. I pulled the letter out and read it again before turning my attention back to the article. It said that Miss Murray was holding her regular monthly surgery in Newbiggin Sports Centre the following evening. It wasn't necessary to make an appointment. When I returned the paper to the kitchen, Sally and Jess had moved on to the funeral of Mattie Watson, who used to keep the pub next to the post office. I'd never met Mattie, but by the time Sally went I felt I knew him as well as they did. If I'd had any relatives of my own he'd have felt like a favourite uncle.

When I got to the sports centre the next day, there were already half a dozen people in the queue ahead of me. I was the youngest by about thirty years. Shona was using one of the meeting rooms as an office and we sat in a corridor outside. I felt as if I were waiting

for a job interview, nervous and strangely competitive. I eyed up the other candidates, thinking that
none of them could have as interesting a reason to
see Shona as I did. A smart young woman who didn't
identify herself asked for my name. I gave it half
expecting a reaction, if not from her, then from the
listening people waiting – *Eh, aren't you that lass that
found the body in Delaval?* But there was nothing.
Thomas's murder was already old news.

'Shona's running a bit late,' the young woman said.
'The trains again.' Her voice was pleasant enough and
she flashed a smile, but she didn't look at me. I said I
didn't mind but she was still looking at the sheet of
paper in her hand and I'm not sure she heard.

I sat on an orange plastic chair of exactly the same
design as the one in the interview room at the police
station, took out my library book and got lost in a
Celtic dream world of a beautiful maiden and her
seven brothers who were turned into swans. OK, so I
like fantasy, right? I know it's sad, but it's harmless
and I don't care. When my name was called I looked
up and saw with a start that all my competitors had
disappeared. Even the young PA had gone. Shona
Murray had put her head round the door to call me. I
recognized the red hair from the television. She
seemed tired but she managed to smile and look at
me at the same time. Perhaps she was relieved I was
the only one left. I followed her into the room.

She didn't sit behind a desk but on a low easy
chair by a coffee table. When I went in she was
arranging her skirt around her. It was long and full
and already crumpled. She motioned for me to take a
seat beside her. I was reminded suddenly of my forced

therapy sessions with the elderly psychiatrist. The layout of the room was much the same. So was the initial question; each time it seemed he'd forgotten who I was and what I was there for.

'Well, what can I do for you?'

I'd always been tempted to give a flip reply: *Sign my sick note and tell the court I'm complying with the order*. I never had, though. In some situations you have to be prepared to go with the games. With Shona I wanted to play it reasonably straight. When she came out with the question I paused for a moment, then answered, 'I'm the person who found Thomas Mariner's body in Seaton Delaval.'

Her interest until then had been professional and courteous. I was aware now of something else. She was more alert.

'I read about it,' she said. 'It must have been terrible.'

'Had you ever met him?'

She didn't answer directly. 'He wasn't my constituent.'

I pushed it. 'But you *had* met him?'

'I visited Absalom House, the hostel where he was living.' She paused. 'It's an interest of mine. Young people who've dropped out of formal education.' She was more confident talking about herself than about Thomas.

'The police think I might be implicated in his murder.'

'And are you?' I admired that. She might have been talking to a murderer but she kept her cool. She didn't shout for her PA. If there was a panic button in the room she didn't go for it.

'No. I'd never met him.'

'I can't be seen to interfere with a police investigation. Not at this stage. That's what solicitors are for.'

I didn't say that in this case a solicitor was the problem.

'I realize that. That's not why I'm here.' *Except if I can find out who did kill Thomas it might let me off the hook.*

'Why, then?'

This was the part I had to embroider a bit. I could hardly admit to having opened Shona's letter to Thomas.

'Thomas had a girlfriend. She's young. Seventeen. They'd had a row and she didn't have time to make up with him, so she's feeling really wretched. She needs an explanation, you know? Some sort of closure.' It was American jargon at its worst but Shona seemed to accept it. 'She asked me to help. I'm a social worker.' It was true, wasn't it? Just because I was no longer practising ... 'She said that Thomas had written to you. She's got it into her head that it could have some sort of bearing.'

For a moment Shona sat very still. 'Any correspondence between a member of the public and me must be confidential.'

'Of course.' I held out my hands. *Look, this isn't me asking. I'm just a go-between.*

'But you would be able to tell the police?'

'Do the police know that Tom wrote to me?' The question was sharper than she'd intended.

'They don't trust me with that sort of information.'

She smiled again. 'No, I imagine not. And I imag-

ine your interest is more about getting them off your
back than helping Tom's girlfriend.'

I smiled back, but I was wondering why she didn't
want to go to the police. She hadn't refused to tell
them the details of the correspondence but I sensed
her reluctance. Surely she couldn't be involved in any
way with Thomas's death? I'd never believed in conspiracy theories.

'Did you know that he'd moved from Absalom
House?' I asked.

'No. Not until I read the report in the paper.' She
looked up at me. 'How were you involved with him?
Professionally?'

'He had problems with his mother and stepfather,
but, as I said, I never met him.'

'I only met him once.' She was speaking slowly.
'He made a big impression. Part of it was that he was
different from most of the lads there. Well spoken,
you know. He said his mum was a teacher. I wondered how he could have ended up there. But the
others were trying to show off in a loud, lippy sort of
way and he was quite cool. For someone so young, he
had style. And he seemed to take to me. The power
thing probably. People always think MPs have more
power than we actually do. It was an informal visit
and we had quite a long chat. I was trying to persuade
him to go back to college. His GCSEs weren't bad.
With a bit of support he'd have got a university place.'

I had a sudden weird thought. Thomas's social
worker could have placed him with Jess. She could
have worked the same magic with him as she had
with me. He wouldn't have had to show off, then. And
if he'd been living with us at Sea View, I'd have looked

after him. I'd have stopped him being murdered. It was ridiculous but the dream of that parallel universe made me feel more responsible for his death than I had all along.

Shona was continuing. 'He asked what the law was on whistle-blowing. Who should he go to for protection? That's what he said. He was very melodramatic, very mysterious. "If there's something worrying you, tell me now if you like," I said. But he wouldn't. "Not here. Not in Absalom House. You don't know who could be listening." The melodrama again. "Write to your MP, then," I said, and I remember writing down the name of the Tyneside MP on a scrap of paper. But he told me he didn't want to tell a middle-aged man. What could he understand?'

'So he wrote to you?'

'Yes,' she said. 'He wrote to me. He made allegations, but they were vague, imprecise. Nothing I could really use. I thought perhaps he was attention-seeking after all. Like all those other lads at the hostel. He just had a more sophisticated style.'

'So you didn't believe him?'

'Not all of it, certainly. Perhaps there was some truth hidden away in there. It was hard to tell. I needed proof before I could do anything.'

'Who was he writing about? Someone at work?'

'You don't really expect me to tell you.' Her tone was light but I could tell she was still thinking about the boy. He'd got to her. 'It took me a long time to reply,' she went on. 'I mean, he got an acknowledgement from my office saying I'd received his letter, but I was actually away on holiday and there was a mountain of stuff to get through before I got round to answering him. And it took me a while to remember him. I meet so many people. He probably never got my letter. It depends when he moved, I suppose. I sent it to the hostel. Perhaps he just thought I couldn't be bothered.'

'Will you still have the letter he sent to you?'

'Sure. It'll be on file somewhere.'

'You might want to show it to the police,' I said. 'Inspector Farrier in Blyth.'

'Sure,' she said again.

But she didn't write down the name and I wasn't convinced she'd actually do it.

Chapter Eighteen

Once Harry Pool's yard had held rail freight but the branch line had closed decades before and the area next to the derelict track had been turned into a small industrial estate. He had the biggest unit, the one nearest to the road. There was a high brick wall with spikes on top, iron gates painted buttercup yellow. The gates were open and I could see a warehouse with office space to one side and a couple of lorries parked up. They were yellow too, with *Harry's Haulage* painted in green on both sides.

All that was much as I'd expected. What I'd not expected was the group of people gathered just inside the gates. They weren't truck drivers and they didn't look much like potential customers either. There were about a dozen of them, enjoying the sunshine and a chat but just starting to get a bit impatient. From their clothes I'd have put them down as the well-meaning middle classes. They could even have been social workers. Until I saw the microphones, I thought they might be holding some sort of demonstration. Then I realized they were all from the press.

It hadn't occurred to me that Thomas's death would still be news, not of sufficient news value anyway to make all these people hang out at his employer's. Although it was irrational, I thought they might guess who I was. I imagined them chasing me down the street, asking me their questions, waving their microphones in my face. I was about to slip away and come back another time when Harry Pool appeared. A metal staircase led outside the building to a first-floor office. There was a platform at the top with a guard rail around it and he stood there, looking down on us. I recognized him from the photograph I'd seen at Archie Mariner's. He was a heavy man with the high colour which made me think he'd be a good bet for a heart attack.

The reporters stopped talking about their holiday plans and bitching about their bosses and shuffled to silence. I didn't have any sense that they were excited. This was routine. I joined the back of the crowd. No one took any notice. Harry leaned against the hand-rail and started talking. He had a loud voice which carried, despite the background noise of traffic in the street beyond the wall. He spoke clearly and briskly but, like the waiting journos, there was no engage-ment with his subject. He reminded me of an old-fashioned union leader, just before he was going to sell his membership down the river.

'As the regional representative of the Road Haul-age Association, I've called this news conference to remind the public of the plight of Mike Spicer, the lorry driver from Berwick, who's still being held in a Belgian prison.'

So, nothing to do with Thomas after all. He'd stumbled slightly over the driver's name. I thought perhaps Harry needed reminding about the facts too.

'Mr Spicer was accused of carrying illegal immigrants over the Belgian border. He has asserted from the moment of his arrest that he had no knowledge of the men's presence. He had complied with all relevant national and EU regulations. The seal around his load was intact when he checked it in Bucharest.'

A lass with an untidy perm waved her hand. Harry turned to her with a show of patience.

'Can you explain how the illegals got on board, then, Mr Pool?'

He gave her a disdainful look, as if to say that he'd been through this a dozen times before and if she'd been up to her job she'd have done some research beforehand.

'We think a ratchet strap was used. The wagon in question was a tautliner, which is put together in sections. The strap is strung around the cargo. As the strap is tightened by the ratchet, the sections are squeezed until a gap occurs, allowing access to the load without the seal being cut.'

You could tell that the lass didn't understand a word, and Harry didn't care whether she did or not. They were all going through the motions.

'This law-abiding citizen is being imprisoned for a crime he did not commit. We must maintain pressure on our politicians to fight for his release.' He looked around, daring someone else to interrupt, then nodded his appreciation when they remained silent. 'Thank you, ladies and gentlemen.'

He walked down the stairs towards them. The metal clanged with his weight at each footstep. I expected some of the reporters to approach him individually with further questions, but they'd lost interest already. They started to move to the cars which they'd left in the street. Harry walked past me to a plum-coloured Jag with a personalized number plate, parked with its nose to the warehouse. He drove off, waving to the few remaining people as he passed through the gates. Then the yard was empty.

I waited for a moment. Now I wasn't sure what to do. The plan had been to get into conversation with one of Thomas's mates, take him out at lunchtime and buy him a pint in return for a bit of gossip about the company. Clearly that wasn't going to work. There was no one here to approach. All the drivers seemed to be out. But there must be someone in the office. Harry Pool wouldn't have left the place without a body to answer the phone. I climbed the metal stairs, trying to keep the noise to a minimum, and knocked on the door.

'Yes?'

It was a grey-haired man who couldn't be far from retirement. He wore glasses which had slid to the end of a thin nose. He looked at me over them. It was a look of appreciation. He didn't get many young women knocking at his door. His eyes moved greedily over my body before resting back on my face. He saw I knew what he was up to and seemed a bit sheepish. He was a sleaze-bag, but a sleaze-bag with some decency.

'I wondered if I could speak to you.' I was wearing a short skirt. I sat where he could see my legs. Although I say it myself, they were looking good, still honey-coloured from the remains of the tan.

'How can I help you?' I knew already that I'd made his day.

'I was here for the news conference, but I could really do with some more background.'

'I don't know. Mr Pool's not here.'

'Would it be possible to speak to you? I mean, I'd like to do a sympathetic feature but without a bit more information it won't be easy. And you seem responsible for the day-to-day stuff.' This role of reporter was coming to be second nature.

He sat at a crowded desk, one of two pushed together. There were piles of paper everywhere. A closed door led to another office. I guessed that belonged to Harry. He'd want his own space.

'What do you want to know, like?'

'I suppose the everyday details. I mean, that's what brings an article to life. I'd like my readers to understand the pressures which might lead to *some* companies breaking the law.'

The phone rang before he could answer. It was a customer wanting a rushed load of children's clothing to be delivered to Aberdeen. As my friend sorted it out I looked at him admiringly, as if I couldn't help but be impressed by his efficiency. When he replaced the receiver he leaned across the desk and held out his hand.

'Kenny Baxter,' he said. 'Now, how exactly can I help you?'

I didn't give my name. 'Just tell me about Pool's company, about what goes on here. If you have time to talk, of course.'

'This is always a quiet period, once the first loads have gone out. There might be some interruptions, mind. I'm here on my own.' He lowered his voice.

'That lad who was killed by druggies in Delaval worked here. I'm having to do his job as well as my own.'

'No! What was he like?'

'He was canny enough.' His voice was wary and I could tell any more questions about Thomas would raise his suspicions.

'It must have been dreadful.'

He nodded seriously and he started talking. An hour later I was still there, and I knew of more scams which went on in the transport business than you'd have thought possible. But throughout it all Kenny insisted that none of that went on at Pool's. Harry was always legit. He was famous for it.

Kenny talked with the passion of the enthusiast. This could have been his hobby, not his work. You had the impression that he'd be here at eight every morning even if he weren't being paid for it. I envied him. I'd felt like that about the secure unit.

'What you have to realize – this is a competitive business,' he said. He didn't have any teeth at the side of his mouth and he spoke with a sucking noise. 'And there's a lot of cowboys. Owner-drivers, like. No one looking over their shoulders to see if they're keeping within the rules. Not like I keep an eye on the lads. If the ministry inspectors come here, they know it's all shipshape.'

And despite the piles of paper and the mucky coffee mugs, it did seem as if there was an order to his chaos. He showed me his system in loving detail. 'These here are the vehicle defect forms.' He pulled a floppy book of forms from a drawer. 'Every shift the driver has to fill out one of these before he starts. Not

just if he finds a defect, either. That's what happens
in some places. Not here. It's every shift. Then there
are the tachographs.'

'The spy in the cab,' I said.

'The lads can't drive for more than four and a half
hours without a break.' Obviously he didn't think my
interruption worth mentioning. 'And not more than
nine hours in a day. Or if they do they have to make
up the rest time later.'

'Isn't it possible to fiddle them?'

'They can try,' he said grimly.

'Would you always be able to tell?'

'It'd have to be good to get past me.' He paused.
'But I can see the temptation. Especially on the international runs. You're always boat-chasing. If you miss
your boat, it can throw out your schedule by hours.'

'I wondered why truck drivers are so bloody
impatient.' It was supposed to be a joke, but he wasn't
amused.

'There's a speed limit,' he said. 'Enforceable.' He
paused before admitting, 'But sometimes they de-fuse
the speed limiters.'

'So the lorries can go faster?' I wanted him to
know I was interested. I *was* interested. I'd been
intimidated like everyone else in a small car by trucks
thundering behind me at more than seventy miles an
hour.

'None of my lads would try it,' he broke in quickly.
'But you can see why people do. Like I said, there's a
lot of cowboys.'

I thought he was winding down, but he'd only just
started. It was as if he was the champion of the honest
haulier. Everyone else was on the make and the fiddle.

He took a moment to catch his breath and to take a mouthful of tea, which must have been long cold.

'Then there's fuel! How much a litre is diesel?' He was in full flow now and he didn't wait for an answer. 'Well, I'll tell you. Sixty-three pence *plus* VAT. But red diesel is thirty-two pence and you don't pay VAT on that. We buy red diesel for use in the yard, for the fork lifts and the machinery. You're not telling me that your cowboy doesn't use red diesel in his tanks.'

'The authorities must test for it,' I said tentatively. 'And if it's red . . .'

'Ah!' He was triumphant. 'But in Ireland it's green.'

'So?' I thought even a colour-blind inspector would be able to tell it was dodgy.

'It starts off as green, but you can filter out the dye by running it through fertilizer. It's smuggled across the Irish Sea.' His face was lit up by excitement. Like some Bible-bashing preacher, he was delighted by the extent of the wickedness involved. I'd met cops like him when I was young. Other people's depravity was a justification for their existence.

The phone rang again. A driver was stuck in a traffic jam on the M18. Could Kenny tell the customer he'd be late? I wondered cynically if the tachograph could tell the difference between a traffic jam and an illicit encounter with a lonely housewife nearer to home. When Kenny came off the phone I put the point, more tastefully, so as not to shock him. I had the impression he'd be easily shocked.

'Not the tachograph,' he answered with a straight face. 'But GPS – you know, satellite positioning. That would tell you. And Harry's talking about putting that in here soon.'

BURIAL OF GHOSTS

Before I could escape I had to hear again about how incorruptible Harry was.

'That's why they asked him to be RHA rep. He's got the reputation for being straight. And it pays off in the end. It's good for business. Must be. The customers know he'll play fair with them. They come back to him again and again. It's his reputation that's kept him afloat when the competition's going bust.'

I didn't know where Harry Pool was and I didn't want still to be sitting here when he returned. I didn't think he'd be taken in by my story as easily as Kenny.

Sitting in the bus on the way back to Newbiggin I went over everything Kenny had told me. There was certainly scope for a scam at Harry's Haulage, some illegal dealing for Thomas to discover and report to Shona Murray. But it must be clever to keep Kenny in the dark. I was sure he'd told me the truth as he saw it. If Pool *was* operating some elaborate fiddle, he had a lot to lose. His reputation was important to the business.

The bus was slow and gave me plenty of time to think. By the time I got back to Sea View I thought I wasn't the only person in the frame for Thomas's murder. If Farrier had me in for questioning again, I could put together a plausible case against Harry Pool too.

Chapter Nineteen

A day later I bought a car from Ronnie Laing. He phoned me at Jess's at nine in the morning. She was out and for a while I was tempted not to answer, but the caller was persistent and the noise was irritating. Jess was on her weekly trip to Asda. It was a social event. She met four mates there and ended up having fancy coffee and sticky buns with them in the café where once I'd been caught thieving.

So, eventually I picked up the phone and it was Ronnie Laing. I knew his voice at once.

'Hello, Lizzie. That is Lizzie . . .' His voiced tailed off nervously, leaving a question. I'd never given him my second name.

'Beswick,' I said. Jess's name. 'Lizzie Beswick.'

Why did I lie? I thought he might not have made the connection between me and the young woman who'd discovered his stepson's body. And I didn't want him to. The sensible thing would have been to put down the phone and to stay away from everyone who'd ever known Thomas Mariner. But I couldn't. I was too close to it and I couldn't see clearly. I continued briskly, 'How can I help you?'

'This is Mr Laing. From the garage on the coast

road. I think I might have found you a car. A little Peugeot. Diesel. Brilliant economy. Good price.'

He gave me the details. There was no stammer. Perhaps it was easier for him to speak on the phone. I found I was writing down the information on the notepad on the hall table; afterwards I couldn't remember what he'd told me and was glad of the notes. It seemed to me then that his voice changed. He stopped being a salesman. His tone was more confiding.

'Well?' he asked. 'Are you interested?' Perhaps he was just selling something else. Perhaps I'd got him all wrong and he was a more skilful salesman than I'd realized, more subtle.

'Yes.' I could hear a breathy nervousness, hoped he hadn't picked it up. 'Yes, really, I think that I might be.'

'I can bring it round to you if you like. Let you have a test drive.'

But I didn't want him knowing where I lived and we left it that I'd call round as soon as I could fix up a lift. When I replaced the receiver I was shaking, not just with nerves but with excitement. And what did that say about me?

I phoned Dan at the hostel, hoping to con a lift from him – he owed me a favour – but I got through to Ellen, who told me it was his day off. She brought up the subject of Thomas before I did. She'd recognized my voice.

'You must write a piece,' she said, confusing me for a moment. I'd forgotten I'd told her I was a journalist. 'How many young men have to die before something is done?'

Then I remembered her son had been attacked on the streets and had died too. Thomas's death must have brought all those memories back. She must have realized she sounded a bit crazy because she apologized. 'We're all on edge here. You must have seen about the boy who was killed in Seaton Delaval. He used to be one of our residents.'

'How terrible.' Trite and pathetic, but she seemed not to notice.

'I find it so hard to let them go anyway,' she said. 'I mean, I know they have to move on, be more independent, but I hate it. I worry so much for them. After this it will be a thousand times worse.' She paused. 'But can you imagine what his mother will be going through?'

For the first time since finding Thomas I tried to understand. How would you feel if a child you never wanted, who was always a nuisance, died? I decided guilt is what you'd feel. A searing explosion of guilt.

'Do you think I should go to see Mrs Laing?' Ellen asked. 'Or would that make things worse?'

I muttered something about not being in a position to give advice and replaced the phone before she could drag me any further into her distress. But I couldn't stop thinking about it and repeated Ellen's question to myself. Should *I* go to see Kay? If I did, what point would it serve? For me or for her? Before I came anywhere near an answer, Jess staggered in, the fingers on both hands white, where three carrier bags in each had cut off the blood supply. I wasn't expecting her back so soon. She'd caught an earlier bus than usual, missing out on the coffee and buns. Perhaps she thought it wasn't safe to leave me alone

for too long. She was starting to make me feel suffo-
cated. I understood what was going on. As Ellen had
said, it was hard to let go. But I was an adult and Jess
wasn't my mam. I needed to get away from her and
Sea View before I said something hurtful. I needed a
car.

We hadn't seen much of Ray since Thomas's
death. I don't think he and Jess had fallen out over
me. He was too besotted by her to do anything to
cause a disagreement. Perhaps he'd just felt he should
spend a bit more time running his business, otherwise
he'd go bankrupt and there'd be no cash then for visits
to folk clubs or trips into the hills.

'The bloke from the garage phoned,' I said to Jess.
She had her head in the larder, putting away the tins
of tuna and chopped tomatoes. 'He thinks he's found
me a car. I wondered if Ray would be free sometime
to give it the once-over.'

She was in a quandary then. She didn't want me
to have a car. If I had a car, who knew what other
scrapes I might get into? How many dead bodies
might I stumble across? But she wanted Ray and me
to get on. If he sorted me out a good deal, perhaps I'd
be grateful to him and I might not kick up too much
of a fuss if she moved him in.

'I'll give him a ring,' she said, emerging bum first
from the pantry. 'See how he's fixed. He's only working down at Sandy Bay. Put the kettle on, pet. He'll
probably fancy a brew when he gets here.'

No competition, then. Ray would win every time.
I'd got what I wanted and I still didn't like it.

It was a sunny day with a gusty wind, the sort of
day that makes schoolkids flighty and wild. As soon

as I was out of the house I had the urge to run. Along the beach and far up the coast, away from Jess and Ray and the neighbours across the lane who were peering out from behind their nets to see the lassie who was caught up with that murder case. But I didn't. I got into Ray's van and drove south with him towards the city, proving to Jess and myself that I was sane and well behaved.

When I got out at the garage Ronnie appeared at the office door immediately, as if he'd been waiting for me. I noticed again how small he was, then forgot it at once as he came closer. There was that smile and a handshake and I was hooked once more. A boy had died and I was a suspect in a murder inquiry but none of that mattered because a middle-aged man seemed to find me attractive. And at that moment I didn't even see anything wrong with it. I was an addict who'd had another hit.

It didn't occur to me then to wonder why he was at the garage in the first place. It was less than a week since his stepson had been stabbed. Even if he didn't care about Thomas, shouldn't he have been at home comforting his wife? All I could think of then was that I wanted to touch him again. I wanted to slide my hand from the back of his fingers to his wrist, then up the sleeve of his jacket, stroking the fine hair against the way it was lying. Which was sick, of course. He was a married man, old enough to be my father. But there was something about him which provoked that reaction. I would see it again with other women. Despite his apparent shyness, he had an energy which was contagious, which made the people who were with him feel more alive too. You could see it in the way he moved. He had a controlled power. You must have seen those slow-motion wildlife films on the telly, of wild cats moving across grassland. That's what he made me think of. He had a great body. Anyone would have been impressed by it. And I tell myself now that I was vulnerable, under stress, in need of comfort and reassurance.

He was speaking. 'I've already had one offer.'

I must have looked blank, stupid.

'For the car. I couldn't take it, of course. Not after having promised it to you.'

'Oh.' I managed a grin. 'Right.'

'You are still interested?'

'Sure.'

'I can take you out for a test drive if you like.'

I looked over to the office. I had supposed he must have someone else working for him. The garage was surely too big to run single-handed.

'I'm on my own this afternoon,' he said, as if he guessed my thoughts. It still didn't tell me how many people worked for him. 'It doesn't matter, though. I'll just lock up. To be honest, my heart's not really into selling today. There's been a death in the family.' He looked out across the busy dual carriageway as if he were lost in thought.

'I'm sorry.' I stepped back and tried to put a bit of distance between him and me so I could think more clearly. 'Look, I can always come back. There's no rush. If you'd just prefer to go home . . .'

'No,' he said quickly. 'I couldn't face that either. I'm better off here. I need to keep busy. It doesn't do to brood.'

'Was it someone close?'

169

For a moment I could almost believe I didn't know. I suppose that's what acting's all about. You have to believe yourself into the part. Perhaps that's where Dan goes wrong. I turned to listen to Ronnie, but a lorry rattling down the coast road blanked out his answer.

'Sorry?'

'My stepson,' he said. 'He was murdered. We weren't as close as I would have liked, but he didn't deserve that. He was only nineteen.'

I wanted to tell him that I'd found the body and that I'd known Thomas's natural father. It would have been something to connect us and a good story. But I didn't. Some impulse for self-preservation stopped me. The same impulse which made me refuse when Ronnie offered to drop me home after the test drive.

'If your dad wants to go,' he said, 'we can drive you all the way home in this. It'll give you a real feel for the car.'

The thought of Ray as my dad entertained me for a moment. I couldn't really imagine that he'd had a fling with a gypsy when he'd been a young man. But perhaps he had hidden depths. I didn't explain our relationship to Ronnie, though. The less he knew about me the better.

'Nah,' I said. 'I can't be that long. He'll not mind and besides he'll want to check it out before I part with my money.'

I explained to Ray what was happening and he settled down for the afternoon with his Ramblers' Association newsletter and his yowly music. If he resented not going back to work he didn't show it.

It was strange to be driving again. I'd always loved

it. It had come naturally to me. Something about the way the hands and the feet and the eyes all work together. It had been a symbol too of my new respectability because I'd done it properly. I paid for driving lessons from my first wages, bought a car from a mate of Jess's after having asked the RAC to report on it, got it an MOT and a tax disc before taking it onto the road. The kids from the home would have been horrified. Most of them had been driving since they were ten. That first car had taken me all over the county, places I'd only heard people talk about. On days off I'd go exploring, north as far as Berwick, inland to Wooler and Rothbury. A stomp along an empty beach or over the hill, then afternoon tea in a little caff. Brilliant.

I pulled out of Ronnie's garage and drove east towards the coast, thinking too hard at first about the gear changes, fumbling for the indicator though he'd told me where to find it. Soon it was coming automatically, no thought needed. He was right. It was a nice little car.

I hadn't intended to go very far, but we hit the end of the dual carriageway before I'd realized. There was a view of the sea, the wind blowing the waves into white spray and the spire of the big church on the front at Cullercoats. I remembered going to a carol concert there one Christmas with my primary school choir. Ronnie and I hadn't spoken all the way.

'Sorry,' I said. 'I didn't mean to come so far. I got carried away. I'll take us back now.'

'It's a shame about your dad.'

'What do you mean?'

'A day like this. You just feel like driving,' he

171

continued. His voice was suddenly angry, mirroring my thoughts and memories in a way that scared me. 'I mean out of the town. Away from all these people.'

'Yours is a strange business to be in,' I said, 'if you like open spaces. Didn't you ever want to do anything else? Live somewhere else?'

'I've responsibilities. A family to support. And I'm a countryman at heart. Country people need cars more than people who live in towns.'

I didn't know what to say, so I indicated at the roundabout to show I wanted to go back towards the city. He must have realized how intense he sounded, because he snapped suddenly back into salesman mode. 'You drive very well.'

'For a woman?' I wanted to lighten the mood too.

'I didn't say that. Most of the best drivers I know are women.' He paused. 'Why haven't you got a car now? Accident?'

'Nah,' I said. I was pleased that the conversation had taken a less threatening turn. 'Nothing like that. I've been abroad for a while. That's all.'

'You're very lucky. I've always wanted to travel. I managed a bit when I was younger. Now it's not so easy. Where did you go?'

'Morocco.'

'Really? A friend of mine said Morocco was his favourite place and he'd been all over. You might have heard of him. The gardener. Philip Samson.'

I was too shocked to say anything. At the time I couldn't take in the implication that Philip's world and Thomas's had met through Ronnie Laing. All I felt was another stab of loss.

Chapter Twenty

My first solo trip in the car was back to Wintrylaw. It was a compulsion. Something I'd been planning at the back of my mind since the interview with Farrier. My memory of Philip's funeral glittered, sharp and hard-edged as cut glass. I remembered the silhouette of Dickon wading out from the empty beach towards the horizon, Joanna's foot on the spade in the churchyard, Stuart Howdon's face as he mouthed the words of unfamiliar hymns in the little dusty church. But according to Farrier my memory was unreliable, tricked by the chemicals in the brain. I needed to check that the details of the place were as I imagined them, that the wild flowers in the wood, the house with the slate roof tiles and tall chimneys weren't a fiction I'd created.

I decided to take a picnic. That seemed enough to keep Jess off my back. Perhaps she thought a woman who took the trouble to make a pile of cheese and pickle sandwiches was unlikely to get into mischief. I couldn't see the logic myself, but it convinced her.

'Will you be back for your tea?' she asked. She was expecting Ray for the afternoon and I thought the question wasn't prompted so much by concern for me but because she wanted to know how long they'd have on their own together.

'No.' I was feeling generous. 'I'll stop on the coast somewhere. That place in Amble maybe. Get some fish and chips.'

I hadn't told her I was intending to go back to Wintrylaw, but she must have had some last-minute premonition that this wasn't just a day out because she shouted after me when I was halfway across the yard, 'Just take care.' Guilty, perhaps, because she'd put her enjoyment ahead of my safety for once.

It was a Saturday. The weather still and hot again, like the day of Philip's funeral, and it was probably the sunshine which had prompted me to make the trip. I couldn't expect Wintrylaw to match up to my memory in mist or rain. I'd started off in jeans and T-shirt but just before leaving went upstairs and changed into the white dress. It was loose around my hips and I thought I must have lost a little weight. It's good for the figure, being the suspect in a murder inquiry.

I wanted to find the back road into the estate, to take the secret, unused track between the stone pillars and through the wood. Ray would have pointed out the spot on the map but he still hadn't arrived and once the picnic was packed I wanted to be off. The map wouldn't mean much to me and I thought once I was in the area I'd recognize the landmarks – the overgrown hawthorn hedges and the way the trees came right down to the lane.

In the event I must have approached the house from a completely different direction. I suppose it was the road along which Howdon had driven me to

Morpeth, but we'd gone so quickly then that I'd not
taken in any features of the countryside. And on that
day the route had been deserted; all the other mourners had left before us. Today, the lane was packed
with traffic, all moving slowly in the same direction. I
followed a silver Range Rover, then turned a corner
and had to brake sharply behind it and a queue of
cars. There was nothing to do but wait and inch
forward with the flow. None of the other drivers
showed any curiosity about the hold-up. There was no
resentment. No blaring of horns. Almost there was a
carnival atmosphere. From my wound-down window
I heard distant music. In the Range Rover two little
girls were strapped in the back. They turned to wave
down at me. They had pink ribbons in their hair and
sparkly make-up. Even they seemed resigned to wait
patiently for the traffic to clear.

Eventually the cars began to move. We turned
another corner and there was a view of the house,
caught in full sunlight, framed on one side by the
church and on the other by trees. In my memory I
always saw it from another angle, but it was the same
place. A little shabbier and not quite so grand perhaps,
but don't we always enhance the pictures in our heads
over time? There was no fiction, here at least. I could
see now what had caused the queue: all the cars were
turning into the drive and at the gate stopped to pay
an entrance fee. Wintrylaw was hosting some sort of
event or open day. At least it provided an excuse for
my being there and wandering around the grounds. It
couldn't have worked out better.

As I approached the gate myself I realized it was
the church's summer fair. A notice painted onto a

piece of tarpaulin and strung across the drive explained it. *In aid of St Bede's roof repair. £5.00 per vehicle.* The woman collecting the money apologized for the steepness of the entrance fee. 'We were hoping to encourage car sharing. Joanna's idea. Philip was a great environmentalist. And it does include tea.'

She had cropped grey hair and was wearing a loose jacket of velvet patchwork, strangely exotic for the occasion. Her voice was familiar. I thought she was the elderly woman I'd heard discussing Philip's Cornish garden at the funeral. I drove on and was waved into a parking space by a teenage lad with a scowl and acne. He had a power complex and made me reverse and come in again close to the neighbouring car. So close that I had to squeeze out, holding the edge of my door. I didn't want chipped paint this soon. There was an immediate smell of crushed grass which took me back to school sports days and the Newcastle Hoppings, so I forgot the hassle with the teenage lad and felt like a kid again.

In Newbiggin, St Bartholomew's has a summer fair. They hold it in the primary school hall. There's a ten-pence entrance fee and the Brownies run a lucky dip with sweeties and pencils and lollipops as prizes. The other stalls play a variation on the theme of jumble – white elephant, bric-à-brac, toys and books. The Mothers' Union provides tea in plastic cups and fairy cakes with thick white icing and hundreds and thousands. I get dragged along by Jess because one of her Asda friends is Brown Owl. They're pleased if they make fifty quid.

This summer fair was in a different class. I stood for a moment to get my bearings and wondered if my

mind was playing tricks after all. It was as if I'd
wandered into one of those bizarre, dreamlike television ads which win all the media prizes. A sinister
white-faced man walked past on stilts. A woman in a
leotard and a bowler hat rode a mono-cycle down the
drive. The theme for the event was circus and everyone had bought into it. The two little girls from the
Range Rover were dressed in pink tutus and spangled
tights. They walked away from me, hand in hand with
their mother, who had a boa of pink feathers. The boy
with acne wore clown's trousers and braces. Everywhere there were acrobats and lion tamers and ring-
masters. I turned slowly, letting my skirt spin out,
taking it all in, impressed by the grandiose folly of
it, by the effort which had gone into creating the
spectacle.

Of course there were stalls. This was all about
raising money. But they were decorated with bunting
and they sold homemade sweets, plants and paintings.
This was a classy craft market with street theatre
thrown in. I wondered briefly if Dan was here, in one
of his disguises. It would be his sort of thing. Beside
me a band began to play. They were of all ages and
wore red waistcoats and red bow ties and played that
rumpy-tumpy, brassy music you get on a fairground.
I would have been glad to see Dan. Now I was here I
wasn't sure what I hoped to achieve, and the music
and the costumes were disturbing and left me disconnected. The cars kept coming and the crowds were
getting thicker. I walked past the stalls at random,
picking up objects every now and again to appear
interested, and to stave off the panic. There was a
milk jug with a blue luminous glaze which I'd have

ANN CLEEVES

liked to buy for Jess but I'd spent so much to get in
that I couldn't afford it.

They were serving teas in a large striped tent
shaped like a big top. I was making my way towards
it, thinking I would have my free tea then escape,
when I came to a stall run by the Countryside Consortium. They weren't selling anything, but they were
handing out leaflets, car stickers and helium-filled
balloons with SAVE OUR COUNTRYSIDE in big black letters. And they were recruiting members. That seemed
to be their main pitch. They were doing a roaring
trade too. While I waited, three people filled out forms
and cheques. I watched from a distance for a while. It
was possible that Ronnie was there. Perhaps he had
first met Philip at an event like this. Apart from an
interest in country affairs, I found it hard to think
what else they might have had in common. The
thought of bumping into him again made my heart
race. I told myself it was ridiculous, but it did no good.

After circling for a quarter of an hour I sauntered
over. I didn't think Ronnie was manning the stand,
but it was hard to be sure. The Consortium workers
all wore animal masks – shaped-paper cutouts held on
by elastic which hid the tops of their faces except for
their eyes. A bear peeled away from his position at
the back of the table and came to stand beside me. I
pretended not to notice him and studied a leaflet
about the importance of field sports to the traditional
English countryside.

'Can I help you with anything?' The voice was
young, well educated. I turned and looked at him. He
wore khaki shorts and a white polo shirt. Sandy hair
was caught up in the thin elastic of the mask, but I

couldn't get any impression of the shape of his face. His eyes were brown. I didn't think I'd know him again. Pinned to the shirt was a green badge – Marcus Tate, Volunteer. Marcus had shared a house with Thomas in Seaton Delaval. He'd worked for the Consortium during his gap year; now he was back, helping out. Filling a space left by Thomas? If he hadn't been murdered, would Thomas have been here, working in the house where his father had lived?

He was waiting for me to speak. 'Just curious.' I paused, then confessed, 'I'm a townie myself, actually. Interested but ignorant.'

'A lot of our members live in towns. Their support is vital.' He had the enthusiasm of the evangelical Christians who came to the door occasionally to convert me, though *they* didn't dress up as bears. Jess always invited them in and gave them tea, so I'd have noticed. I smiled encouragingly and waited for him to go on, but he was too clever to push it. 'The facts speak for themselves,' he said. 'Take the literature and come back if you're interested.'

'What would I be signing up to?'

'As much or as little involvement as you wanted. The membership fees support our work. We're grateful for that.' He smiled, acknowledging that the money was what they were after. His teeth were straight and even. 'Your membership buys certain privileges too – discounts at country house hotels, restaurants, camping shops, that sort of thing. Since foot and mouth, things have been tough for rural businesses. If you wanted a more active role – helping out on farms, supporting our research in a practical way – that would be welcome, but it's not a condition of joining.'

179

'And fund-raising?'

'Of course. Every charity is always on the scrounge. There's no obligation to dress up, though.' The smile again. 'And in fact we're very fortunate. We have a number of generous corporate sponsors.'

'Can I think about it?'

'Sure.' If he was disappointed he was too professional to show it.

'And you'll be here all afternoon?'

'No. I'll have done my stint soon. Someone else will be here to help you. Or if you'd rather . . .' He took one of the brochures I was holding and scribbled in the margin. 'That's my mobile number. If you have a credit card I can join you up over the phone.' His voice was insistent and it seemed an odd thing to suggest. I wondered if he knew who I was and wanted an excuse to talk to me without an audience. Someone else wanting ghoulish details about knives and blood. But how could he? There'd been no photograph with the newspaper reports of my discovery of Thomas's body and *I* wasn't wearing my name on a badge. Perhaps there was a competition among volunteers to see who could recruit most members. He could even have been on commission. There was another queue to get into the tea tent. When I looked round from my place in the line he'd gone, disappeared into the crowd.

Chapter Twenty-one

Although there was a queue to get into the tea tent, inside it was peaceful and ordered. No self-service or plastic beakers here. The canvas filtered the noise from outside and, after the glare of the afternoon sun, the light was hazy. I seemed to see the scene in soft focus, as if from a long way off. There were small tables covered with gingham cloths, a posy of flowers set in the centre of each. It could have been a tearoom in Harrogate, mid-week, locals only, if the waitresses hadn't been wearing fishnet tights and top hats. One of them approached me. She was plump and I thought she'd be stuck with the pattern of the net on her thighs for days.

'There's a seat over there if you don't mind sharing.'

She pointed to a table where a couple were in conversation. The woman was dressed as Pierrot in a quartered silk costume in pink and white. Her hair had been tied back from her face, which had been painted white too, with delicate black triangles above her eyes and a black teardrop on her cheek. It was Joanna Samson. I couldn't tell if her companion had dressed up for the occasion or not. He had on a tweed jacket in loud checks of various shades of brown and mustard. It was just what the owner of a tacky, provincial circus would have worn, but it could well have been Stuart Howdon's idea of casual weekend chic.

'That'll be fine,' I said.

When I approached the table Joanna gave me a look which could have been bemused half-recognition or a polite welcome to an intruding stranger. Howdon had his back to me and continued to talk. It was something about papers to be signed. His voice was hectoring. I remembered what Dickon had said about hating him. What hold could he have over Joanna? Why did she put up with his bullying?

'We'll need some sort of decision,' he said. 'Honestly, Jo, things can't go on as they are.'

Something about her face made him fall silent, but still he had his back to me.

'You don't mind if I join you?'

He hesitated for a moment – perhaps he recognized my voice – then he did turn and he shrugged an acceptance of the inevitable. He gave no sign that we'd ever met. He had some nerve.

It wasn't the place for a scene. Once I wouldn't have bothered about that. Now I wasn't up to telling a woman who'd been recently widowed that her husband's illegitimate son had been brutally murdered. Not in front of a crowd. I did wonder if the police had been to see her to discuss a possible link between Philip and Thomas, but it didn't seem likely. Farrier hadn't believed my story in the end and he was kind enough not to want to deliver that particular bombshell. Why cause her grief for nothing?

I drank tea and ate scones and jam. The conversation between Joanna and Howdon spluttered into self-conscious small talk about mutual friends and then about the preparations she'd been making for an exhibition of her work in Morpeth.

'You will come tonight, Stuart?' she said. She made her voice little-girl pleading. 'I know it's only Morpeth, but we've invited some of the nationals. I always get so nervous before a new show. Bring Marjorie if you like.'

'I wouldn't miss it for the world.'

'You are *such* a tremendous support.' She pushed back her chair and stood up, startling us both. 'I must go. I haven't seen Dickon since lunchtime. And there's so much to do.'

She walked out. There was a moment of silence in the tent as people watched her go. She was a celebrity. Everyone knew who she was. Howdon waited until the hum of conversation had resumed before leaving himself.

I found him by a stall selling toffee apples. The smell of caramelized sugar caught in the back of my throat, made my voice husky when I shouted.

'Mr Howdon!'

He hadn't expected me to follow. Had he thought I'd accept his refusal to recognize me and slink home without facing him? Anyway, I took him unawares.

'Yes?' He turned sharply and the ridiculous jacket flapped open. His paunch was large and fleshy.

'What are you playing at?' I kept my voice even but it was hard to keep control. I had an urge to kick out at the fleshy stomach. I wanted to wind him and break down his pretence. I wanted to make him cry.

'I'm sorry. Have we met?' He furrowed his forehead. The bushy eyebrows met in the middle.

183

'You know fine well we have!'

'I'm sorry, you'll have to remind me. My memory's dreadful. Age, my wife says.' He smiled jovially as if he expected me to appreciate the joke.

'Lizzie Bartholomew.'

'No, I'm afraid it doesn't mean anything.'

When I'd first met Howdon I'd dismissed him as an oaf, a besotted family retainer. Now his skill at this deception made him frightening. It really was hard not to believe he was telling the truth and I didn't know what to do. He stood there, as children galloped past to buy toffee apples, appearing to humour me, tilting his head forward politely to hear what I had to say. The only sign of discomfort was a sheen of sweat on his forehead, but it was a very hot day.

'We went to your office. For Christ's sake, I sat beside you at Philip's funeral.'

'You knew Philip?'

'Of course I did. I was only there because you wrote to me.' I was shouting. I knew it would do no good, but I couldn't help myself.

'I'm sorry, young lady. I'm afraid you're making a terrible mistake.'

He turned and walked off towards the house. It was only as I watched him bobbing through the crowd that I wondered if there was an intended threat in his final words. I suppose I could have chased after him, but I'm not sure even now what good that would have done. I stood and looked after him and felt as helpless as I'd ever done. I felt tears coming. I hate crying in public. It's pathetic and you look red-eyed and ugly, and people always think it's because you've been dumped. I had a horror of bumping into Joanna again too. If she saw me crying, I suspected she'd be sympathetic, and that would make things worse. People were starting to leave and already there was a queue of cars at the gate waiting to turn into the lane. I was too restless to sit and wait for the line to move. So I turned my back on the stalls and the kids with faces sticky with candy floss and the dressed-up parents, and set off towards the church.

When I got to the lich-gate I turned back. I couldn't see the garden with the stalls and the tents, but the fairground music, unbearably jolly, bubbled on. I thought the thick walls of the church would block it out. There I'd sit in the cool and the dark and sort things out. But when I turned the ring handle on the big arched door there was no movement. The building was locked.

I sat on the step in the full sunlight and shut my eyes. My head spun. It was like when you've been drinking. All afternoon and all evening, moving from bar to bar, shouting and laughing, never still for a moment. And when you finally lie down to sleep, the moving continues. We call it the whirling pits. Perhaps everyone does. It's like you're on one of those old-fashioned roundabouts in kids' playgrounds. The ones you scoot with one foot to get moving. That's how I felt sitting on the step of St Bede's. And in that moment I could believe again that Farrier was right, that the meeting with Howdon and the commission to trace Thomas, all that was a dream. I'd made it up in a drunken stupor and it was spinning round and round in my head.

'Hello.' A friendly voice. I opened my eyes. Dickon stood there, wonderfully normal in shorts and a striped T-shirt. No fancy dress.

'Hi.'

'You're the lady who was at Dad's funeral.'

'You remember that?'

'Of course. We met on the beach. You'd been to Morocco. You met Dad on a bus.'

The sunlight was full in my eyes, so I had to squint to look up at him. It meant that he was the only thing I could see sharply. Everything else was a fuzzy yellow background to his face.

'If someone came and asked you,' I said carefully, 'would you tell them I was here that day?'

'Which someone?'

I hesitated. 'The police.'

'Why would they want to know?' He was very serious. It was like talking to an adult. And you could tell he'd been brought up to respect the police. I'd have to remember that.

'I told them I was here and they don't believe me. It's not their fault. They need to check.'

'Like an alibi?' He was suddenly very excited. 'You want me to give you an alibi?'

'Yes.' I tried not to smile. If he thought I was laughing at him he'd be offended. 'Exactly like that.'

I considered telling him it was a secret, just between us, but it didn't seem right to ask him to keep stuff from his mother. Besides, that was me being paranoid. Whatever games Howdon was playing, he wouldn't put pressure on a little boy. Dickon stood there looking down at me, the halo of light still around him. Philip's other son. He was probably curious about what the police thought I'd done. I didn't want him to run off. I might start to believe I was imagining him as well.

'Have you had a good afternoon?' I asked. 'Or is it a pain having all those people in your house?'

He shrugged and looked over his shoulder, distracted by more exciting possibilities, the beach perhaps, a secret den. Living here, his childhood must be like those I'd read about in books – *Swallows and Amazons*, Enid Blyton. There would be adventures every day.

'I found a dead squirrel,' he said. 'I collect skulls. I need to boil it down, but they won't let me into the kitchen.'

'Is it a big collection?'

'I keep it in a suitcase under my bed. I'll show you sometime. There are wings too. And a tawny owl pellet.'

'I'd like that.' It was a lie of course, but he seemed pleased.

I took the foil-wrapped package out of my bag and offered him a cheese and pickle sandwich. He took it and sat on the step beside me.

'Did your dad have a friend called Ronnie?' I asked.

'Ronnie Laing?'

My mouth was full of bread. I nodded and waited for him to give more details in his own time. But he didn't have a chance to go on. The shadow of a figure was thrown from the gate towards us. We were both startled and looked up. It was Flora. She must have been playing in the band, though I hadn't noticed her there, because she was wearing the uniform waistcoat and bow tie. She looked older than she had at the funeral. The waistcoat was tight and she already had the figure of a young woman. Her long hair was plaited down her back. She walked towards us. Her face was pink from too much sun.

'There you are,' she said disapprovingly. 'I've been looking everywhere for you. Mummy wants you back at the house.'

'Why?'

'You did promise to help. It's the party to launch the exhibition tonight. You know how she gets.'

'Has the Fat Controller gone?' He looked at me. 'That was what Daddy called Mr Howdon.'

'I don't know.' She frowned. She didn't like him talking to me about family things. 'You'll have to come anyway.'

He stood up reluctantly, scattering crumbs and slivers of cheese.

She turned, knowing he would follow her, a young dictator. She hadn't acknowledged my existence with a glance or a nod. I might have been invisible. Dickon gave me a little wave and ran after her. She marched along the path, her long plait bouncing up and down, glinting silver, the newly developed bum swaying.

I stayed where I was. The sun had moved behind a tree and it was pleasantly cool. And my head was full of questions. If Philip really was a friend of Ronnie Laing, he must have heard of a stepson called Thomas Mariner. So why had he needed me to trace him? He could have asked Ronnie to make the introductions, or to give Howdon the information he was after. But that would have meant acknowledging Thomas as his son. Perhaps he wasn't ready to do that before he died. I longed for Philip still to be alive. I wanted him sitting beside me in the shadow of the church. I wanted his arm around my shoulder. Most of all I wanted an explanation of all this mess.

Chapter Twenty-two

I walked down to the beach to finish my picnic. The tide was higher than it had been when I'd first talked to Dickon, high enough for me to hear the water sucking back against the sand. Something happened to me there. A change of mood. The righteous indignation I'd felt about being pissed about by Howdon turned to fury. Lisa the nurse would have told me there was other stuff going on as well. Stuff about Nicky and not wanting to be a victim again. Perhaps I knew that even then, but it didn't make any difference. I was seething. I needed an acknowledgement from Howdon that he was playing games. I needed to take control. I sat on the empty beach and thought of revenge.

When I got back to the house all the visitors had gone. The big top was a heap of canvas and rope on the grass. The rubbish bins were overflowing. People were clearing up, but there was no one I recognized. A torn paper mask was all that was left of the Countryside Consortium stall.

Of course, I could have gone straight home. I'd given Jess and Ray long enough on their own. I tried the deep breathing that they tell you relieves stress. I tried to persuade myself that Howdon wasn't worth the hassle. But it didn't work and I didn't really want it to. I thought it was just as well I'd changed out of my jeans and was suitably dressed. It was years since I'd gate-crashed a party.

Joanna's exhibition was being held in a room over a café bar on the main street. The bar was one of those places which makes you believe you're in the Cotswolds or Hampstead, full of expat southerners with loud voices. I'd been there for a meal once with a couple of social workers. They weren't local either. One of them had written a play. Upstairs that day there'd been a poet reading and a woman playing a tenor sax. At the same time. We'd listened for a while, then we'd gone downstairs to eat. The menu had been chalked on a blackboard beside the bar, but I'd not been able to read it because two women had stood right in front of it, debating their choice of wine. Showing off. Performance art to compete with the poet. I'd been well behaved and only caused a minor scene.

I parked next to Safeway's and walked through an alley. A pack of adolescent girls prowled up the mid-dle of the street in search of a pub which would serve them. I checked my appearance in a shop window, pulled my fingers through my hair. There was a faint green stain on the back of the dress – seaweed from a rock or lichen from the church step. I hoped the lighting inside was dim. Otherwise I'd have to stand with my back to the wall.

Joanna had hired the whole place for her party. There was a young man with an open-necked shirt and a game-show host's smile collecting cards at the door.

'Oh, shit!' I said, putting my hand to my mouth. The arty middle classes like bad language. 'I didn't think about the invitation . . . Look, it's Lizzie, Lizzie Bartholomew. You can always check with Joanna. Or Stuart if he's here . . .' I smiled. My voice was ditzy, apologetic. *I'm a girlie. Decorative. I don't do organized.* And I don't want to brag, but you'd have sworn I was born south of Sunderland.

He smiled back. 'No problem. Drinks and canapés down here. The exhibition's upstairs.'

There was no natural light in the bar. It had an old-fashioned feel which I'd not noticed on my previous visit, candles in bottles, a natural-wood floor, cane chairs. Perhaps the décor had recently changed and rustic Mediterranean was in fashion again. It was so dark in there that I thought I could have gone topless without embarrassment. I hadn't needed to worry about the stain on my dress. A woman in jeans and a skimpy top stood in the light of the doorway carrying a tray of drinks. I took an orange juice. My anger didn't need fuelling with alcohol. The juice had that bitter aftertaste which meant it had come out of a long-life carton. Every expense spared.

I looked around for Howdon. I didn't have a game plan. I wanted to know what he was playing at. I wanted to see his face when I said, *Strange you don't remember me. Ask Dickon. He does.*

I walked to the end of the room. It was long and narrow. Everyone seemed to be smoking. As my eyes grew accustomed to the gloom, I picked out groups of people who seemed to be there for the free party, not the photos. The bar's usual Saturday night clientele. I wondered how many others the charmer on the door had let in without invitations. There was no sign of Joanna or Howdon. I set my glass on the bar and made my way upstairs.

The exhibition space was larger than I'd expected, much bigger certainly than the bar below. It must have spread over the neighbouring shops. Again the light was artificial. There were black blinds at the windows. The photographs were lit by a series of ceiling spots. And there were a lot of photographs. They hung on the walls and on freestanding screens which partitioned the room. I was impressed. I'm not sure what I'd been expecting. Not something this professional. A lad was standing at the top of the stairs. He handed me a folded sheet of printed paper, a catalogue or programme, with the titles numbered. It said which of the pictures were for sale and gave a list of prices which made me whistle under my breath. It said that a percentage of any profits would be donated to the Countryside Consortium. It didn't tell us how big a percentage.

The exhibition was called *A Landscape under Threat*, though as far as I could tell the specific nature of the threat wasn't explained. Despite myself, I got hooked into the images. I knew what I was there for but I found myself distracted. The pictures disturbed me. They were all in black and white. Some were enormous, huge landscapes with chiselled valleys. Some were little and the subjects were domestic – not in any sense family snaps, but they seemed as accessible as that.

There were a lot of people in the big room but they spoke in reverent whispers. If background music was playing, it was so faint that I couldn't hear it. The screens acted like the walls of a maze, guiding us through the room. Howdon could have been there, hidden just round the next corner, but I didn't hurry past. My attention was held by the pictures and I stopped before each one. They had all been taken in Northumberland. There was a sweep of sand dunes with a brooding, thunderstorm sky. A field of fat lambs surrounded by grey dry-stone walls, lit by a low evening sun. A swollen river sweeping past a barn. Then there was a scene which was familiar. It showed sunlight slanting through bare winter trees onto a narrow lane. I'd seen it before on Ronnie Laing's wall. If it wasn't a print of the same photo the shot must have been taken at the same time on the same day.

I got so caught up with the shapes on the walls that it took me a while to work out why I found the images disturbing. I mean, they were attractive, pleasing, so why did they make me feel uncomfortable? Because they weren't real. Even when I recognized the place in the picture, the *sense* of place was wrong. I thought it wasn't true that the camera never lies. I mean, the physical shape of the landscape was true, but the viewer's response to it had been manipulated. Perhaps that's what art's all about. Perhaps I was being naïve. But I'm straightforward. I don't like being messed with.

The pictures of the coast, for instance. In a storm like that, there'd have been litter blown against the grass. There's always litter. In the distance there should have been one of those concrete bunkers they put up in the war to stop the German tanks rolling up the beach. Even further away I'd have shown the cokeworks at Lynemouth or the chimneys of Blyth power station. And none of her farmhouses had satellite dishes, or scrappy machinery in the yard, or black polythene covering silage. There was no sign of foot and mouth, no *Keep Out* police notices. If this was a threatened landscape, why hadn't she shown that dump at Widdrington, where the carcasses were buried and the lorries leaked blood? What I'm saying is that this isn't a pretty landscape and she'd made it look pretty. It made me think she had a fairy-tale vision of how the world and her life should be. Philip's illness and death must have come as a shock. She wouldn't have been expecting something like that.

I turned away from the picture I'd seen on Ronnie's wall and there was Howdon, standing in a corner with a glass in his hand, talking in a low voice to a man I'd never met and a little woman in a purple jacket and a purple skirt with thin pleats, like the umpires at Wimbledon wear. She had a thin rat-like face and a complexion drained of all colour. She shouldn't have worn purple. She had a long-suffering look, which made me think she was Howdon's wife. He hadn't noticed me and suddenly he began to laugh. It wasn't loud. A restrained chortle which he held in with his handkerchief. Perhaps the man had told him a joke. Perhaps he'd told one himself. Anyway, that laughter pushed me over the edge. I could believe it was me he was laughing at. I lost it.

'What the fuck do you think you're playing at?'

I've told you I don't usually swear. I like to think I don't need to any more. But I needed to then. The words rang out in that quiet room. I could imagine them bouncing off the walls and the high ceiling, the sound waves like ripples, but getting bigger not smaller. No one intervened. Thank God for English embarrassment.

He looked over at me. He could hardly pretend I didn't exist. Not with such a big audience. For a moment he didn't know how to respond. He stood with his mouth open – a cartoon fish.

'Who is this, Stuart?' The woman. She thought I was his mistress. Perhaps he had a history of screwing around. I wouldn't have been surprised. If he felt the need to justify the affairs, he'd have told himself he'd lost the love of his life to Philip Samson, and he needed the comfort. That was the sort of pathetic man he was. 'What's going on?'

Her voice was firmer than I'd have expected from her appearance. She might put up with infidelity but not with a scene at a friend's party. Not a grand friend like Joanna. And she'd sensed that he'd recognized me. I could tell. She wouldn't let him pretend otherwise.

'Stuart?'

I wanted to scream, *Christ, I'm not his girlfriend. Credit me with some taste.* But that would have implied that she had none and my quarrel wasn't with her.

'Your husband lied about me to the police,' I said, lowering my voice, keeping it calm, fuming inside.

'Stuart?' she said again, impatient now. She might have been talking to an annoying and not very bright child.

Still he couldn't find the words to reply. I yelled at him, 'I was arrested for murder. And it's all your fault.' Pathetic. Like a kid in a school playground. But the scary thing is that if I'd had a knife I'd have had a go at him.

At last he regained his powers of speech. 'No, no. I never meant that.'

'Well, what did you mean?'

'He was trying to protect me.' It was Joanna in 1930s film-star mode. Every time I'd seen her, there'd been a different style. I couldn't get a grip on her. Tonight she was in a long sheath dress. Her lipstick and nails were red, the red of fresh blood. It was quite an entrance. Everyone was looking at her. They pretended to stare at the pictures, but none of us were fooled. I thought then that she was enjoying the attention, but perhaps I was wrong, because she took my arm. 'Let's find somewhere to talk,' she said. 'Somewhere quiet.'

There was a little room off the main space, an office with a desk, a computer and a couple of chairs. No window. She must have changed there; someone had propped a full-length mirror for her against one wall and there was a make-up bag on the desk. She showed me through the door and disappeared. I wondered if she wanted Stuart there to hold her hand, but she returned almost immediately with a bottle of wine in a cooler and two glasses.

I told her I was driving but I took one glass. That was all. When I left her later, the bottle was nearly empty. She must have been drinking steadily, though I didn't realize at the time. Her voice was quite reasonable throughout.

'Did you know he was married?' she asked. 'In Morocco.'

'I guessed.' Immediately. In the bus.

'Look, I don't blame you for what happened. I just

wondered if he mentioned me.' Her eyes were hungry.

He'd said she'd deny him nothing. I wasn't sure that was what she wanted to hear. He'd said she was a saint and even then I'd thought I'd heard an implied criticism.

'It was just one night,' I said. Not lying.

'You made an impression all the same.' She was trying to make a joke of it, but there was still that look in her eyes.

'How do you know what happened in Marrakech?'

'Philip told me.' She stared at me steadily over her glass. 'I didn't mind. How could I? He knew he was dying. It was only natural that he would want to have as many experiences as possible. I should be grateful to you. I find that difficult, of course, but I certainly don't resent you.'

'Did you know about Thomas?'

'No.' It seemed hard for her to admit it. 'I never even guessed.' She refilled her glass. 'Stuart explained it all this afternoon. It unnerved him bumping into you at Wintrylaw. He told me about the instructions Philip left with the will, about the boy being murdered.' She looked up at me again. 'Stuart was distraught. Really. It can't be easy for a solicitor to lie to the police.'

I didn't say that in my experience solicitors lie all the time. She was an innocent. She probably even believed in God.

'He didn't want me to find out that Philip had had an affair in Morocco and he didn't want me to know about the child. He was thinking about me and the children. Our children. Honestly.'

Like I said, she was an innocent.

Chapter Twenty-three

Inspector Farrier rang at lunchtime the next day to say that as far as he was concerned I was no longer a suspect in the Mariner murder. Joanna had promised that Howdon would go to the police, but it had happened more quickly than I'd expected.

'Stupid prat,' Farrier said. 'I'd like to do him for wasting my time, perverting the course of justice, but he's persuaded someone more important than me that it was some kind of mistake. A misunderstanding.'

Joanna had said 'misunderstanding' the night before at the exhibition, but I'd heard the quotation marks. We'd both taken the irony as read. Just before I'd left the room in the gallery, where she'd sat like a leading lady before opening night, drinking the last of the wine, I'd asked, 'Why do you put up with him?'

'Who? Stuart?'

'Yeah. The Fat Controller.'

That had made her start for a moment. Perhaps she was thinking of Philip too. 'Because he's kind. Really. He'd do anything for me. He's a sweetie.'

But I'd remembered what Dickon had said about his mother hating Howdon and I wasn't taken in. If she was the sort of woman who needed admirers to feel good about herself, there'd be plenty of other men

199

to play the part. I'd heard the way the rugby players talked about her at the funeral. Howdon had some power over her. I wished I knew what it was, but only in a vague, curious way. It didn't seem personal any more.

When I replaced the receiver after talking to Farrier, I supposed I should celebrate. I was in the clear. The trouble was that I had nobody to share the celebration with. Jess was out with Ray and anyway I couldn't spend all my time with a mother substitute. It suddenly hit me how lonely I was. It hadn't always been like that. When I'd worked at the unit I'd had lots of friends: colleagues, people from university who'd stayed in town. I'd done all the usual stuff – drank too much, danced, laughed. Since Nicky I hadn't wanted company. Now, for the first time, I missed it.

So I thought I'd celebrate alone. I drove up the coast to Craster, left the car there and walked out to Dunstanburgh Castle, grey sprawling ruins surrounded on three sides by the sea. The headland was almost empty. A stiff westerly blew against the incoming tide and helped clear my head. I walked back along the beach and hit the pub in the village in time for an early supper: crab soup, then smoked salmon from the smokery over the road sandwiched between chunks of home-baked bread. I made the food last. I didn't want to hurry home.

When I got back to Sea View I was still feeling a bit low. It hadn't been fun being a suspect in a murder inquiry, but it had been exciting. And it had given me an excuse not to think about my future. What was the point of making plans if I was likely to be arrested at any moment? Now everything seemed flat and I was restless and disengaged. Jess and Ray were sitting in the living room, cuddled up together on the sofa, listening to music. Not folk this time but that sort of jazz where all the notes slur into each other, so it makes you think of a drunk telling stories, being mellow and nostalgic. No one else was in. The bad lads were out causing chaos in town.

'There's some wine open in the kitchen,' Jess said. She was as mellow and sleepy as the music.

I poured myself a glass, then went back and joined them. It was nearly dark but they'd not bothered to close the curtains. A light buoy was flashing in the bay. Three sharp flashes then a gap. I sat cross-legged on the floor and looked out at the water.

'That solicitor's realized he's made a mistake,' I said, without turning towards them. 'He's told Farrier.'

'Eh, pet, what a relief!' She didn't ask how I knew. She didn't even care that much that Howdon had lied. She was so full of happiness that there wasn't much room for a response to my good news. I was pleased for her. Really, I was. But I was jealous too. I wanted to be curled up on a sofa with someone who made me feel that way. I didn't want to feel empty and bitter and frustrated.

'They've released his body,' Jess said suddenly. 'That lad, Thomas. It was in the *Journal*. His funeral's next week.'

I decided then to go to the funeral. There seemed no reason not to. I thought that for me it would be the end of the matter. If Philip's funeral had marked the start of my troublesome relationship with the Samsons, then Thomas's would mark the finish. I didn't tell Jess. She'd have thought it was an intrusion, sick even. *Why, Lizzie, a funeral's a time for families, pet. Families and close friends. You didn't even know him.*

But I knew his father, I thought. And that makes me family in a way. None of the other Samsons will be there. I'll go to represent Philip. Of course, that wasn't the real reason. My motives were more mixed up than that. Not nearly so noble. It was about missing the excitement, and wanting to see Ronnie Laing again, and feeling that until I knew who killed Thomas I wouldn't be able to enjoy the money Philip had given me. All that besides a sense that by not finding Thomas alive I'd let Philip down.

Thomas's funeral was in a new Methodist church not far from where the Laings lived. It was built of red brick. Inside the brick was exposed and hung with banners, a bit like the ones the unions carry on gala day. The banners were in bright primary colours and letters cut from felt spelled religious texts. It wasn't like being in St Bartholomew's. I left my car at Nell's house and walked to the church with her and Dan. I'd phoned Dan up the day before to find out if they were going.

'Nell's keen,' he'd said. Then, 'Why on earth do you want to bother?' I could tell he'd be glad of an excuse to get out of it but he'd go because of Nell.

'Oh, you know, to show my respect.' I still wasn't sure I had a real answer and that was as good as anything.

It was a close and overcast day, with thunder flies

swarming under the trees outside the church. We waited at a distance and watched the mourners go in. There were a number of well-dressed women in early middle age. The Methodist Wives, I thought, there to support Kay and to eye up each other's black frocks. Thomas's grandparents, Mr and Mrs Mariner. Mrs Mariner was already patting her eyes with her hanky and Archie was doing his best to comfort her. He had to take her arm to help her up the steps. Harry Pool with Kenny and a couple of lads from the yard. Ellen from Absalom House in a snot-green velvet skirt and jacket, her hair freshly dyed. A young man wearing an expensive suit who could have been Marcus Tate. Without the animal mask it was hard to tell. As they climbed the white stone steps, everyone wiped the thunder flies from their faces and their clothes, and shook their heads to clear them from their hair.

'Well,' Nell said, 'are we going to stand here all day?' And she led us in behind the stragglers and we flapped and shook the flies away just as the others had.

We sat near the back, sheepish, as if we had no right to be there. The church seemed mostly to be full of Kay's friends. Apart from the boys from Harry's Haulage and Marcus, I thought we were the only people Thomas would have bothered with. When I turned round once, halfway through the first hymn, I saw Farrier across the aisle from us, singing lustily. He must have come in at the last minute. He didn't seem shocked to see me. He winked.

I didn't see Kay and Ronnie until they followed the coffin out. They had been sitting on the front row with the little girls. It appeared that Thomas would be cremated. There would be a brief service but only for close family. I thought Ronnie saw me as he walked out, holding the hand of a little girl on each side. He gave a brief glance in my direction – shocked recognition, disbelief. Then something else which I couldn't place immediately but which could have been fear. Almost a hunted look. Why would he be frightened of me? I waited in the church until all the other mourners had left, blocking the pew so Nell and Dan couldn't move either. I didn't want to meet Ronnie there, and I certainly didn't want to see him in Kay's company.

When we did get outside the hearse had gone.

Harry Pool wiped his forehead with a handkerchief. His face was even redder than I remembered, glistening with sweat.

'I don't know about you lot,' he said. 'But I could use a drink.'

So we all trooped off to the pub on the corner, which was one of those soulless, cavernous places, built in the 1930s but more recently done up in mock Victorian, with two different wallpaper prints and dark furniture and hunting pictures. And even that had started to look shabby. It had just opened for the day. It had that morning smell of last night's beer and last night's cigarettes. We must have seemed an unlikely crowd to the barmaid, who stood, her bum leaning against the wall, languidly rubbing glasses with a tea towel. Harry Pool got in the first round. He'd loosened his tie and undone the top button of his shirt, but he still seemed breathless and wheezing.

'And you, lass,' he said to me when he asked what I was drinking, 'how did you know the boy?' He seemed not to remember my visit to the yard. It wasn't surprising. I'd just been one of a crowd of reporters.

I was going to say I knew Thomas's father, but stopped myself just in time. Whatever my views on the matter, it wasn't fair to Kay to spread around information about Philip.

'I didn't really,' I said. 'More a friend of the family.'

'Aye,' he said. 'Like me.'

So we sat down at the tables and at first we looked awkwardly at each other, not speaking. Dylan's 'Knocking on Heaven's Door' was playing on the jukebox. It seemed to be playing all afternoon. Harry Pool came back from the bar with a tray loaded with drinks. I remember that Ellen was drinking whisky. That surprised me. The rest of us were on the beer: the lads on bottled lager, everyone else on hand-pulled bitter.

'I think we should drink to Thomas,' Harry said. He was still standing, leaning forward onto the table as if he needed the support. 'No one deserves to die like that. Specially not someone with his whole life ahead of him.'

We all raised our glasses, solemnly, like a toast at a wedding. 'Thomas,' we said. One of the lads stifled a nervous giggle. If he was mentioned after that it was only in whispered conversation between individuals.

It seems now that I was drunk after the first pint. Perhaps it was the strangeness of the occasion. Perhaps it was a mistake to mix the alcohol with my medication. I can remember snippets of conversation freeze-framed like in a home movie, but in my memory the background's always blurred, and I don't know the order in which the discussions occurred or their context.

At one point Ellen was talking to me. It must have been close to the beginning of the session, because I was still sitting next to her. There were empty plates on the table. I think Harry must have ordered sandwiches for us all, though I don't remember eating. I looked at her mouth moving. She was wearing scarlet lipstick, which had leached into the face powder around her lips. The effect was geographical – tributaries feeding into a lagoon in the desert, with her mouth as the lagoon. I was still staring when I realized she was waiting for an answer to a question I hadn't heard.

'Sorry?' I said. Dylan was knock, knock, knocking in my brain.

'We need to talk. Thomas was special.' Even though I was focusing on her, I had to strain to make out the words. She didn't want to be overheard. It was one of those secret Thomas conversations. 'He was troubled.'

'I was going to write something.' By this point I was expansive. The fiction that I was a journalist seemed a huge joke. 'An article.'

'Yes, yes.' The words came out as a double hiss. She gripped my arm with her hand. 'Come to Absalom House. Any time. I'm always there. We'll talk.'

Then she whirled away and the next time I noticed her she was at the other side of the table, smoking a cigarette, holding it in a stagy way between two fingers, her head slightly tilted back, looking at Harry Pool through the smoke.

Nell and Dan sat together throughout the after-noon, but they never seemed to be speaking to each other. A few times Nell looked at me with that intense and piercing stare which she seemed to have adopted as part of her style, like the chopped hair, and once, when we met outside the Ladies, she asked, 'Who was that man in the church who winked at you?'

I'd forgotten about Farrier. He must have disap-peared immediately after the service, or perhaps he'd been invited to the crematorium with the family. I could imagine him being a source of comfort to them.

'He's the detective in charge of the murder investigation.'

'Do they know anything?' Her voice was as urgent, as pressing, as Ellen's grip on my arm had been.

'They've accepted I had nothing to do with it. That's all I care about.'

'No,' she spat back. 'It's not all you care about. It can't be. I can tell. We have to know why he died. Don't we?' She didn't wait for an answer. She made her way back to Dan so carefully, her body so upright, that I know she was pissed too.

Harry's lads were less demanding in conversation. One must have been older than he looked because he'd just got his HGV licence and was already talking about the trips to Europe for the firm. He was excited at the prospect of the long drive alone, but nervous too. He'd already been on some of the usual routes with a more experienced driver – Spain, he said, and Poland. I asked him what he carried back from Poland. Vodka, I wondered, jam, fruit? But he seemed unsure about that. Everything was in containers, he said. How could he tell?

The last encounter I remember was with Marcus. He approached me, carrying a drink for us both, and sat beside me on a padded bench which ran along the wall. He had taken off his tie. One end of it flapped out of his trouser pocket. He was playing at being drunk but even then I didn't think he was. I could see through the act with the sudden flash of perception you sometimes get even when you can hardly stand. He rested one arm along the window-sill behind me, not making contact with my shoulders but very close.

'I recognize you. You were at Wintrylaw.'

I don't know why, but I pretended not to understand what he was talking about. Perhaps it was just too much effort. Anyway, I didn't answer.

'I was the bear,' he said. He formed circles with the thumbs and middle fingers of each hand and held them to his eyes. 'I wore the mask. You were going to join up.'

'The Countryside Consortium.' As if it had all just come back to me.

'What are you doing here?' He leaned forward diagonally across the table so our faces were almost touching. 'Did you know Thomas?'

'I found his body.'

He jolted away from me, but I didn't know how much of a shock that actually was. Because he was playing at being drunk, I didn't trust the reaction.

It was at that moment that Harry Pool stood up. He said he was going to call it a day. He had his wife to get back to. She'd been stuck with the grandchildren all day. And we followed him out. He'd brought us together and we couldn't continue without him. Marcus and I were last out. I found his arm round my shoulder, his hand resting gently on my neck. I didn't have the energy to push him away. And anyway, I really quite liked it.

We stood on the pavement to wave the others down the road. The next thing I knew I was in a taxi on my way to Seaton Delaval, to the little house where Thomas had died. I don't remember there being any discussion about it, but perhaps that's not fair. There may have been. I do remember standing with Marcus on the doorstep, watching him grope in his pocket for a door key. When he couldn't find it he tipped the plant out from the pot on the window-box and took the spare key from the bottom. And I remember being violently sick in the gutter.

Chapter Twenty-four

Still holding the point of the knife against my skin, Nicky reaches out and switches off the light. Suddenly it's dark. I feel my pupils widen in response, but there's nothing to see. There are security shutters on the window. I've always been scared of the dark.

He puts an arm around my chest and pulls me down so I'm lying on the bed. He's lying beside me, very close. I can smell him. One hand presses me against his body, the other holds the knife. He's whispering into my ear. His lips brush the lobe and the touch makes me start. He's telling me what he intends to do with me. I try to block out the words. As he speaks I feel his erection through the cotton of his sweat pants against my thigh. He unbuttons my shirt, fumbling in the dark, one-handed, then he moves the blade of the knife towards my breast, lightly scratching the skin, not drawing blood.

There are footsteps in the corridor outside.

'Don't move.' The words are so quiet that even with his mouth against my ear I can hardly make them out.

The footsteps disappear.

We both know they'll be back.

*

I was in Thomas's bed. It was the same evening, still light. Marcus was standing in the doorway. I knew where I was immediately, and in the same instant I recognized that if I moved my head I'd throw up again. The next sensation was panic. What was I doing there? What had I done? I could remember stumbling into the house, holding on to Marcus. The shock of being here. Then nothing but the flashback. Carefully I slid one hand down my body. Still dressed. Relief. No sex. I'd only taken off my shoes before getting into bed. The nausea of the hangover came back and I shut my eyes.

'Tea?' Marcus's voice seemed to come from miles away. From Norway. If not further. I could believe that the grey North Sea and several oil rigs were coming between us. I forced myself to look at him. He was smiling as if he'd been following my thoughts, as if my embarrassment amused him.

'What's the time?'

'Nine. Nine-thirty.'

'I should phone home.' I'd told Jess I'd be back soon after lunch. She'd be wondering, worried. It wasn't her place to worry, but she'd be sending Ray out on a search party if she didn't hear soon. Even worse, she might phone Lisa.

'Sure,' he said. 'Tea first.' He had a mug in each hand. He sat on the end of the bed. I shuffled back so I was sitting upright and felt better, more in control.

Someone had done a seriously good job of cleaning the room. There was a new carpet, cheap grey nylon cord. The wall must have been painted. It was brighter than the others and there were no posters. All the

211

same, it couldn't have been much fun getting rid of the blood.

'Sorry,' Marcus said. 'I didn't know where else to put you. And earlier you were in no state to care.' Again he seemed to have developed telepathic powers. 'Once the police had finished, my dad paid for a cleaning company. This is my first day back here.'

'Don't you mind?'

'Not a lot that I can do about it. My dad won't pay for anything else. I suppose I thought the sooner I came home the better. The same principle as getting back onto a horse after you've fallen off.'

'Isn't your father worried about you staying here on your own?'

Marcus shrugged. 'The police think Thomas was killed by druggies looking for something to steal. He must have disturbed them. They're not likely to come back.' He paused and added, 'My father's a businessman. He wouldn't find it easy to sell the house while people remember the murder. So I'm stuck here. For a while at least.'

But I wasn't really listening to that. I was thinking the disturbed burglar theory was impossible. There'd been music playing, loud enough to hear from the street. Even someone out of his head would have realized the house wasn't empty. And then I thought Farrier wasn't that dumb. Either a different officer with the deductive reasoning of a gnat had been talking to Marcus, or the police were spinning him a line for their own purposes. I felt suddenly uncomfortable, vulnerable.

'Where were you that day?' It came out spiky and accusing. Not sensible in the circumstances.

'At the university.' He didn't seem offended by the question. 'A lecture, then a tutorial.' He smiled. 'There were lots of witnesses.'

'I didn't mean . . .' But then I broke off. Of course I had meant. I'd needed to check that it was imposs- ible for Marcus to have killed Thomas. I still only had his word for it, but I felt too ill to keep up being scared.

'The police said Thomas wasn't in work the day he died because he had flu. Was that true?'

'I don't know about flu, but he wasn't well. Some sort of virus. He was asleep when I went out that morning.'

Perhaps that was why he didn't answer the door when I first arrived. Later he'd woken and put on his music. Had he still been in bed when the murderer came? No, because he'd been wearing jeans and a sweatshirt. Had he got up to let the killer in?

Marcus left me to wash my face and hands and then I phoned Jess. I told her not to worry. I'd had a couple of drinks, so I was going to stay the night with a mate. At that point I still hoped to get home, but it was better not to promise. She'd be fidgety all night and she'd wait up. I wasn't in any fit state to drive. I wasn't sure I could face public transport and I wasn't going to cough up for a taxi all the way back.

Marcus was in the kitchen, beating eggs in a glass bowl with a fork.

'Scrambled eggs OK?'

I nodded, surprised that I felt so hungry.

The kitchen was at the back of the house, small but well equipped and tidy for a student place. I remembered the chaos of boots and shoes I'd seen in the hall on my first visit, the carpet thick with dust, and thought perhaps the cleaning company had been let loose in here too. Or perhaps Marcus didn't mind muck but he was naturally orderly in the kitchen. I've known men like that. It occurred to me, watching him standing there, still dressed in the suit trousers and white shirt from the funeral, that this was the son Kay Laing would have liked. I wondered if she'd known Marcus when he was a child. Dan had described them as school friends.

'How did you know Thomas?' I was leaning against the door frame. If I'd gone into the kitchen I'd have been in the way.

He glanced up. He had that clean, scrubbed, wholesome look of well-educated English boys. No zits. Short hair with a bit of curl in it. A skin the colour of pale toast, pink at the back of the neck where the sun had caught it.

'We were at infants' school together. The two terrors of the class.'

Like Archie Mariner and Harry Pool, I thought. Still friends sixty years on, though one had made a fortune and the other struggled to live on a pension.

'When I was eleven my father sent me to King's. You know, the private place in Tynemouth?'

I nodded.

'We'd moved up the coast by then anyway, and Thomas and I had already lost touch. We met up again later. School's less important as you get older. We bumped into each other at parties. Whitley on a Friday night. Everyone you've ever met seems to be there when you're sixteen.'

'And was Thomas still a terror?'

'Oh, not so very much. No more than anyone else. The only difference was that he didn't mind being caught.'

'Do you know his stepfather?'

He gave himself a chance to think about that, buying time by bending to lift a pan from a low cupboard. 'I've seen him around.'

'At the Countryside Consortium?'

'He's not very active,' Marcus said. 'There are lots of supporters.'

It wasn't much of an answer but I let it go. He had his back to me now because the eggs were cooking and he was standing over them with a wooden spoon, teasing them away from the edge of the pan as they began to stick.

'How did you get involved?'

'Through my father. My parents separated when I was six. I stayed with my dad. Later he moved in with another woman. She has land up the coast. She doesn't farm it herself but she keeps a couple of horses there and she held on to the house. I suppose she's the enthusiast. He deals in property, a glorified estate agent really, but he considers himself a cut above the rest. He wouldn't normally touch a place like this with a bargepole, but he could see it would do for me. His interest is in big houses, country hotels. When the landed gentry want to flog off part of the estate, they go to him. I'm not sure how committed he is to the cause. He doesn't hunt, for example. My stepmother's horses terrify him. I think he saw joining up as a shrewd business move, a way of keeping in with the right people, networking.'

'And you?'

He didn't answer for a while. He was buttering toast. Then he concentrated on tipping out the eggs. Even from where I stood, I could tell they were perfectly cooked, golden and creamy, the curd just firm. He handed me a plate and cutlery and followed me through to the living room. We sat on easy chairs each side of the mantelpiece, the plates perched on our knees. I wondered if he and Thomas had sat like this to eat.

'For me it was just a job,' he said. 'I wanted a year doing something practical. My degree's in business administration. My father spoke to someone, fixed it up. He's good at that. And it was useful experience, a year in an office, pretty well running it, in charge of fund-raising at the end.'

'And what was it for Thomas?' I asked.

'Ah,' he replied. 'For Thomas it was a crusade.'

'I don't get that. I wouldn't have thought it would be his thing. I mean, he was brought up in the town. Wasn't he into music, clubs, shops?'

'Sure. All of those. But he liked the *idea* of the countryside, the fantasy. England's green and pleasant land. You know. I told him the reality wasn't like that, but he had this dream of living in the hills, self-sufficiency, not being bugged by his mother or anyone else.'

I thought it sounded ludicrous, but there was something chilling in Marcus's description of the dream too. There was a touch of the wild American survivalism in there as well as *The Good Life*. Patriots and shotguns along with the organic carrots. But perhaps I'd got it all wrong. Perhaps a love of the countryside was in Thomas's blood, inherited from Philip. That thought moved me naturally to Joanna. I meant to ask if she was one of the Consortium's supporters, but Marcus got in with a question of his own.

'Why did you come here? The day you found Thomas's body, I mean. What brought you to the house?'

'His family was concerned. They didn't know where he was living. I'm a social worker. They asked me to trace him. No fuss. Unofficially.'

He accepted my explanation but he said, 'Ronnie knew.'

'Sorry?'

'Ronnie knew that Thomas had moved in to help with the rent. I told him. Not long before Thomas died. I felt really bad about it afterwards, because Thomas hadn't wanted anyone to know he was here. It was a big thing for him. He'd almost sworn me to secrecy. The typical grand gesture that he really liked.'

'What happened?'

'There was a CC pro-hunting rally in town. By the Monument. I wasn't taking part. I don't actually believe in hunting. I went out with my stepmother a couple of times and couldn't see the point. And now I'm not working for them . . . But I was in town anyway and I watched from the pavement with everyone else. Ronnie was in there, taking it all really seriously. I mean he was marching, head up, not shuffling along like the rest of them. He saw me, recognized me as a mate of Thomas's. He came over and asked if I'd seen anything of him lately. I told him I'd asked Thomas to move in.'

'Why did you tell him? If Thomas had told you not to?' I can't stand a grass.

Marcus looked awkward. 'It's hard to say no to Ronnie Laing.' I thought that was just an excuse but I didn't say anything.

'When was that? Exactly?'

'I don't know. A week or so before Thomas died.'

'Ronnie didn't say anything to Thomas's mother.' I remembered how Kay had looked when she scribbled her work number on a scrap of paper, asking me to let her have news of her son. And she'd given me the hostel address. She hadn't known he'd moved on. I told myself that Ronnie was trying to protect his wife from anxiety. She'd think Thomas was safe if he was in Absalom House.

'He didn't like having Thomas around,' Marcus said. 'I can understand it in a way. He could be a pain and Ronnie likes a quiet life. You know, needs his own space.' Suddenly it seemed Marcus knew more about Ronnie than he'd originally let on.

'Why's that?'

But Marcus just shrugged. He wasn't going to give anything more away about Ronnie.

'Tell me about Thomas.'

'He tried too hard. It was like he could never relax. He had to be entertaining, playing to the crowd, making sure people liked him.'

'Exhausting,' I said.

'Yeah, for him and for us. I think that's why Nell dumped him. He wore her out.'

'How did he take that?'

'He was absolutely sure he'd get her back.'

We looked at each other. We both understood the

folly of his certainty, both felt sad that we'd never get a chance to be proved wrong.

'What were you doing at Wintrylaw that weekend? Why help the Consortium if you don't believe in what it stands for and you don't work for them any more?'

'I believe some of it.' He was defensive. 'Anyway, they were paying. A percentage for every member I joined up.'

'That's why you were so keen to recruit me?'

'Of course.' He gave a smile which was arrogant and disarming all at once. 'Why else?' He stood up. I watched him carry the plates into the kitchen and stack them neatly beside the sink. He called through the open door, 'Coffee?'

'Why not?' I thought perhaps I should offer to wash up, but I still wasn't sure I could stand without the dizziness coming back. And he'd brought me here, hadn't he? I was his guest. He filled a machine with water, spooned coffee into a filter paper and switched it on. The smell of coffee dripping into the jug helped clear my head.

I asked, 'Did Thomas ever talk about his work at the haulage yard?'

'Not much. It wasn't like a vocation, was it? He was there for the pay cheque, like me at the Consortium.'

'Did he seem worried by anything that was going on there?'

'What sort of thing?'

'I'm not sure. Health and safety issues? Drivers working too long without a break? Lorries not being properly serviced?' *Red diesel? Green diesel?*

What else would have made him talk to Shona Murray about whistle-blowing?

'There'd been something going on between him and his boss.'

'What sort of thing?'

'I don't know. A row. A misunderstanding. At one point Thomas talked about leaving. I told you he was a dreamer. He was going on about setting up in business on his own. Then it all seemed to blow over.'

'You've really no idea what it was about?'

Marcus didn't answer. 'What's going on here?' he said. He brought in the Pyrex coffee jug and two mugs and put them on the carpet between us. 'I mean, what has it got to do with you?'

He seemed very young and unformed standing there, looking down at me. He'd experienced so little I thought there was nothing for me to get to know. A pretty face. Perhaps that's why I was tempted to confide in him. He couldn't understand what I'd been through, so it didn't matter. It was almost like talking to myself.

'I'm interested,' I said. 'I try not to be, but I can't help it. The police had me down as the killer for a few days. They almost had me convinced I'd done it. I suppose I think I've got a right to know what happened.'

'You should let it go,' he said roughly.

'What do you know about it?'

'Nothing. But if you don't it'll become an obsession. No one can live like that.'

I thought, What can you know about obsession? What can you know about anything with your sheltered life, and your riding, and your daddy who has enough money to buy you a house and clean away the remains of your murdered friend?

Then I thought I was being unfair. I stretched out and poured the coffee. He took a mug and sat down. The question I'd failed to ask earlier came into my mind. 'Is Joanna Samson one of the Consortium's supporters?'

'She's the patron.'

'What does that mean?'

He shrugged. 'She's a well-known photographer. She lets them put her name on the letter heading, holds fund-raisers, garden parties.'

Like the queen, I thought. She'd enjoy that.

'Do you know her?' he asked.

'I knew her husband.' Just saying that made me feel good.

He leaned down and poured more coffee. The mugs were matching, white with royal-blue bands.

'Have you ever heard of Stuart Howdon?' I asked. 'Is he involved too?'

He twisted the mug, his long fingers splayed across the rim, moving it backwards and forwards over the carpet. 'I've told you. You should let it go.'

'Do you know who killed Thomas?'

'Of course not.'

'Why did you bring me here?'

'Perhaps I fall for older women. Something to do with my mother having walked out when I was so young.' I could tell he regretted the flip remark as soon as it had shot out of his mouth. 'I'm sorry.' He paused a beat. 'You were drunk. You wouldn't tell me where you lived. I didn't want you driving.' He broke off again, this time for longer. 'Honestly. I told you, this is my first day back. I couldn't face coming back here alone after the funeral.'

'Is there anywhere else you can go? Or I could probably stay tonight, if you like.'

He shook his head. 'It was just then, coming in through the door. Knowing he wouldn't be here. It's not that we were close. Not specially. Not any more. But we'd been friends for a long time.' He stood up. 'I'm OK to drive. I'll take you home.'

I let him, though nobody else connected to Thomas's murder, except Dan, who for some reason didn't seem to count, knew I lived in Newbiggin. I made Marcus park at the church and said I'd walk from there. It wasn't raining but way out to sea there was a storm; a crack of lightning lit the horizon. He'd got out of the car to say goodbye, opened the passenger door to let me out. The perfect gentleman. I had the impression there was something more he wanted to say, but he just stood awkwardly, next to the open door. I pulled his head towards me and kissed his forehead, then his lips lightly. I suppose I was still drunk, but it seemed the right thing to do.

Chapter Twenty-five

That night Marcus died. An accident apparently.

I found out about it the next day. I'd gone to Whitley to collect my car from outside Nell's house. On the way there on the bus I'd noticed the inside lane of the Spine Road was closed, but I'd put it down to bridge repairs. There have been roadworks along that stretch for as long as I can remember. Back at Sea View Jess was cooking chilli; you could smell it from the yard, and hear her singing through the open window, so I knew Ray would be there. Chilli's his favourite and Jess only sings when she's content. They asked me to eat with them and I said that I would because I like chilli too. As I've said before, I've got no pride.

She grinned at me, pleased that we'd be playing happy families. 'It'll be ten minutes. I've got the rice on.'

It would be brown rice. Ray was a health freak and brought it from the wholefood place on Gosforth High Street.

I wandered through to the living room and flicked the local news on the telly. There was a new lass reading the headlines. Young. Bonny. Blond, short hair. I was going to call through to Jess to ask what had happened to the old bald guy who used to do it, when a photograph of Marcus came up onto the screen. He was wearing a white V-necked jersey and looked as if he'd been playing cricket or tennis. I stood there staring at him while she described the accident. He'd driven his car off the bridge on the Spine Road, the high bridge which crosses the River Wansbeck, just before it runs into the sea.

Then Marcus left the screen and there was a shot of his car, hardly recognizable, on the side of the river bank. The incident must have taken place in the early hours of the morning, the reporter said. There were no witnesses. Then she went on to describe the visit of the Princess Royal to a nursery school in Alnwick and Jess called me through for my tea.

What I felt first was a terrible sense of loss. It was entirely selfish. Marcus might have become a friend and now I wouldn't have the chance to know him better. At that point I didn't consider his death objectively. It didn't hit me then that, coming so soon after Thomas's, it might be more than a terrible coincidence. I didn't feel in danger myself.

I didn't mention the accident to Jess and Ray. I didn't want to talk about it. The next day there were more details in the *Journal*. The paper had made the link between Marcus and Tom and talked about a tragedy. But the implication was that it had been Marcus's fault. The tone of the report was sanctimonious. Blood tests showed a high alcohol level. It was understandable that he'd been drinking on the night of his friend's funeral, but reckless. Someone else could have been killed.

I couldn't take it in. Nothing seemed to fit. I'd left

Marcus at eleven-thirty and there were plenty of cars on the Spine Road then. He'd been drinking earlier in the day, but not as heavily as the rest of us and he'd stopped six hours before. He'd had nothing with me in the house in Delaval. His driving when he'd taken me home had been anything but reckless. He had a new car, properly new, not like mine, another present from Daddy, and he was being very cautious. No way would he have been speeding. Then the old fear came back. Perhaps I wasn't remembering it properly. Perhaps the confusion was mine. More paranoia.

I was tempted to go to Farrier. I could have explained that Marcus was fine when he left me. But that wouldn't have explained the alcohol level in his blood. Where had he been? It had been too late for the pub when he left me. Besides, I didn't want to tell the inspector that I'd been with Marcus just before he died. I could picture him raising his eyebrows and giving me his kind, fatherly look. *What is it with you and young lads, Lizzie Bartholomew? You're the kiss of death to them.* I wouldn't have blamed him. If I'd have been a detective it'd have me suspicious. Besides, all my instincts told me it was crazy to get mixed up voluntarily with the police.

So for two days I sat in Sea View and brooded about it. As Marcus had said, I was given to obsession, even in my well-behaved medication-taking days. If not an accident, then suicide or murder. Suicide because he'd been responsible for Thomas's death? Or murder because he knew too much about it? I sat at the kitchen table and wrote notes. My writing was very small and cramped, not my usual style at all. I recorded my conversation with Marcus, word for word, as best I could remember it. There'd been a row with Harry Pool, Ronnie Laing had known that Thomas was living with Marcus but hadn't passed on the information to Kay, Tom had seen his work at the Countryside Consortium as a crusade. Was there anything else? Anything I'd missed?

Jess hovered around me at this time, brewing tea and feeding me home-made cake, growing more concerned. On the third day she brought herself to speak. 'You should get out, pet. I'm no company for you. Go and spend some time with your friends. What about that nice lad who brought you the flowers?'

She meant Dan. I presumed he'd still be working in Absalom House. With Ellen. Like a shock, I remembered the conversation we'd had in the pub on the afternoon of Thomas's funeral. 'He was troubled,' Ellen had said, as she gripped my arm. Perhaps he'd talked to her, given her more than the few hints he'd dropped to Marcus Tate.

She answered the phone herself when I rang the hostel.

'It's Lizzie Bartholomew,' I said. 'I wondered if I might come and talk to you. As we agreed.'

'Yes, yes.' The same double hiss which was a habit of speech, almost a nervous tic. 'As soon as you like. Whenever you can.'

'Can I buy you lunch somewhere? It might be easier to talk away from Absalom House.' There'd be fewer interruptions, I thought. No one to overhear. No Dan to stir up memories.

She suggested a coffee shop in Cullercoats, not far from the sea front. We arranged to meet at twelve; she had a meeting in the afternoon. I offered to

226

postpone to a more convenient day but she was insistent. 'Today,' she said. 'I want to meet today.' When I replaced the receiver I felt lighter, as if a terrible headache had begun to clear. Relief, perhaps, at being able to walk away from my writing. Jess watched me leave the house with a mixture of anxiety and pride, like a mother sending her child to school for the first time. She was pleased I'd taken her advice but not sure I was fit to be let out alone.

Ellen was already there when I arrived. I saw her hair from the street. She was at a table in the bay window and seemed lost in thought. She didn't notice me until I joined her. It was one of those places where all the staff and most of the customers are over fifty. Restful, but irritating if you're in a hurry. We ordered coffee and sandwiches and then we were left alone for twenty minutes to talk.

'You said that Thomas was troubled. What did you mean?' I had a notebook and pen. It wasn't just that I wanted to look the part. I didn't want to take any chances with my memory.

'I'm not sure this should go into the article,' she said. 'Not specific details. It wouldn't be fair. To him or his family.'

'Off the record, then.' I said, closing the notebook.

'Thomas came to me for advice,' Ellen said. 'He was concerned that our conversation should be confidential. I haven't been to the police. It hardly seems relevant to his death. But it makes a general point which I'd like you to put in your piece. It shows what a responsibility parents have for their children, even when they're older. It shows how careful we have to be. How thoughtful. We can't take them for granted.'

I wondered again about her own son. What had she done to drive him onto the streets. Probably nothing. Nothing terrible. But she'd felt guilty for thirty years.

'I wouldn't submit anything without showing you first.'

'He didn't get on with his stepfather.'

So, I thought, tell me something I don't know.

'I *had* gathered that.' I said it gently, though. Social work had taught me patience. People have to tell their stories in their own ways.

Ellen took a packet of cigarettes from her bag. She set it on the table and looked at it. 'It made him fantasize about his natural father. Who he might be. Thomas had got it into his head that it might be a man of some importance, some wealth. He was desperate to trace him.'

'Had his mother never told him his father's name?'

'Never. All the time he was growing up, he was just told it was someone she'd worked with when she had a part-time job. The grandparents had been given the same story. According to Thomas, they'd assumed the father was a student too, but his mother wouldn't even confirm that to him. Thomas couldn't let it go. He pushed and pushed to know.'

'Is that why she threw him out of the house?'

'He believed that had something to do with it.' Ellen paused as a flat-footed middle-aged woman approached. She was dressed in the sort of nylon overall I'd made Jess throw away. In slow motion she put a pot of coffee and two cups and saucers on the table, then walked off. Ellen watched until she was out of earshot and continued. 'He felt it as a terrible injustice. He thought he had a right to know, that his father would want to meet him and his mother had deliberately kept them apart.'

'Perhaps she was doing it to protect Thomas. If she knew the father wasn't interested . . .'

'Of course. I explained that. But he couldn't accept it.'

I couldn't accept it either. Philip had been thinking of Thomas before he died. He was a kind man. It might have been difficult for his wife and family, but he would have wanted to get to know the boy.

'I think he'd guessed, or believed he'd guessed, the identity of his father,' Ellen said. 'He hinted as much just before he left Absalom House.' I expected her to mention Marcus Tate's death then, but she said nothing. Perhaps Thomas had never told her Marcus's name, so the report of the accident meant nothing to her. Perhaps she hadn't heard about it.

'Did he tell you his father's name?'

'No,' she said. 'He wanted to be sure before he told anyone. There was someone he needed to talk to, he said, to confirm it. And it wasn't my place to pry.'

She broke off again as the waitress appeared with our food. Thoughts were tumbling into my head. I would have liked to write them down but Ellen would have been suspicious of that. Perhaps this was the explanation for Thomas's interest in the Countryside Consortium. If someone had led him to believe that Philip was his father, he might have seen it as a way of getting close to the Samson family. Joanna's name appeared on all the publicity material. It would be a big step to confront a stranger with the knowledge that you were his son. He might want to see something of the man first.

Ellen set down her tuna sandwich. 'Do you think he found his father before he died?' she asked. 'Oh, I do hope he did.'

'Is there anyone else he might have confided in?'

She shook her head. Her eyes were big and brown. Watery. Cow's eyes. 'He didn't have many friends. Not real friends. So few of them do.'

'There was Nell.'

'I'm not sure he'd have talked to her.'

'Why?'

She didn't give a direct answer. 'I never cared for Nell, even before she left Thomas for Daniel.'

'What was the problem?'

'She's too intense. Driven. And too bright. Thomas never thought he was good enough for her. He couldn't compete.'

'Did he have any good friends at Absalom House?' I was thinking of the dark girls I'd seen in the room next to his. The sisters with the white scarves. Had he confided in them?

'He wasn't there for very long,' Ellen said. 'And of course he was working, out all day . . .'

'Did you ever meet Marcus Tate, the lad he moved in with?'

She shook her head.

'What about his employer? How did they get on?' This was fishing, but I was starting to feel desperate. I wanted to find out if Ellen knew about a row between Thomas and Harry Pool. If Tom had confided in her about personal stuff, his father, she could know what he'd meant in his whistle-blowing letter to Shona Murray.

'Something was going on at work.' It came out in a rush and she seemed to regret her words almost immediately.

'What sort of something?'

She paused and again I had the impression that she wished she hadn't raised the matter. 'I wondered if he was being bullied. The men who turned up for his funeral seemed pleasant enough, but it's possible they weren't all like that. Some days when he got in he was angry. He wouldn't talk about it, but I know he wasn't happy there.'

'Perhaps he was bored, frustrated. It can't have been a very exciting job.'

'There was more to it than that.'

I pressed her for details but she insisted that there was nothing else to tell. She'd worked with young people long enough to pick up the signals. Something at Pool's was causing Thomas stress. She finished eating before I did and hurried off, mumbling something about the trustees' AGM. She seemed anxious to leave. Her attitude puzzled me. I thought I hadn't handled the meeting well. She'd seemed to distrust me. In the pub after the funeral she'd seemed desperate to talk to me, yet today she'd given me nothing but gossip, opinions. I was left wondering if I could believe any of her ramblings. Perhaps she'd wanted to appear more important to Thomas than she'd ever really been. Perhaps she was just a lonely old woman who wanted someone new to share her guilt with.

Chapter Twenty-six

I wished I'd known Marcus better. I'd dismissed him that night of the funeral as a good-looking lad who'd had it easy, who'd had too little experience of the world to know what I'd been going through. Now he was dead and I thought I owed him a bit of attention. Ellen hadn't been able to give me anything and I could hardly bowl up to his parents at a time like this to muddy their grieving with questions. I wouldn't know where to start at the university. All I knew about him was that he was doing a degree in business administration and by now all the under-graduates would be away for the summer anyway. So I thought I'd go back to the Countryside Consortium. It was one of the links between Marcus and Thomas. If Ellen was right and Thomas had worked out the identity of his father, someone at the office might know.

The office address was printed at the bottom of the leaflet Marcus had given me at Wintrylaw on the afternoon of the church's summer fair. I'd expected it to be in Morpeth, the county town where Stuart Howdon had his office, but it turned out to be on the edge of a village south-west of there, part of the flat, undistinguished countryside on the way to Newcastle airport. I found it on the map, next to a main road. I must have driven past it on a number of occasions.

I went the day after my meeting with Ellen, and as I approached it along a straight road I realized I'd been there before, not to the Consortium office, but to the complex where it was housed. A big sign advertised it in advance: Warren Farm. A set of farm buildings had been converted to business use, built round a central court which must once have been the farmyard. There were retail units, craft workshops, a restaurant. I'd brought Jess here after a jaunt out in my first car. We'd browsed round the shops and stopped for lunch. The café was in the main farmhouse – all stripped pine and exposed beams – and I still remembered the chocolate cake as something special.

I pulled into the courtyard. Although it was sunny and the road had been busy, there were only a couple of other cars there. Perhaps that was because it was mid-week, early in the season, but the complex had a depressed air which I hadn't noticed on my previous visit. One of the shops was holding a closing-down sale. It occurred to me that the business people running this place would be supporters of the Country-side Consortium. They'd moved out of farming but the new venture didn't seem to be a brilliant success either. They'd be looking for someone to blame.

That this was a natural home for the Consortium was confirmed as soon as I got out of the car. Ahead of me in the small rank of shops was a taxidermist. The window was dressed as a woodland scene, with a stuffed fox surrounded by dead leaves and two unnaturally plump pheasants perched on a log. I presume they were pheasants. It would have appealed to the hunting set, and I thought Dickon would be fascinated, but it made me feel squeamish. I walked quickly past. The next place – selling waxed jackets and a huge selection of rubber boots – was closed. Then came a shop with a blinding display of brightly coloured sweaters in the window. The door was open. A woman sat inside knitting. She set the needles aside as she saw me approaching and looked up eagerly. I didn't know which would be most disappointing for her – if I pretended to be interested in the stock but didn't buy, or if I asked immediately for directions. I stood in the doorway.

'I'm looking for the Countryside Consortium,' I said apologetically.

She pointed out the way and went back to her knitting.

The office was on the first floor above the row of shops, built into the slate roof. It was reached by a narrow wooden staircase. I stood at the bottom, putting together a scrappy cover story – something as near to the truth as I could make it – then I went up. The door at the top was glass with *Countryside Consortium* etched into it. I looked through into a long, narrow office furnished with half a dozen desks and computers. One wall was covered with posters. Everything seemed very glossy and new, more prosperous certainly than the rest of the centre. At first glance the room seemed empty and I thought it must be shut, perhaps as a mark of respect for Marcus. Then a middle-aged woman came into my field of view. She saw me peering through the window and for a moment seemed as startled as I was. She looked me up and down and seemed to decide that I meant no harm.

'Come in,' she called. 'Do come in.'

I pushed on the door but it was locked on the inside and she came to open it. We stood staring at each other. The woman was plump and small with flyaway greying hair and dowdy clothes which made her seem older than she probably was. She seemed excited, but flustered, to see me. I'd had the same response from women in the charity shops Jess dragged me into. For some of them this was their first foray into the world of work.

'Oh dear,' she said. 'Oh dear.' I wondered if everything she said would be repeated. I decided to take advantage of her confusion.

'Is Marcus in? He told me to get in touch if I decided to join.'

She stared at me in horror.

'I mean, he's not a friend or anything,' I went on. 'But he was at the fair at Wintrylaw and he told me all about the Consortium.' When she didn't answer I persisted, 'I have got the right place? He said he worked here for a year.'

'Yes,' she said finally. 'He did. He was a lovely boy.'

She was frozen to the spot and I took pity on her.

'I hope this isn't an inconvenient time.'

'No, no, not at all.' But the smile was fixed with panic. Something about the look reminded me of the bird in the taxidermist's window. 'You see, I'm the only person in at the moment and I'm just a volunteer.' She hesitated. 'Marcus is dead. I'm surprised you

235

didn't see it on the news. A dreadful road accident, they say.'

'How awful! You must have been very close. Working in the same office. Sharing in the same ideals.' I was laying it on thick, but she was taken in by it.

'Oh, yes. We're all very committed to the cause.'

I didn't want to ask her about Thomas or Ronnie. I couldn't pretend to a credible chance relationship with them too. So I tried an indirect approach. 'It must be a good place to work. It makes a difference, doesn't it, if you can believe in what you do.'

'Oh, yes,' she said again. 'We're very happy here.'

'None of the niggles and bitchiness you get in most offices, then?'

She answered without hesitation. 'Dear me, no. Nothing like that.'

If Thomas had written to Shona Murray about events at the Consortium, it seemed unlikely that this plump volunteer would know anything about it.

'Wasn't Philip Samson one of your workers?' I made my voice as gushing as I could manage without throwing up. 'I used to love his television programmes. Tell me, what was he like in real life?'

She was tempted to lie, I could tell. But in the end her conscience got the better of her. 'I never actually met him. He was a supporter of course and his wife, Joanna, is here all the time. But Philip never got involved with the day-to-day work of the office.'

So, if Thomas became a volunteer here in the hope of meeting his father, he would have been disappointed.

'I do hope you'd still like to join us,' she said. 'I can help you with that.'

'I think I should.'

'We volunteers try to do our best.' I wondered how many real staff were usually employed here, but it seemed tactless to ask. It would imply that I didn't think she was up to the job. 'Just take a seat and I'll find a membership form.'

She turned and pulled open a drawer in one of the big filing cabinets. The brown jersey skirt was stretched and baggy around the bum. She lifted out a file and returned to the desk.

'I wish now I'd joined the organization when I was talking to Marcus,' I said. 'So he realized he'd talked me into it. He almost persuaded me then, but you know how it is. You need time to think about these things.'

'Oh, I do agree.' She bent earnestly across the desk towards me. One of the walls was made up almost entirely of windows and the sun was streaming in. I caught a whiff of smelly armpit. 'We none of us take the Consortium lightly. It's a difficult decision to make to become involved. But we do have to come together over these important issues. I see it as a moral fight. I don't think that's putting it too strongly. We can't let our enemies have their own way. We simply can't.'

She wrung her hands. It seemed an extreme response. This was interesting. Thomas had talked about a crusade. What had fired them up to this point?

'Enemies?' I asked lightly, not mocking her but sounding as if I needed to be convinced.

'Oh, yes! There are people all over the countryside who have a vested interest in seeing the Consortium fail. Politicians, conservationists, woolly-minded liberals . . .' She paused. She wanted to add to the list but she was running out of steam. 'Ramblers!' she cried triumphantly.

'I see.'

Obviously I sounded sceptical, because she really started to wind herself up then. 'Let me tell you, young lady, that two young men involved in the struggle have died recently. One of them was your friend Marcus. The police might see that as a coincidence, but I don't.'

If she was hoping to shock me into listening to her seriously she succeeded. While the idea of a vendetta against the Consortium seemed ludicrous, it was an angle I hadn't considered before, and there was a logic, a simplicity in her theory, which was appealing.

'Do you really think they were killed just because they worked for the Consortium?'

'Yes,' she said firmly. 'I do.'

'Who by?'

Woolly minded liberals? Ramblers?

'As I've told you. Enemies of the cause.' Her eyes were wild. She believed absolutely in what she was saying. But then, some people had believed that foot and mouth had been introduced by Greenpeace to get back at the farmers.

'If you have any evidence,' I said carefully, 'you should go to the police.' What I really wanted, of course, was for her to share any evidence she had with me.

She opened her mouth to speak, but before the words came out there were footsteps on the stairs. I turned to see Marjorie, Stuart Howdon's wife, looking very Conservative Ladies Luncheon Club in a blue silk dress. For a moment she seemed not to recognize me and directed her attention to the woman on the other side of the desk.

'How are you coping, Doreen?' she asked brightly. 'Any more queries from the press?'

'If they ring I just say that no one's available to speak to them at present.'

'Good girl.' As if Doreen had been six. Then she turned her focus to me. 'What are you doing here?'

'This young lady wants to become a member.' Doreen beamed.

'I don't think so. I don't really think Miss Bartholomew shares our aims and objectives.' She stood back, leaving the way to the door clear for me. It was a hint and I took it.

I waited in the car for more than an hour, hoping that Marjorie would leave and I could get more information from Doreen, but there was no sign of her. By now, I thought, as I drove off, Doreen would have been persuaded that I was one of the enemies of the Consortium and I'd get nothing from her anyway.

Chapter Twenty-seven

When I got back from Warren Farm I turned my attention to Harry Pool. If I could find out where he lived, I could talk to him at home. It would be quieter there and we wouldn't be overheard. But he was ex-directory. Everyone seems to be these days. I don't know why, but it became really important to track him down. Perhaps it was because I hadn't discovered anything useful at Warren Farm. It ate away at me. Tom had been uneasy about something going on at the yard. Marcus had mentioned that first and Ellen had confirmed it. A sensible voice, somewhere behind my eyes, said, *Tell Farrier. This is his work, not yours. Let it go.* But being out, sniffing around, was better than sitting in Sea View brooding, and at least it would get Jess off my back.

At four o'clock I was parked outside the haulage yard, waiting. Just up the road was a church hall where some dance classes must have been going on. Cars came along and dropped off little girls in shiny black leotards, their hair pinned up so they looked all bare and skinny. There were even some lads, Billy Elliot wannabes. The parents waited and watched them safely in before driving away. No one noticed me. I was just another mother waiting for a five-year-old ballerina. It might sound strange, but sitting there for all those hours, I wondered for the first time what it would be like to have kids. It had honestly never occurred to me before.

Harry didn't appear until six-thirty. The dancers were older now. Young teenagers in leg warmers, leggings and baggy sweatshirts. Some made their own way, giggling and gabbing up the road, but there was still a steady stream of doting parents. By then I was desperate for a wee. I thought there must be a toilet in the hall, and I was about to gamble that he wasn't at work that day, that he was out, touting for business, when the nose of his Jag pushed through the gateway and pulled up just on my side. He got out and swung the big iron gates together, locking them before getting back into the car and driving off.

He took the road to the sea front, then indicated south at the Playhouse. I slipped through the lights just in time and followed him, two cars back. We drove past the clubs and the pubs where the teenage dancers would hang out in a couple of years' time, where they probably hung out now, on a Friday night, all tarted up, with an older boyfriend to get in the drinks. It was strangely dark for a summer evening. No rain but glowering cloud, giving an unnatural feel. Like there was an eclipse or something. Some of the neon signs were on, flashing, and some of the cars had switched on headlights.

They were digging up the road near Cullercoats harbour and the traffic was slow. It wasn't hard to keep up with Harry Pool in his plum-coloured Jag. He turned away from the sea just past that big church, the one where I'd sung Christmas carols when I was still making an effort to be good. The road was a cul-de-sac so I shouldn't lose him now and I didn't want him to see me. I parked on the front next to a shut-down hot dog stand and went up the street on foot.

He'd already parked on the drive of a big three-storeyed house. It was detached, all gables and porches, older and classier than I'd imagined. I'd pictured him in a brick monstrosity, like something from an American soap, on a new estate. Mrs Mariner hadn't exaggerated how much money he must be making. This was a long way from the little street in North Shields. He got out of the car and clicked the key fob to lock it. He didn't look at the street. There was another car in the drive, a small VW with chil-dren's seats fitted in the back. He went into the house and shut the door behind him. I walked past slowly but I couldn't see anything interesting. The only room visible from the road was a sitting room, quite grand, with a piano against one wall and a big bowl of flowers in the fireplace, and that was empty. I bottled out of ringing the bell. I hadn't worked out what to say. There was a distant rattle of a metro train. The line must run past the back of his house.

I started back towards my car but at the main road turned onto the flat area of grass they call the Links. I thought it might be possible to get to the back of the Pool house. There were a couple of kids kicking a ball around and a woman being pulled by a dog on a lead. I stuck my hands deep in my jeans pockets and walked as if I was lost in thought, like I'd had a row with my boyfriend and needed to be alone. No one took any notice. The kids picked up the ball and ran off. The woman disappeared towards the Sea Life

Centre. I gave a quick look round, then climbed the fence onto the metro line embankment. The fence was wire mesh, high but buckled in places. It had been climbed before. The other side was wild, trees and shrubs had been allowed to grow thickly together to repel vandals and graffiti artists. No one would be able to see me, even if a train went by. I undid my jeans and crouched to have that piss, taking care not to sting my bum on the nettles, but so desperate by then that nothing else mattered.

The houses by the church were separated from the embankment by a big wall with glass cemented into the top. I thought they'd have burglar alarms and security lights too. I stood by the wall, knowing that Harry Pool's back garden was on the other side, but all I could see were the upstairs windows. I thought I could hear children's voices, but I couldn't tell if they came from a neighbouring garden. It was dead frustrating, not being able to see in, and in the end it was too much for me. I threw my jumper onto the top of the wall and rooted around in the undergrowth for something to stand on; all sorts of rubbish had been thrown in there. In the end I found a plastic bin. It was split down the side, but firm enough to hold my weight when I turned it upside down. I was able to haul myself up far enough to look over.

At my end of the garden there was a fruit cage and some apple trees, which broke the line of the wall and gave me some cover. Then a vegetable plot, then down a couple of steps to a lawn and flower beds, with a patio next to the house. Everything very tidy. The lawn had stripes down it. Not Philip Samson's style at all. I'd been looking in books and magazines since I'd found out what he did for a living and he liked wilderness, everything blurred together, over-grown. The embankment was more his sort of place.

Harry Pool was sitting on the patio, watching the children whose voices I'd heard earlier. They must have been his grandkids but they were just as much at home as if they'd been in their place. I remembered the children's seats in the VW and thought that Harry's wife must look after them while their parents were at work. Harry had mentioned that after Tom's funeral. There were two of them, a girl aged four or five and a younger boy, still unsteady on his feet. They were playing on a yellow plastic slide and occasionally Harry got up to help. A French window from the house was open. A light had been switched on in the room inside and a woman was laying the table. Because of the light I could see her clearly. She was middle-aged but still very smart, younger than Harry by about ten years. Something disturbed her in her task because she left the room by a door I couldn't see. A little later she returned and walked to the French window.

'Come on, you two. Your mummy's arrived.'

Harry chased them inside but didn't follow them. He sat down again and lit a cigar. I could smell it above the garden smells of cut grass and honeysuckle. A little later the woman joined him and sat beside him on the white, wrought-iron bench. The neigh-bourhood was very quiet and I could just make out what she said.

'Supper's ready when you feel like it.'

He seemed lost in thought and didn't reply.

'You look sad tonight.' I saw her take his hand. She

was wearing white linen trousers. Her hand on top of his rested on her knee. 'What is it?'

'Nothing,' he said. 'Nothing at all.'

He stood up and they walked hand in hand into the house. I slid down the wall, pulling my jumper behind me. The glass had snagged a hole in the sleeve. It was only Matalan but it was a favourite and I was well pissed off that I'd ruined it for nothing.

I phoned him the next day at the yard. I still didn't have a proper game plan but I did have a vague script in my head. He didn't answer himself. I spoke to Kenny, who didn't seem to recognize my voice.

'Mr Pool please. It's personal.'

I could sense Kenny's curiosity but he didn't say anything. There was a moment's silence then, 'Harry Pool.' Booming, so I had to hold the receiver away from my ear.

'Mr Pool, this is Lizzie Bartholomew. We met at Thomas Mariner's funeral.'

'Aye,' he said. 'So we did.'

'We had met before actually. I was one of the reporters when you gave the news conference at the yard about Mike Spicer.'

'Were you, though?' Noncommittal. Amused, rather than hostile, I thought.

'I wondered if I might do a more in-depth piece.'

'Bit young to be a hardened reporter, aren't you? What are you? Some sort of trainee?'

I adapted the script in my head. 'Yes. I have to submit a piece for college. I mean, obviously I hope I can sell it too. But it'd be really great if you could spare the time to talk to me.'

I knew I sounded overeager, but it didn't matter.

A student hoping for an exclusive would be. And how old did he think I was? Eighteen? Nineteen?

'Why not?' he said. 'You'll not make a worse hash of it than the professionals.'

'When can we meet?'

'Might as well get it over with. Can you make it today? Not at the yard. I've got to be home this afternoon anyway. I'll give you the address.'

I almost said it was OK, I knew where he lived, but I shut up just in time.

So at two o'clock I was back in Cullercoats, driving along the sea front towards the big house next to the church. And this time I could park outside and walk up the gravel drive and ring the doorbell. The VW wasn't there and, though Harry didn't say, I guessed his wife was out. When he opened the door he was in shirtsleeves with a mug of tea in his hand. I wasn't important enough for the grand lounge at the front with the piano and the flowers, or even the dining room with the French window. Instead he took me into a big kitchen, which was just what you'd expect – quarry tiles on the floor, everything fitted, a long pine table. He waved the teapot at me and, when I nodded, poured out a mug. He pushed a tin of biscuits across the table towards me.

'Help yourself,' he said. 'What I know of students, they're always starving.'

I'd dressed carefully. A trainee, trying to make an impression. Knee-length skirt and cheap white shirt. Hair pinned up.

'You said you were a friend of Thomas's family,' he said casually. He sat at the table opposite to me. 'How do you know Kay, then?'

Panic. It couldn't be through work. She was a
teacher and I was studying journalism. 'Church,' I
said. 'We met at church.'

'My,' he said. 'And I thought Methodists didn't
drink. You put away enough the day we buried
Thomas.'

'It's more my parents' thing,' I admitted. 'The
church, I mean. I don't often go now.'

'Kay was a bit prim even when she was your age,'
he said. 'She was a Sunday school teacher when all
the other lasses were out enjoying themselves. We
knew her very well at one time, Bridget and me. She
baby-sat when the children were small.' He looked up,
smiling. 'And now they're grown up with kids of their
own.'

I took another chance. 'It must have been a shock
when she found out she was pregnant.'

'Aye, so it must, but we're not here to talk about
that. There was gossip enough at the time.' He smiled
to take the edge off the rebuke. 'We're here to talk
about poor Mike Spicer. Now tell me, Miss Bartholomew. What do you want to know?'

'Before we look into the details of Mr Spicer's case,
would you mind giving me some details about your
company? How you came to set it up, that sort of
thing. You're the Road Haulage Association representative and the background would give readers a great
understanding of the pressures on the industry.'

Most people like talking about themselves. Harry
Pool certainly did. 'I took redundancy from the shipyard,' he said, 'and I could see there was no chance of
more work in that field. It seemed a good time to set
up on my own. I'd always liked the idea. I started off

with one wagon, doing local runs down to Teesside and up to the Borders. Then I sold my car to buy a second, a bit bigger, a curtain-sider. Now I've a mixed fleet of twenty-five and we've a certificate for international work.'

'So you run the risk of bringing illegal immigrants into the country too, like Mike Spicer?'

It was a random question to support the fiction that I was doing a follow-up piece on the Spicer news conference, but Harry Pool's attitude changed. He didn't lose his temper, nothing like that. But he suddenly became alert. Before he'd been laid-back, humouring a student, now every word was spoken with care.

'What exactly are you implying, Miss Bartholomew?'

'Nothing. Just that working overseas must involve more risk, more complications. Not just because of the dangers of unknowingly carrying asylum seekers.'

He conceded that I was right. There was a lot of red tape. 'We had to think very carefully before expanding into Europe. Previously we occupied a niche in the market. Big companies don't like delivering to the Borders. There are no motorways and transport time is slow. Obviously there's a lot more competition now, and not just with British firms.'

'They have lower fuel costs?'

'Much lower.' He quoted some of the figures I'd heard from Kenny. 'The price of fuel is crippling for a medium-sized business like ours. How can I compete with local firms in Germany and France?'

'Don't the French hauliers have higher overheads?' I asked. 'National insurance? Tax?' I'd been reading up on the subject. I hadn't wanted to look a complete prat.

'Maybe they have.' He would have preferred to be allowed to continue unchallenged. 'If they have to pay them. A good accountant and you can get round most of that. There's no avoiding the duty on diesel.'

'Isn't there? I'd heard there was a black market trade in the red diesel farmers use.'

'That's all talk and rumour.' For the first time the good humour slipped. I didn't tell him the talk and rumour had come from Kenny. 'Reputable hauliers couldn't afford to get mixed up in that.'

'Someone must buy the stuff, though. I read that it's smuggled in. Through Ireland, they say.'

'Shady outfits with nothing to lose. Not me. I prefer to play it straight. That's why I'll have nothing to do with convoys and blockades.' He looked pointedly at his watch. 'Is there anything else? I'm expecting an important call.'

I closed the notebook. 'How did Thomas feel about all that?'

'What do you mean?'

'The convoys and protests. He was a Countryside Consortium supporter. They backed the fuel protesters, didn't they. They see cheap fuel as a countryside issue.' According to the leaflets Marcus had given me at Wintrylaw.

Harry didn't seem inclined to discuss the finer points of the argument. 'I didn't care what Thomas did in his own time. In my time he was there to work.'

'Did he enjoy it?'

He gave an awkward laugh. 'Does anyone enjoy work at that age? I know damn fine I didn't.'

'But nothing was bothering him? He got on OK with everyone?'

'Of course. We all did. They're like family, my lads.'

He stood up. I felt I was being chased away, as he'd chased his grandchildren back to their mother the night before. As he shut the door behind me, I heard the phone ring.

It was as I was on my way back to the car that I realized how relieved he'd been to see me go. He didn't seem to notice that he'd given me no new information on the Spicer case.

Chapter Twenty-eight

I had a shock when I got back to Sea View. There was Inspector Farrier sitting in the kitchen, drinking tea and chatting to Jess like he was one of the Newbiggin Mafia and they'd been friends for ever. I'd got right into the room before they saw me. Farrier looked up first. His face creased into a cross between a smile and a wink, but Jess was so wrapped up in what she was telling him that she didn't notice me. 'Our Lizzie's a sensible girl, Inspector. A bit headstrong at times, but that's hardly surprising, is it, after all she's been through? And really, she's not been a peck of bother since she arrived.'

I could feel myself blushing, at least my skin turning hot. Farrier was enjoying every minute. He grinned and that's when Jessie realized I was there. She was startled – 'Hey, man, Lizzie, don't creep up like that.' But not embarrassed. She made an excuse about nipping to the shop to pick up extra milk, but Farrier said he'd been sat all day and maybe I wouldn't mind a walk either. We could pick up the milk on our way back.

I let him out through the front door. He admired the little garden and the view, but I wasn't listening. I was thinking about what he could be doing there. He

must have found out that I'd left the pub with Marcus
Tate that evening before he died. There were a couple
of lads in waders fishing from the beach, and a father
and daughter flying a kite, but no one to overhear us.
A breeze was blowing from the water, gusting so the
kite swooped and dived, and we started walking along
the sea wall. It wasn't sunbathing weather.

'I should have been round before,' Farrier said, 'to
apologize in person. I believed Howdon. I couldn't see
what he had to gain by lying.'

'He's a lawyer. You should have known better.
It's what they do for a living.' It wasn't that I didn't
appreciate the gesture, but I felt awkward. Apology
doesn't come naturally to policemen and, despite the
warm and fuzzy image, that's what Farrier was. Then
I realized. 'You've not come all this way just for that.'

'I had a phone call from your MP,' he said. 'Shona
Murray. You went to see her.'

'I had to do something.' Defensive, because I was
sure he was going to warn me about meddling. 'You
thought I was a murderer.'

'No,' he said, so softly I could hardly hear the
words above the water breaking on the rocks and the
wind. 'I never did.'

I wanted to believe him. 'Did she show you the
letter Thomas wrote?'

'Aye. It took her a bit of time to get round to it,
the silly woman, but she got in touch eventually.'

'I told her to. I gave her your name.' It's not my
style to crawl, but I needed the brownie points. I
wanted him to tell me what was in the letter.

He stopped, leaned his back against the painted

railings. 'You could have come to me, Lizzie. I'd have chased it up for you.'

I looked at him. Couldn't help it. I could hardly walk on without him. He was dressed like a student who's come to learning late, in middle age. There were a few of them at university. Nerdy jeans, too baggy round the legs, a hand-knitted sweater, ribbed, beige with little brown flecks. In the winter he'd probably wear a duffel coat. Whenever I'd seen him before he'd been in a suit and tie, and I couldn't work out what the scruffy gear was all about. Was this his day off or had he dressed down on purpose, a way of persuading me to lower my guard?

'What do you want from me?'

I knew I sounded rude, but the persuasion was starting to work. I could feel myself being seduced by the fatherly voice, the patience and the kindness. I'm a sucker for older men. Look at Ronnie Laing. I've got the discrimination of a rabbit. Manic depressives are always being taken in by unsuitable people.

The wind was making his eyes water. He took a white hanky from the jeans pocket and wiped them.

'I want to know who else you've been talking to, what else you've found out.'

'Picking my brains?'

'Yes. Just that.'

'Why isn't this official, then? Why aren't you with the skinny cow with the notebook? Why not get me down to the station, take a proper statement?'

'Is that what you'd prefer?'

'I just want to know where I stand.'

He didn't answer.

'They still think I did it, don't they? They think it was done by a crazy, so it must be me.'

'Some of them think that,' he said. 'Not me.' He looked out at the sea. 'Did you ever meet Marcus Tate?'

'At Thomas's funeral.' It was a relief. I thought I'd have a chance now to share my anxieties. Suddenly I didn't feel quite so lonely. But he didn't follow it up, he just started walking again. I stood where I was and shouted after him, not caring now who could hear. 'Marcus Tate . . . Do you really believe that was an accident?'

He stopped and turned. 'There's no reason to believe otherwise.'

'But you?' I was screaming and not just to be heard above the tide. 'What do you think happened?'

'Why don't you tell me what *you* think?' His voice was measured, but I wasn't taken in. He'd stuck his neck out coming to see me. He was as obsessed by the case as I was. He'd have his own reasons for that – things to prove at work, old scores to settle – but he was committed to digging away until he found reasons he could believe in. It kept him awake at night too. A sharp gust of wind blew a shower of spindrift. I could taste the salt on my tongue.

'Do you fancy a coffee?' I asked. 'There's a new place along the prom that does a decent cappuccino.'

He'd been tense, standing there, waiting to see if I'd confide in him. He nodded uncertainly, not sure whether or not he'd got an answer. Let him wait a bit longer.

The café was on a square, part of the same development as the new promenade. Brick and block paving and Victorian-style street furniture. Bland and unimaginative, it had nothing in common with the original east coast fishing village. I wondered if the architect had been there since it was built, if he woke up with nightmares. I knew Steve, the lad who ran the café. He'd sunk his redundancy from Ellington pit into the lease of the building and the purchase of a seriously impressive Italian coffee machine. He'd probably bought into the council's dream that a couple of wrought-iron lampposts would bring the tourists flocking. I'd been there on the opening night and he'd talked about turning it into a classy, cosmopolitan place, hiring a chef to serve Mediterranean food in the evenings. But it wasn't going to turn him into a second Harry Pool. Anyone could have told him that people from outside wouldn't leave their cars unattended in Newbiggin at night.

Surprisingly, though, the locals loved the place. It was somewhere to meet. Young mums gathered there after dropping kids at nursery, and teenagers dropped in on their way back from school and imagined they were sophisticated. That afternoon it was like a scene from an arty European movie. Steve's unemployed mates were in, looking dark and brooding, chain-smoking, posing until the lasses from Ashington College arrived back on the bus. Farrier and I moved outside. There were a few rickety garden tables and chairs on the square; he stuck out umbrellas when the wind wasn't so strong. The sun had come out. Farrier had paid for the coffee. He'd asked for a receipt. I supposed he'd claim it back as informant expenses. I didn't like the idea of that. Hated the thought of grassing.

'So this is informal?' I said.

'Confidential. The information you give will never be traced back to you.'

'What did Thomas write in his letter to Shona Murray?'

'You can't expect me to tell you that. It's confidential too.'

'No deal, then.'

We faced up to each other across the table. A couple of gulls were fighting over some discarded chips on the other side of the square.

'I need,' I went on, 'a gesture of good faith. You must be able to understand that. I know some of it. I know he was intending to become a whistle-blower.'

'You know most of it, then.'

'Who was he going to shop?'

Farrier shrugged, as if to say that I'd won and much good may it do me. 'He didn't give Ms Murray any details. Honestly. Nothing useful. He said he suspected "a prominent member of the community" of breaking the law. Before he gave her evidence he wanted an assurance that his position would be protected.'

'What position? His position at work?'

'I don't know. Really, Lizzie. Why else would I be here, grovelling to you?'

He was hardly grovelling, but he seemed genuinely frustrated by the lack of information. I wasn't sure if he was telling the truth about Thomas's letter to Shona, but I'd probably had all he was prepared to give.

'Have you got anything on Harry Pool?'

'He's no criminal record.'

'That's not what I asked. You must have done some checking. Whistle-blowing implies work, doesn't it?'

He wiped a smear of foaming milk from his top lip before saying cagily, 'We haven't turned up anything significant.'

'He lives in a bloody big house,' I said. 'Even for someone with his own business. Especially when hauliers are supposed to be going bust because of the high fuel charges.'

'Have you been to see him too?'

I nodded.

'And?'

'He didn't admit to stabbing Thomas to death, if that's what you're asking. He makes a big effort to come over all law-abiding and respectable. Condemning the fuel protesters. Standing up for the other members of his trade body. All that.'

'But?'

'Dunno if there are any buts. Maybe he's really a nice guy.' I paused. 'Did you know that he'd fallen out with Thomas, a month or so before the murder?'

'No. Who told you that?'

I paused again. 'Marcus Tate.'

'Did you talk to him at the funeral, then?'

'Everyone went to the pub afterwards.' That was true, wasn't it? I still didn't want to give too much away. 'You should have come.'

'I wasn't invited. What else did Marcus tell you?'

'Not much.' I remembered the notes I'd made in Sea View at the kitchen table, could see the spidery writing. 'That Thomas saw his voluntary work for the Countryside Consortium as a crusade.'

'He was young,' Farrier said. 'Everything's black and white at that age.'

I would have liked to ask him what *he'd* been passionate about as a kid. Instead I said, 'What do you know about the Countryside Consortium?'

'Not much. It's a pressure group for the country-side, isn't it? Pulled together after foot and mouth. Landowners working to limit rights of way, small busi-nessmen, people interested in field sports. It started in the north but now it's a nationwide thing. There was a rally at Westminster not long ago. Huge numbers turned out. They're talking about putting up candidates for parliamentary by-elections.'

'Ronnie Laing is a supporter.'

'I suppose that's how Tom Mariner got involved, then.'

'No. That's what's so weird. Tom hated his stepfather.'

'I should go,' Farrier said suddenly. Perhaps his wife would have his tea on the table. Perhaps he had an appointment with the thin-lipped Sergeant Miles. I didn't care.

'Have you been to Wintrylaw, talked to Joanna?'

'Yes.'

'I don't understand why Philip asked me to find Thomas. He and Ronnie Laing were friends. He must have known about a stepson.'

'Na. Not if they were the sort of friends who only had an interest in common. We're not like women. We don't share our life stories over the first pint.'

He looked at his watch. I didn't want him to leave.

'Aren't you interested in what else Marcus told me?'

'Sure.' Being polite, playing the game.

'Thomas was devastated when his girlfriend dumped him but he was convinced he'd get her back.'

'Was he?' At least there was a spark of surprise. 'I interviewed Miss Ravendale. A very tough young lady. She didn't strike me as someone who'd change her mind. Hasn't she got a new boyfriend? You were sitting next to them at the funeral.'

'Dan Meech. I was at college with him.'

'Were you now? Neither of them was very forthcoming with me. They don't like the police. Fascist pigs. They didn't quite say so. Well brought up. Manners. But they made it clear.' He hesitated. 'Are you likely to see them again?'

'No plans to.'

'Might be useful to know why Thomas was so sure they'd get back together. Was she seeing him, do you think, behind Dan's back?'

'I wouldn't have thought that would be her style.'

'If you do get anything out of her, you'll let me know?' Then he stood up, without waiting for an answer.

We walked back along the sea wall. The fisherman were still there, but the little girl and her father had gone.

Just before we got to Sea View I said, 'I was with Marcus Tate the evening before he died.'

Dumb, I know. Perhaps I just wanted Farrier to take more notice of me. It didn't work at first. He didn't even stop walking.

'You said. You all went to the pub.'

'After that.'

Then he did stop. 'What happened?'

'I was pissed. He took me back to the house in Seaton Delaval. Later, he drove me home. It was eleven, eleven-thirty. He wasn't drunk. There was no way he drove that car over the bridge. Not then.'

He didn't say anything. He just stared, and it was like he was trying to get his head round the facts, trying to make sense of it.

'I suppose you want me to make a statement.'

'No. Never mind that yet. Does anyone else know you were there?'

I shook my head.

'Don't tell anyone, Lizzie. Promise. And forget what I said about Nell Ravendale. Just keep your head down. Go away for a while. I don't want any nasty accidents happening to you.'

He touched my arm lightly and walked away.

Chapter Twenty-nine

Farrier was being kind when he suggested that I leave Newbiggin for a few days and I should have taken his advice. But isn't kindness the biggest turn-on in the world? His concern for me surprised and touched me and I didn't want to run away. His casual suggestion that I might speak to Nell took on an importance that he hadn't intended. I felt I'd be doing him an enormous favour. It would please him. I imagined him throwing his arms around me in a hug, spontaneous and father-like. Those were the pictures I was running in my head. Pathetic, huh?

I was still taking the pills. I don't want you to think I was delusional. Not at that stage. But stress is a factor and Marcus Tate's death, his face pressed against the windscreen as the shiny new car fell towards the River Wansbeck, haunted me. I told myself that he would have been unconscious by then, but I pictured him fighting to free himself. Nicky always seemed to be lurking at the back of my mind too at that time. The flashbacks were occurring more frequently, taking me unawares during the day as well as at night. It was better to imagine Farrier, scruffy and safe in his ill-fitting jeans, telling me how brave and clever I was. Those thoughts kept the nightmares at bay.

So I phoned Dan.

'Hi,' I said. I'd got hold of him first try in Absalom House. 'How're things?'

'Shit,' he said. 'Ellen's even more manic than usual and Nell's still into this guilt thing about Thomas. I think there's stuff she's not telling me.'

'It must be hard for her.'

'Yeah.' I expected him to go on to say it was hard for him too, but he showed uncharacteristic restraint.

'Do you think it would help her to talk to me about it?'

Social work training's brilliant. It gives you a cliché for every occasion and the bottle to deliver it straight. He took the question seriously. Perhaps he was thinking that if he could persuade Nell to talk to me it might stop her whingeing at him. But perhaps I was being hard on him.

'It might,' he said at last.

'Maybe we could meet up for a drink sometime.' I was careful not to be too pushy. Much better if he thought the suggestion had come from him.

'You doing anything tonight?' he asked.

'Nothing important.'

'I'm running a session for an after-school club at Acting Out. Nell's going to help. You could meet us there. Sevenish?'

I said that sevenish would be fine.

Acting Out operated from a small community arts centre in North Shields. Once it had been a church and I remembered it still had that religious smell of damp prayer books and old ladies' clothes. I'd been there a few times before. Dan had first become involved with the group when he was a student and he'd dragged me along to watch him in performance or prancing around with a load of kids. It was where we'd first had sex. I wondered if he remembered the occasion or if I was just one in a string of conquests, and we'd all become blurred in his memory. I suspected that Nell would stand out.

I still remembered it in detail. He'd been helping to rehearse a bunch of older kids for some musical they were doing and by the time it was over it was late. I was bored and wondering how I was going to get back to Newbiggin. They trooped off to the pub to catch last orders, expecting that we'd follow them, but we didn't. Someone had been sorting through a pile of junk, looking for costumes, and we ended up on that. Perhaps that's where the smell of musty clothing in my memory came from. The tangle of velvet skirts and threadbare woollens protected our knees and elbows from the wooden floor.

Inside the building hadn't changed much. The kids were just leaving when I got there, yelling and swearing as they barged out through the double arched door. No one stopped to let me in. I wanted to shout a lecture about manners, but at their age I'd have been just the same. In the lobby posters advertised forthcoming events: a local blues band, a folk festival, Acting Out's summer play for kids. There were photos to go with that. Dan looked sinister in a top hat, false moustache and long, black cloak. Like an old-fashioned undertaker, I thought, though I'm sure that wasn't what was intended. The play had a green theme and his character was called Professor Pollution.

As I took a flyer on the folk festival to give to Ray

and earn some brownie points from Jess, I saw another poster. It caught my eye because there was a picture of Wintrylaw in the background, faded and slightly out of focus as though seen through a sea mist. The print was bold against it. *Country Delights. An evening of music and poetry. Hosted by the Countryside Consortium at Wintrylaw House.* I made a note of the date.

Dan and Nell were perched on the stage in the main hall. The house lights were off and they were lit by a green spot which made them look like aliens. Someone was in the lighting box running a technical test, but Dan had nothing to do with it. He was talking to Nell. From the back I couldn't hear what they were saying. They were frozen in the green light, turned towards each other. The setting made the contact seem dramatic and intense, but the conversation could have been aimless, banal. All I could tell was that there was nothing funny. Neither was laughing. When the door swung to behind me with a bang they stopped. The hall was still dark and they couldn't see who'd come in.

'Hi, Lizzie!' Dan called. 'Is that you?'

I walked to the front to join them.

'What are you doing here?' Nell asked. Direct but not unfriendly.

'Dan suggested we meet up for a drink.'

I was surprised. I'd thought he'd have prepared her. She looked at him and seemed to guess what I was thinking, then smiled. It was as if she was letting him off the hook. He hadn't had the guts to tell her he'd set up the meeting, but she understood.

'I've got to lock up,' he said quickly. 'You two go on. I'll catch you up.'

'Dan's pissed off because I can't stop talking about Thomas,' Nell said.

'I don't care,' I said. 'I'll talk about him too.'

She jumped down from the stage. 'We'll be at Connie's.'

He nodded, as if that was what he'd been expecting.

Dan's usual taste in pubs was basic. He liked drinking holes, street-corner places where the same elderly men sat over their pints of mild and the only food available was a dusty bag of pork scratchings or a jar of cockles. Connie's was different. It was a café-bar on the fish quay, part of a big building which had once been a chandler's. It had slowly whirring ceiling fans and a jungle of plants in pots, a lot of bamboo and pale wood. Connie's had tables outside but Nell led me in. It reminded me of the place in Morpeth where Joanna had held her exhibition, not in the style of the décor but the clientele. It was the sort of place where I felt intimidated by the smart clothes and the knowing voices. But Nell acted as if she owned it. Seventeen and so cool.

'Have you been here before?'

I shook my head. A kind of admission that I didn't move in the right circles or know the right people.

'Connie's Thai. Fat Sammy had the place before. It was OK. Nothing special. Then he went on holiday and brought her back. Bought her, according to rumour. Thought she'd be a nice, subservient, Oriental wife. Stay in the background, wash up, clean, save on staff costs. But it didn't work out like that. She took over, introduced her own menu. She bullies him.' She leaned against the bar. 'We'd better have a bottle, hadn't we?'

'I'm driving. I'll only want a glass.'

She wrinkled her nose. 'There's not so much choice by the glass.'

'White and cold, it'll be fine for me.'

We sat by the window. Nell chose the table. Perhaps she wanted warning of Dan's approach. Perhaps she just wanted to enjoy the view.

'I can't get Thomas out of my head,' she said. 'My parents talk about counselling.'

'It might help.'

'I think it's normal to think about him,' she said. 'Someone you've cared about dies as violently as that, you're going to be upset. It would be stranger to forget.'

'Did you still care about him?'

'Of course.'

'But enough to go out with him again?'

She looked at me. There was a crust of green paint just above her eyebrow, like a toad's wart. 'What do you mean?'

'Were you still seeing him? Sleeping with him? Even after you were going out with Dan.'

She stared at me as if I were a monster. Kids can be such prudes. I've noticed it before. It's the middle-aged who have affairs and screw around. Kids are intense. They take fidelity seriously. They talk about love as if it means something.

'Of course not. What do you take me for?'

From behind the counter came the sound of orders barked in broken English, the crash of crockery.

'Why did you dump him? Was it just because you'd met Dan?'

'No.' She paused, sorting out her thoughts and her words. 'He was all drama and mystery. It was impossible to tell what was real.'

'So you never led him to believe that you'd go out with him again?'

'What is this about?' She was imperious. Again I was astounded by her confidence. Perhaps it was having parents who believed she was a creative genius, a boyfriend who worshipped her. But I had the feeling that even with all that I'd never have faith in myself. Not as she did.

'You wanted to talk about Thomas. I'm talking. Did you ever have any second thoughts about dumping him?'

'Not really.'

'What does that mean?'

'It means that if I'd known he was going to die horribly and suddenly like that, I wouldn't have left him. I'd have hung on for a few months. It would have made life much easier. I'd have got more sympathy, wouldn't I? Instead people don't expect me to care. They put me down as cruel and hard-hearted.' She looked suddenly wretched. 'I *do* care, you know. But it wouldn't have worked out between us.'

'When did you last see him?'

'A couple of weeks before he died.'

'What happened?'

'He was waiting for me outside school. I was late

getting out. There'd been an English exam. Shakespeare. And afterwards we were talking with the
teachers. The usual post-mortem. He was there, waiting. Patient. He could have been there all day, and I
had the feeling that if I hadn't come out then, he'd
have waited until the morning to catch me on my way
back in. I knew it was me he was there for. I could
tell by his face when he saw me walk out of the gate.
But I said, "Hey. What are you doing here?" Friendly
but casual. I didn't want to encourage him. "Why
aren't you at work?"'

She shut her eyes. Perhaps she was getting the
picture clear in her head. Perhaps she just wanted to
shut it all out.

'He was really excited. Eager, bouncing around
like some puppy or something. Wanting you to pat his
head and tell him he was a good boy. "You won't
believe what's happened, Nell. You won't believe what
I've found out." And it was too much. He was always
too much. That was what attracted me in the first
place and that's what I couldn't cope with in the end.'
She looked up at me. 'I expect you think I'm a
heartless bitch.'

I shook my head. 'How could you possibly know
what was going to happen?'

'I knew he was desperate to talk to me, but I
couldn't face it. I'd had the shitty exam and another
in the morning to revise for and I knew how it would
be. He'd go over the same stuff again, about how he
hated Ronnie and about how things might have been
different if he'd had a real father, and he'd suck all
the energy out of me. At the start I found it flattering.

That he needed me so much. But I couldn't take it any more.' She composed herself to complete her story. 'A friend drove out of school. She stopped and offered me a lift. I just shouted to him, "Sorry, Tom, can't stay and chat." And we drove off. That was the last time I saw him. That's the picture I have of him. Staring after me as if I'd just spat in his face.'

'Did he try to get in touch with you again?'

'He left a message on the answering machine at home. It was much more controlled. Quite weird. *Sorry to have missed you the other day, but probably it's as well we don't meet until I've got something definite to report. Be in touch soon.* That was it. Weird, as I say. One of the reasons I wrote to him was to make it clear that I wouldn't go out with him again. That I hadn't wanted to hurt him, but I wasn't going to change my mind.'

'Did you tell Inspector Farrier about the meeting and the message?'

'It didn't come up. He just wanted to know where I was the morning Thomas was killed. And it's not the sort of thing you'd discuss with a stranger.'

I didn't ask her what she'd told Farrier, though I was curious. He'd have checked out any alibi. And I didn't really think she was capable of stabbing Thomas with a knife. Her guilt was more subtle than that.

'Do you have any idea what Thomas was on about? What he'd found out?'

She hesitated, and for a moment I thought she might have something useful and important to say, then she shook her head. 'Something about his father perhaps. It was a real obsession with him.'

That would fit in with what Ellen had told me. But why would Thomas's discovery that Philip Samson was his father have triggered his murder?

Nell was gazing through the leaves of a giant umbrella plant out of the window. Suddenly her face relaxed and she stopped being angry and haunted. Dan was walking along the pavement towards the bar, moving easily round the people, taking the last of the evening sun. He caught her eye and stopped, tentative, wondering if he'd given us long enough to talk. She smiled and waved at him. He came into the bar and started to pull over a chair to join us, but I stood up to make my excuses. I'd have only been in the way. I was almost at the door when something occurred to me, a question which had been niggling away at the back of my mind since I'd chanced on the news conference at Harry Pool's yard and which took on a sudden and surprising relevance.

'Those Eastern European girls at the hostel, where exactly did they come from?'

I didn't think Dan had heard. He was looking at Nell, eyes glazed, thinking of sex.

'Romania,' he said in the end. 'I think that's it. It could be the Czech Republic. They don't have much English.'

'Were they placed by social services?'

He was still finding it hard to concentrate. 'You know what Ellen's like. She'll take anyone. No questions asked.'

Chapter Thirty

I didn't know anything about asylum seekers. Only what I'd read in the papers and seen on the news, and there was precious little factual reporting in that. And I didn't mind the paucity of fact. It saved me having to think through the issue clearly. My sympathy lay with the immigrants. Of course. What else would you expect? I'm a social worker, all liberal conscience and fuzzy sentiment. Just the sort of person Doreen at the Consortium despises. And there was more to it than that. A lot of the Eastern European immigrants are Roma, gypsy, and I have some fellow feeling. If the popular Newbiggin myth is to be believed, we could be related. When I hear people slagging them off, I take it personally.

I phoned a mate who worked for social services. A sort of mate. She'd trained with me, but she knew all the right games to play and she was already a team leader. That meant she didn't have to visit grubby flats any more, or think up new excuses for not drinking tea, or play with the snotty kids of her clients. It took a bit of persistence to get through to her and when she did make herself available her voice was wary. It only occurred to me later that she probably thought I was on the scrounge for a job.

'Lizzie. Hi. It's been a long time. How are things?'

'Fine,' I said, trying to sound it, only managing that mad jollity which sounds natural to infant teachers.

'We should meet up sometime.' That was the last thing either of us wanted. She'd be embarrassed to be seen with me and she'd always bored me rigid.

'Really, I was just after a favour.'

'Yeah?' The tone had turned distinctly chilly.

'Some information. It's something I'm working on. A kind of project. It's about asylum seekers.'

'Oh, right.' She was too relieved to ask what kind of project.

'Is North Tyneside one of the official dispersal areas? If so, do you know who's in charge of resettlement?'

This was a test of her competence, a sort of challenge. 'I haven't heard of the borough becoming involved. County Durham is, of course. I've read about the problems there. Let me ask around and phone you back.'

She did. Almost immediately. She was like that. Conscientious, the sort of student who always got her essays in on time. Mine usually were given higher marks, though, and that's why she didn't like me. She told me smugly that it was as she'd thought. No formal resettlement programme in our area, no one specifically responsible for immigrants. 'Sorry not to be more help,' she said as she replaced the receiver, not sounding at all as if she meant it.

Of course, that didn't mean the sad-eyed girls weren't legitimate residents of Absalom House. They could have been students. They could have been born here. But I was starting to weave a fantasy in which they had starring roles, and I was already so committed to it that the social worker's reply was pleasing.

I'd put together a story in my head, lying sleepless in Sea View watching the beams from the light buoys bounce off the ceiling. This is how it went: Harry Pool was smuggling people into the country. That's why his attitude towards me had changed when I'd asked him about bringing in asylum seekers. That's why he wasn't putting more effort into defending Michael Spicer. He wanted the issue to go away. His trucks went to Eastern Europe, didn't they? A trade in illegals would explain his affluence, the big house in Cullercoats, the flash car. Smugglers made a fortune. The papers I'd read on the subject all said that. And once the people were here perhaps Ellen helped them, the younger ones at least. As Dan had said, she'd not ask any awkward questions or check papers too carefully. She wouldn't want them ending up on the streets and dying like her son. Perhaps she was so eager to see me, that day in Cullercoats, not to give me information, but to find out how much I knew.

And perhaps Thomas had found out about it. He was in a better position than anyone to put together what was going on. He worked in the office at the yard. Even if Harry had tried to keep him out of it, there could be overheard conversations, mysterious phone messages. Nobody had ever said that Thomas was dumb. He'd work it out. Maybe he'd even seen the lorries come back and watched them unload. I ran it in my head, saw it like one of those cheesy cop shows they have on the telly on a Sunday night, all shadowy lighting and eerie electronic music. I pictured Thomas hiding behind a stack of containers, watching the dark figures climb over the tailboard of the truck. And he was living at Absalom House, so when the immigrants turned up there he'd not be taken in by whatever cover story Ellen and Harry had hatched up for them.

You can't blame me for getting excited, for being seduced by the theory. I mean, it was beautiful. Everything slotted right into place, even Marcus's idea that Thomas saw himself with a new future at work. Perhaps Harry had offered to cut him in on the deal. Perhaps Thomas had tried blackmail. OK, it didn't explain Marcus's sudden death, but perhaps that was an accident after all.

The only problem was, I couldn't see Harry or Ellen stabbing him. I mean, Ellen, come on! There might be something scary about her appearance. That dyed hair and scarlet lipstick always made me think of vampires. But she was a sweetie. She was genuinely fond of the kids in her care. She couldn't knife anyone to save her life, especially a lad who'd reminded her of her son. And I'd seen Harry playing with his grandchildren. Perhaps I'm a sentimental fool, but he didn't strike me as a violent man. That afternoon when we'd all been in the pub after the funeral threw me too. Could he possibly have gone through that charade if he'd been the cause of it? I didn't think so.

My first instinct was to go to Farrier and share my theory. The thought gave me the same feeling as when I was about to hand in an essay to my tutor at college. *Please like it. Please approve. Of my ideas and me.* Then I thought that was pathetic, and I needed something more concrete to give him anyway. At the back of my mind was the fear that, as he'd warned me off meddling, he'd be cross. He'd only be pleased if I had a really solid piece of information to hand to him, not a wild accusation against two respectable people. Otherwise, like all the other cops, he might think I was crazy.

I decided on a trip to Absalom House. It might be possible to speak to the foreign girls without bumping into Ellen or Dan. And in Sea View I was restless. I couldn't settle to anything. My prowling around the house was starting to worry Jess and she'd begun muttering about it having been a long time since Lisa had been round, and maybe I should ask her in for coffee.

She stopped me on my way out. I thought she was going to ask an unsubtle question about when I was due to see the psychiatrist next, but all she said was, 'Are you doing anything next Friday night?' It slipped out really casually and I was preoccupied, or I'd have taken more care in the answer.

'I don't think so.' I was fishing through my bag for my car keys.

'Oh, that's good. There's a ceilidh. Some friends of Ray's are getting engaged. You're invited too. It'll be a chance for you to get to know them all.'

And she beamed, delighted, so how could I refuse?

I arrived at Absalom House late in the morning and it was quiet, as I'd hoped. Dan had told me that most of the residents were expected to take on work or training. 'It's not just a doss house,' he'd said, giving me the party line. But surely the sisters wouldn't be at work or college. Not yet. Not if they were hiding from the authorities. I tried the front door, but it was locked. The windows at the front of the house were covered by net curtains and I couldn't see in without going right up to the glass. It was a busy street, a sunny day, and I didn't want to draw attention to myself.

Absalom House formed a block in the middle of a terrace and there was no access to the back from the street. I had to walk round the end of the terrace to a narrow lane, just wide enough for a car to pass through, which gave access to gardens and ramshackle garages. I made my way along it, trying to look as if I belonged, past a shed full of pigeons and a fierce dog on a long chain. I knew when I'd reached Absalom House because of the glass lean-to built onto the kitchen. There were double wrought-iron gates leading onto tarmac. No cars. Then a patch of overgrown garden. I let myself in and listened. No sound except for the barking of the dog, still furious because I'd walked past its territory.

The door into the lean-to was unlocked. It was in full sunshine and inside it was steamy, smelling of vegetation and compost. There were Gro-bags of tomatoes on the window-sill, on the floor pots with the sort of tropical plants you get in conservatories, a couple of white wicker chairs and a table. It would be a pleasant place to sit in the winter but now it was unbearably hot. I could see into one end of the L-shaped kitchen. It was much cleaner than when I'd sat there drinking tea with Dan. Suddenly a large woman in a long white apron came into view. She was vigorously wiping down surfaces with a cloth. I

felt the shot of adrenaline, as if I'd drunk five espres-
sos in one gulp, and tried to breathe deeply to relax
myself out of the panic. What if I *were* caught? I had
an imagination, didn't I? Surely I could come up with
a story for Ellen and Dan. I couldn't quite think of a
plausible one now, but something would come to me.
The woman wrung out the dishcloth and hung it over
a tap, then untied her apron, rolled it into a ball and
stuck it into her bag. I was still shaking, convinced
that she'd use the back way out into the lane, even
when she disappeared from view again. I gave her
five minutes, then went to the door so I could see the
whole of the kitchen. She'd gone.

The kitchen floor was still tacky underfoot where
it had been mopped. There was a smell of disinfec-
tant. In a corner a washing machine grated and
churned. The rest of the house seemed quiet. I looked
out into a long corridor. At one end was the front
door, at the other the big room where the kids played
pool and watched television. The hum of the washing
machine seemed a long way off and there was something unsettling about the silence. It wasn't natural,
like a school in the holidays or a pub before opening
time.

If the girls were in the house, where would they
be? I left the safety of the kitchen and moved down
the corridor towards the common room. There were
other closed doors on the way and I listened at each
one. Nothing, not even the shuffle of papers or the
clunk of a keyboard. The common room was empty.
It was a gloomy, shabby room with a smell of stale
smoke, but the woman I'd seen in the kitchen had
been there too. It was tidy. The carpet had been

hoovered and the pool cues lay in line on the table, the magazines piled, edges together, on a veneered coffee table.

I remembered the startled faces of the girls as Dan had led me on his conducted tour of the house. They hadn't been here, with the other kids. They'd been peering out of their room on the first floor. I thought that's where they'd be now. I imagined them hiding out there, bored and scared, listening to the alien sounds of a world they didn't understand.

I ran up the stairs and along the first-floor landing. I'm not sure what prompted the hurry, the sudden sense of urgency. The fear of more bodies, more blood? I was still tormented by the thought that if I'd not put off my visit to Thomas's, if I'd not drunk coffee that morning, I might have reached him while he was still alive. All the time I was trying to get my bearings, to remember the only time I'd seen the girls who looked so similar that they could be twins, the glimpse through the door just before it closed. When I found it I recognized it immediately. A wide door, painted pale yellow, next to a fire extinguisher and a sign pointing to the emergency exit. I knocked. There was no answer. I listened but heard nothing and knocked louder.

'It's all right.' A whisper, but in this silence it seemed to echo. 'I just want to talk to you. I'm a friend.'

I turned the door handle and pushed. It caught for a moment on a shred of frayed carpet, then opened. No one. No blood-spattered walls, no cowering girls. No sign that they'd ever been there. The beds had been stripped. The duvets were neatly folded on top of the pillows. There were no clothes in the wardrobe and, though I searched the drawers, under the bed and in the bathroom, there was nothing which might give me an identity or a clue to where they'd gone.

I went back onto the landing and shut the door behind me. The anticlimax had left me washed out, so when I heard the front door open and voices in the hall below me, the response wasn't fear but a petulant irritation. I just wanted to go home.

'I really think we should tell them.' It was Dan, the tone wheedling, as if this was an argument which had been going on for a long time. He was in it for the long haul.

'No.' It was Nell, sharp and assertive. That confidence again, which made me want to weep with envy. If I'd spoken to Dan like that, would he have cared more about me? 'Not yet. There's too much to lose.'

'But if you're right . . .'

'I don't *know* if I'm right. It's a guess, speculation. When I *know* I'm right we can come to a decision.'

I could have wandered down the stairs. *Hi, you two. I was just looking for you.* I could have asked them what the row was about. I could have asked them where the Romanian girls had moved on to. But I was still shaking and drained, and I couldn't face them yet. I didn't want to explain what I was doing there. I waited until I heard them go into the kitchen, the water filling the kettle, the click as it was switched on. I hurried down the stairs and slipped out into the street.

Chapter Thirty-one

I'd parked my car at the end of the road, tucked behind a brewery lorry which had been delivering to the hotel on the corner. I got in but I didn't drive straight home. Although the lorry had moved away I didn't think the car would be recognized from Absalom House and I sat there and waited, going over the girls' disappearance, slowly becoming more relaxed. It was lunchtime. A few lads wandered past, sharing a bag of chips, but they were in school uniform and they didn't go towards the hostel. I didn't care. Perhaps because I could convince myself that this was a purposeful activity, the restlessness had gone.

I'd started to doze when Nell and Dan came out. Dan pulled the door tight behind him. Neither of them looked towards me. I waited until they'd reached the end of the road before getting out of the car. I was stiff and sleepy. It seemed an effort to go after them.

The town was busy. There were holidaymakers and daytime shoppers – workers on their lunch hour, elderly couples, women with babies. Outside the pubs lads with bare chests sat on the pavement and drank too much lager from plastic glasses. And everywhere kids, shirts out, ties off, queuing outside the bakeries and chip shops. My mind wandered. I was still half asleep. Why didn't Nell spend more time at school? Perhaps once the exams were finished the sixth-formers weren't expected back. What were her plans? At the same age, the summer after A-levels, Kay Mariner had become pregnant with Thomas. But Nell was too canny for that. I tried to focus on the couple as they made their way through the crowd. Now I'd started on this, I didn't want to lose them. They walked slowly, hand in hand, as if they were killing time. I just followed. I had no plan of action. I was killing time too. Perhaps jealousy had something to do with it. They were so obviously happy that I took a perverse pleasure in watching them. It was like scratching a midgy bite or sticking your tongue in a loose filling.

They stopped to buy a *Big Issue* from a guy outside Woolworths. I'd noticed him there before. He was one of the cheerful ones who put their heart and soul into selling, but I've always felt awkward around the *Issue* sellers since that time in Blyth and I looked away. When I turned back Nell had seen me and was waving. They seemed friendly and unsuspecting and I felt a bit of a rat for snooping round Absalom House and then following them here.

'We meet again,' I said.

'We were just going for something to eat,' Dan said. I couldn't tell if he wanted me around. At least he didn't ask what I was doing in Whitley.

'Lizzie'll come, won't you, Lizzie?'

Nell put her arm through mine. It was a long time since I'd had such intimate physical contact, but I didn't like it. It reminded me of the time I was arrested as a kid and the policewoman put her arm

ANN CLEEVES

around my shoulder, then pushed my head to get me into the cop car. But I let Nell pull me along.

They took me down an alley through a hole in a rank of shops towards the sea. I'd never been down there before. There were high walls on either side, so we were in shadow, and the path was so narrow that Nell and I scarcely had room to walk side by side. Beyond one wall there was a garden. I could see the tops of apple trees. Despite the crush, Nell didn't let go of my arm. She was wearing cropped black trousers and a thin batik top in purples and pinks; the sleeves were rolled back to her shoulders, which were very brown. Her skin was warm and she smelled of sandalwood. I think she and Dan continued talking to each other, but I don't remember what was said. I was feeling uncomfortable, trapped and panicky, and I had to concentrate on not letting it show.

At last the alley opened out into a cobbled courtyard, just big enough for two tables and chairs. Through an open door I could see a small café where a couple of ageing hippies were drinking coffee from thick yellow mugs. There was a smell of garlic, fresh coriander and joss sticks.

'We'll sit outside, shall we?' Nell said in that tone which made me think again that she was used to getting her own way without question. I'd have argued to go in, just to put up a bit of a fight, but the room looked even more cramped and shadowy than the alley and I couldn't face it. 'What'll you have, Lizzie? The chickpea and olive pâté is very good. And the salads are terrific.'

I said the pâté would be fine. I was opening my bag to find my purse but she'd already fished out a

£10 note from her trouser pocket. 'That's all right. Our treat.' And I wondered what she wanted from me. The night before she'd been sad and dreamy. Today there was a determined cheerfulness which reminded me of the lad on the street pushing the *Issue*. 'Dan'll get it, won't you, Dan?'

He got up without a word and went inside. There were terracotta pots in the courtyard. One of them contained a buddleia with huge pointed flowers which pulled the stems down into arches. There were other plants I didn't recognize; all had big, highly coloured blooms. The buddleia held three butterflies. They hovered over the purple flowers so close to the blossom that they seemed stuck to it. They could have flown away but they didn't.

'Who asked you to trace Thomas?' Nell asked. I wasn't expecting the question and had to think about the story I'd given her before. She looked at me with her intense trademark stare. Was this why she'd brought me here? Why was it so important now?

'His family.'

'Ronnie Laing, you mean?'

I paused. I couldn't see the point in lying. 'No. His real father was trying to trace him.'

'Oh,' she said. 'Poor Thomas. He'd have been so pleased. Did he know?'

I shook my head.

'Did you ever meet Ronnie?' I asked.

She paused. I imagined that she was trying to compose a plausible story, but I had no reason to believe that. Perhaps she was just making an effort to remember. 'Once,' she said. 'Before Thomas left home.'

'What did you make of him?'

'He was very pleasant. I wondered what Thomas was making all the fuss about.' She paused again before adding, 'But then appearances can be very deceptive, can't they?'

Dan returned with the food. He passed a few coins of change back to Nell. 'It wasn't Ronnie who asked Lizzie to find Thomas,' she said. It seemed a significant point for them both. I felt I should follow it up, but she went on to change the subject immediately, talking about her friends and their choice of universities.

'What are your plans?' I asked.

'Art School,' she said. 'Glasgow or London.'

'Does that depend on your results?'

'No.' She was matter of fact, not boasting. 'They've seen my portfolio. They both want me. I just haven't quite decided yet which I prefer.'

'What about you, Dan? Will you stick with Ellen and Acting Out?'

'Dan's ready for a change too,' she said, before he had a chance to answer.

The food was good. It should have been pleasant sitting with the sun on my neck, garden birds calling behind the wall. I couldn't explain my unease.

'Are the girls still in Absalom House?' The question came out more abruptly than I'd intended and Dan seemed startled.

'Which girls?'

'The ones I met when I first visited there. Eastern European. They had the room next to Thomas.'

'No,' he said reluctantly. 'They left last night.'

'Where did they go?'

He shrugged. 'I'm not sure. Ellen found a family to take them. She thought it would be better. Safer. You know Ellen. An old mother hen.'

'What can be unsafe about Absalom House?'

He frowned. 'Nothing. But it's mostly lads there. And Ellen thought they needed more support than we could give.'

'Did she find a local family to take them?'

'I don't know. It was my day off yesterday and she wasn't in this morning. I haven't had a chance to catch up. Why are you interested?'

'Social worker's nosiness. Humour me. How long had they been there?'

'I'm not sure. A couple of months.'

'Long enough to meet Thomas?'

'Yeah, they came just before he left. But you can't imagine they had anything to do with his death. They were quiet. Amazingly shy. The other residents called them the ghosts, because of the white scarves they wore on their heads and because they only seemed to come out at night.'

I finished my meal and then I left. I half expected Nell to stop me, but she just waved me away. They lingered there. They seemed to have nothing better to do. I looked back once and saw them caught in their sun trap, bright and gaudy in the midday light as the overblown flowers.

I planned to go back to Sea View then. Suddenly the idea of Jess fussing over me didn't seem quite so tiresome. We'd drink tea in the shade of the kitchen with the door open to let in the breeze from the sea, and if Ray came to join us I wouldn't even mind that. There'd be something restful about his slow movement and his silences. But as I emerged from the alley into the noise of Whitley Bay's main shopping street, my attention was caught by a familiar figure, so out of place here that it was shocking. Like you'd bumped into your headmistress at a rave.

There was no doubt that it was Stuart Howdon moving briskly down the pavement on the other side of the street, past the banks and the building societies. I recognized the bobbing of the walk, the way he stopped occasionally to catch his breath. He was wearing a grey suit and a striped tie. Even in genteel Morpeth it would have seemed over-formal in this weather. Here, where skimpily clad holidaymakers and loud rock music spilled out of the pubs onto the wide pavements, he looked absurd. I supposed that there must be a meeting with a client, perhaps a business lunch, but even at the first glimpse I sensed something furtive about his movements. That was what I wanted to see. I disliked him and wanted to think the worst of him.

He stopped to wipe his forehead with his handkerchief and looked around him to get his bearings, then set off up the street which led to the metro station. He hadn't seen me; he was, I thought, too preoccupied to notice. There was the rattle of a train and through the arch in the station building I saw it pull up to a stop. It was one of the brightly painted ones, advertising a chain of garden centres. Howdon put on a spurt of speed towards the ticket machines though he must have realized he didn't have a hope of catching it. The doors opened and a horde of people pushed out. There was a school party, a group of five- and six-year-olds in bright red polo shirts shepherded by teachers and parents. It took them a long time to leave and perhaps Howdon could have caught the train if he'd had the right change for the machine, but now he hung back, content to watch. I followed his eyes and saw, framed by the metro doors, Ronnie Laing.

I was astounded. He must be here to see Howdon, but what could the two men have in common? I had found it hard to believe that Ronnie had been a friend of Philip's. This connection made even less sense.

Ronnie looked cool and dapper waiting for the sea of red, chattering children to allow him through. I stood for a moment, trying to gauge my reaction to him. No excitement. No desire to touch him. That infatuation had been part of the illness, as I'd suspected. There was something disappointing in the coolness of my response. Did it mean that if I continued with the treatment I'd never be excited by a man again? I was still brooding about that when I realized how exposed I was, and turned quickly and walked away down a street which faced directly onto the station. On the corner was an old-fashioned launderette with huge cream machines, and posters for washing powder which looked as if they'd been there for forty years. There was a long window which gave a clear view of the station façade. An elderly woman, so shrivelled she was as small as a monkey, must have been in charge of the place. She was asleep on a chair behind a Formica counter. She breathed gently and regularly, like a baby sleeping. When I went in her eyelids fluttered but she didn't wake. No one else was there.

Howdon had been looking out for Ronnie Laing. A meeting had been arranged. I could see that at once.

They shook hands. It wasn't like friends meeting.
They kept a distance between them. I couldn't hear
anything that was said and it's possible, I suppose,
that I'd got the body language all wrong, but I don't
think so. My impression was that Howdon wanted
something from Ronnie. He was the supplicant and
Ronnie was listening, not liking what he heard, and
starting to become agitated.

The conversation lasted no more than ten minutes. They walked a little way towards me and sat on
a wooden bench under some horse chestnut trees.
Another train came in and my view was obscured
for a moment by the passengers who sauntered out
towards the town centre. When the crowd cleared
they were still there. I don't think anything had passed
between them. Howdon's briefcase was still at his
feet. Ronnie was calmer now, almost impassive. His
expression suggested that he was open to persuasion
but that the argument had better be good. As I say, I
could have been reading the encounter all wrong, but
that was how it seemed at the time. Howdon was
squirming, waving his hands, flexing his stubby, saus-
age-shaped fingers. Then he bent to open his briefcase. He took out a file which he handed to Ronnie.
Ronnie read for a moment, handed the papers back
and slowly nodded his head. Howdon didn't respond
immediately, then he seemed so relieved that I
thought he was going to pull Ronnie towards him in a
bear hug, like two Soviet politicians cementing a deal,
but he only relaxed his face into a smile.

Ronnie stood up first. There was the sound of a
train in the distance and he walked briskly to make
sure of catching it. He didn't break into a run, but it

seemed as if he wanted to escape. Howdon shouted something after him. It could have been *Good luck* or *Thank you*. I couldn't make it out. Ronnie frowned slightly, as if he thought Howdon was making a show of himself. The train pulled into the station and he walked on without looking back, without acknowledging the solicitor's presence.

Howdon only got up then. He straightened his trousers and wiped imaginary specks of dirt from his suit. When he started back down the road towards the town, I left the launderette and followed. The old woman muttered something in her sleep as I opened the door.

He headed for the main street, where I'd first seen him. He was in less of a hurry now and stopped to take off his jacket. He held it over his shoulder by the collar. Very jaunty. He slowed down at the entrance to the alley where Nell and Dan had taken me, and I wondered briefly if the two events were connected, if he intended to meet up with them too. Instead he went into a florist's and came out with a big bunch of roses. I imagined them as a peace offering for his wife. She was a woman who would need constant placating. His jacket was back on. It was beyond him to carry it and the briefcase and the flowers. He walked to a side street, where he'd parked his car. He put the roses carefully on the back seat and drove away. He had no suspicion that I'd been watching him. That gave me a feeling of power, but it was unsettling too. It was as if I were invisible, as if I didn't exist.

Chapter Thirty-two

It's dark and I long for the light more than I long to be out of the cell-like room. In the light I'd feel more in control of the situation. If I could see Nicky's face, I'd judge his thoughts, his intentions.

As it is, I'm helpless. There is nothing I can do. He can sense every movement. I open my mouth to speak, but before the words come out, he whispers, 'Shut up.'

The footsteps return. Someone is opening every door on the corridor and calling to the kids in turn, 'Is Lizzie Bartholomew there?'

I recognize the voice. It's Maggie, one of my colleagues. She has cropped hair and big glasses. She sounds slightly worried, but there's no panic in her voice. This is reassuring. I can almost believe it's all a big mistake, a practical joke which will soon be over. Her footsteps come closer.

Nicky pulls me back into a sitting position. The knife is still against my left breast. His breath comes in small shallow pants.

The footsteps stop outside his door. I imagine Maggie's hand reaching for the knob.

'Don't come in.' After the sinister whispers I hear his words as a defiant shout.

'Nicky.' Now Maggie is panicking, but she tries not to let on. 'Have you got Miss Bartholomew in there?'

'If you come in, I'll kill her.'

We both know it's true. He's killed once. He's looking for an excuse to kill again.

He moves the knife suddenly. I feel it like a bee sting. A thin trickle of blood runs down my breast and dries, almost immediately. I begin to sob.

The next time I saw the main players of the day in Whitley – Nell and Dan, Ronnie and Howdon – they were all together in the same place, a coincidence which only added to my sense of the surreal and fuelled my fantasies. I admit now that I was losing my grip on reality. At night my theories to explain the deaths of the two boys grew wilder and more paranoid. I saw a spider's web of cause and effect, individuals all monsters and all interrelated. In the morning I'd wake exhausted and my dreams seemed ridiculous. The flashbacks were vivid and real.

I decided at the last minute to go to Wintrylaw, to the Countryside Consortium fund-raiser I'd seen advertised in the arts centre where Dan worked. There wasn't any specific reason for the trip, though it did occur to me that Doreen the volunteer might be there and she might be persuaded to talk. At that time there was no planning to anything I did. I thought vaguely that Howdon and Ronnie Laing would be around, and hoped I might find out more about what they'd been plotting in Whitley Bay. I hadn't worked out how I might get that information. I'd wing it as I went along. There was the possibility of seeing Dickon again too. I had an ambition to tell him jokes and make him laugh.

It was still only June, but I had a breathless feeling that summer was coming to an end. There had been occasional cool days but generally the weather that year had been unusually still and warm. Now I was looking forward to it breaking. The continual sun took me back to Morocco and Philip. I had the idea that a cold spell would kill off the pain and help me to think more clearly. That evening was still humid and sticky. Everyone was irritable. In Sea View Jess snapped at the bad boys and even at Ray. She seemed glad when I said I was going out; it would mean one less body under her feet.

I wasn't sure what to expect from the event, but I approached the house with anticipation, a childish excitement even. From that first time, when I'd looked down onto the great chimneys, Wintrylaw had been a special place for me. It wasn't only that Philip had lived there. It represented glamour, something I'd never had, and hadn't even realized I wanted. The sort of thing I'd usually sneer at. Tonight I wanted it more than ever and hoped I wouldn't be disappointed.

As soon as I arrived I saw there was no danger of that. The house was in shadow but torches on the terrace and along the drive lit it up like a film set. There was a stage with a PA system on the lawn and people were already sitting on the grass. When I joined them I saw the revellers had grand picnics, hampers, champagne, but at that point they were backlit from the house and nothing more than dark, featureless shapes. I was stopped at the gate, as on my last visit, by the woman who'd been collecting the entrance fee for the summer fair. This time she seemed less embarrassed by the extortionate charges. She took my money and nodded me through, urging me to hurry because the event was about to start.

Joanna was waiting at the terrace steps to greet the last of her guests. She had reinvented herself again, this time as a character from Georgette Heyer. She wore white, something simple and high-waisted, with a muslin shawl across her shoulders. Her hair was up, apart from a few curls allowed to escape from a comb. I wasn't sure if she'd recognize me but she did at once.

'Lizzie,' she said. 'My dear. How kind of you to forgive us. Philip would be so pleased that you've decided to support us.'

The mention of Philip embarrassed me, which is probably what she intended. It reminded me that I had things to be forgiven for too, that I had nothing to feel superior about. She waved towards a table, probably the same trestles which had been brought out for the funeral. There were bowls of punch and the underage waitresses from the Alnwick catering firm were ladling it into glasses. 'You should try some,' Joanna said. 'My own recipe. Delicious.' I wanted to ask her if Dickon was around, but she'd already turned her attention to someone else. We were the latecomers and she was eager for the evening's entertainment to begin.

The performance of music and poetry had been dreamt up as a fund-raiser, but the Consortium seemed to have turned it into a tribute to Thomas Mariner and Marcus Tate. It was almost as if they had become their first martyrs. I didn't see Doreen, but if she'd been there she would have wept. I wondered if Joanna had anything to do with the boys featuring so prominently, or if, once it had been suggested, she felt she couldn't disagree. She could hardly say to the organizers, *Well, actually, this is a bit awkward, because Thomas was my husband's illegitimate son.* If she was bothered by the comments made about Thomas's life she didn't show it. I was watching her for most of the evening.

After the opening music – a selection of madrigals, I think, sung by a big amateur choir from Newcastle – Ronnie Laing made a speech. I'd expected him to be there, but I hadn't expected him to take such a role. I'd have thought he'd have hated the attention. He climbed onto the stage and waited for the crowd to settle to silence before speaking. Perhaps it was because it was a sort of performance, but he spoke quite fluently and his stammer was hardly apparent. I looked round for Kay, but she wasn't there to see how well he was doing. 'I was surprised when I heard Thomas had joined the Consortium as a volunteer. We hadn't discussed it beforehand. I suppose we'd reached a stage when we didn't discuss much at all.' He paused. There were sympathetic smiles. 'But I was so pleased that he did. When he died it gave me something I could remember and be proud of. It made me feel I'd made a contribution to his life.' The crowd got to its feet and cheered. Even I felt a bit emotional. It was only as he was being helped off the stage that I thought Joanna couldn't have confided the name of Thomas's real father to him. He couldn't have put on a performance like that if he'd known Philip was Thomas's dad. I was pleased. I hoped she'd always keep the secret. The information wasn't really hers to share. Later, I think, there was a speech by Mr Tate, Marcus's father, but by then I was watching proceedings from the house and I didn't hear what was said.

My mind wandered as a third-year student from the performing arts course at Northumbria University read from John Clare. The light was fading quickly now and it was hard to make out any of the figures sitting on the grass, but when I turned back to the terrace I saw Stuart Howdon standing next to Joanna. He was whispering in her ear, so close that at one point he had to brush one of her stray curls away from his face. Joanna was looking out to the stage with an attentive smile. It was impossible to tell what she thought of what she was being told. When I looked back again, they'd gone.

There was an interval and the punch was brought out again, and dainty scraps of food which were more decorative than sustaining. I was glad I'd stopped at the chippie at Amble on the way. I'd thought Dickon and Flora might appear at this point, but there was no sign of them until I glanced up at the house and saw Dickon looking down out of a first-floor window. There was nothing wistful about his gaze – I could see clearly because there was a light in his room. He didn't want to be with us. He despised us for putting ourselves through all this.

When everyone else was called back to the stage for the second part of the show I slipped into the house and ran up the big curving staircase. At every moment I expected to hear shouting, a demand to know what I was up to. Dickon's room must be at the end of the house, as he was looking out of the last window. I walked quietly along a straight corridor with a threadbare carpet. I didn't care so much about Joanna, but I didn't want to meet Flora. I could picture her disdain in the face of my stumbling explanations. I hadn't seen her in Dickon's room. If she *was* there, out of view from the garden, he'd have to bail me out.

In fact he was alone in his room, and his door was open so I could see from the landing that I was safe. The television was on – an American hospital drama, with lots of shouting and blood – but he wasn't watching it. He was still perched on the window-sill, looking out. I didn't want to go into the room without invitation and just waited in the doorway until he noticed me. His face brightened and he zapped the telly off. I felt wonderfully flattered.

'I'm waiting for the fireworks,' he said, 'but there's an awful lot of boring stuff to go through first.'

I hovered outside still.

'Come in,' he said. 'It must be over soon and there'll be a good view from here.'

'Where's Flora?'

'She's at her mate's house. A sleepover. She says fireworks are for kids.'

So I sat beside him on the window-sill and looked down.

'Your mother's really good at this sort of thing.' The thought just came into my head. A large woman was singing something classical I didn't recognize. The audience had become a shadowy blur. The woman stopped, bowed, and there was good-natured clapping.

Dickon smiled. 'Really good.'

'I expect it's because she's a photographer. She can see the effect she wants in her head.' Again I was speaking more to myself, but he was lapping up the praise on his mother's behalf.

'She's brilliant at stories too,' he said. 'Though she doesn't have so much time for those any more.'

'It must be hard for her since your dad died.'

'Yeah,' he said. 'I suppose.'

The students were back again, acting a scene from *A Midsummer Night's Dream*. Phrases drifted up to us. The sash window was open at the top. It was the bit about the wild thyme and the sweet musk rose. A soporific dream seemed to have settled over the audience too. Dickon watched for a few minutes, then lost interest. He suggested showing me his skull and wing collection and pointed out a battered suitcase under his bed. I told him I'd rather wait until I had more time to concentrate properly and we stared out of the window again.

'They were talking about you earlier,' he said.

'Who were? Was it your mother?'

'No. Mr Howdon and Ronnie Laing.'

'Oh?' I couldn't quite bring myself to ask what they'd said. And I thought Dickon would probably tell me anyway.

'I didn't hear much,' he said regretfully. 'They were in Daddy's office while everyone else was helping to set things up. It's not fair. Mr Howdon never helps.'

'Too fat.'

'Yeah.' He chuckled and looked out of the window. I could have kicked myself for interrupting, but he continued, 'Mr Howdon doesn't like you much.' There was admiration in his voice. 'What have you done to piss him off?'

'Nothing. Not deliberately, anyway.'

'He said you were a meddling cow.'

'Not very nice.'

'No.' He paused. 'He didn't say cow. He said something worse.'

'Definitely not very nice.'

'He wants to give you money to keep your nose out of their affairs.' That threw me a bit. I hadn't been meddling in their affairs. Not since our ruck at the exhibition at least. I'd been more concerned with Harry Pool and Absalom House since then. Then I thought of course, Marjorie had told him about my visit to Warren Farm.

'I don't know what he's talking about.'

'Ronnie said that wouldn't do any good. You weren't the sort to be bought off.'

So Ronnie knew who I was. But how much did he know? Surely not that Philip had hired me to find Thomas? Or were they all involved? Was there some elaborate conspiracy after all?

'Was Ronnie a friend of your dad's?'

Dickon considered. Friendship wasn't an idea to be taken lightly. 'Dad was sorry for him. He said he'd had a bad time and he'd done really well to sort himself out. Most people would have gone under.'

'What sort of bad time?'

'Dunno. Never asked.'

'Your dad was a magistrate, wasn't he? Could he have met Ronnie in court?'

'I'm not sure. He didn't talk much about court. He

said he wasn't allowed.' He pulled on my sleeve to attract my attention back to the scene outside. 'Do you think the fireworks'll start soon?'

'What do you make of Ronnie Laing?' I asked, because Dickon's opinion was all I could get at the moment.

'I think he's OK. He helped me build a den in the wood. We had a campfire. And he came with me badger watching. Do you know you have to stick coloured cellophane over your torch to stop the light frightening the badgers away?'

'No,' I said. 'I didn't know that.'

'You could come sometime. They haven't got cubs any more but you can get really close . . .'

I interrupted. 'Has Ronnie ever talked about his stepson, Tom?'

'Has he got a son?' That grabbed Dickon's attention for a minute. 'No, he never said. Perhaps he'll bring him over to play.'

I didn't know what to say to that. They'd have been brothers.

The show was coming to a close. All the performers got onto the stage to take a final bow. I wondered if Joanna would make a speech, but she was back at her place on the terrace next to Howdon. Dickon saw me looking at them.

'She doesn't like Mr Howdon,' he said angrily. 'Not in *that* way. She can't do. I asked her why he's always here these days and she said it was business.'

'Do you know what sort of business?' I asked, but the first of the fireworks were being let off and I knew I'd lost him.

'I'd better go,' I said. 'Bye.'

He didn't look away from the garden. 'See you.'

I took a scrap of paper from my bag and wrote down my phone numbers – Sea View, my mobile. 'If you want a chat any time, give me a ring.' It was for my benefit, not his. I couldn't cope with the thought that I might not bump into him again. He took the paper from me and stuck it into his jeans pocket, his eyes still fixed on the coloured lights outside.

I sat with the crowd until the display was over. I didn't want to have to make conversation with Joanna while Howdon was there. The state I was in, I'd only have confronted him and caused a scene. *How much did you think you could pay me off with?*

When the last rocket was fired over the sea, I pushed my way out towards my car. I hoped to be among the first to leave, but everyone else had the same idea and there was a crush of people heading for the car park. That's when I saw Dan and Nell. They were some way in front of me, hand in hand as they always were. Nell was in a long silk skirt. Black or dark purple. I couldn't really tell in the dark. But it was certainly them. There was no mistake about that. Their faces were caught in a car headlight and they looked stern and determined.

I told myself there was nothing sinister about their presence. Dan would still have contacts with the university. He mixed with an arty set. Probably some of their mates were acting and singing. But I wasn't really convinced.

Chapter Thirty-three

The next morning I phoned Farrier, not thinking I'd get through to him, expecting to be fobbed off. But after I'd hung on for five minutes he came onto the line.

'Lizzie?' He sounded concerned, anxious even. 'What's wrong?'

'Nothing.'

There was a silence which implied, *Well, why are you bothering me, then?* I was suddenly awkward and tongue-tied. 'Look, this is probably like teaching my grandfather to suck eggs . . .'

'But?'

'You *would* check if anyone close to Tom had a criminal record, wouldn't you?'

'Depends how close.'

'Stepfather close.'

'What makes you think Ronnie Laing has a criminal record?' The tone was sharp. He didn't sound anything like a friendly grandfather now.

'Nothing specific. I mean really. I suppose it's more a wild guess.'

'You promised you'd keep out of it.'

'I am! I have!' Protesting too much. I didn't like lying to him, but he seemed taken in by it.

ANN CLEEVES

'Yes, we would check family members for past offending.' He was humouring me, mock long-suffering. This time I used the silence.

'Really, Lizzie, you can't expect me to tell you.'

More silence.

'OK, then, to put your mind at rest. Ronnie's clean as a whistle. Never been charged. A model citizen.'

But a model citizen with a troubled past, I thought. Philip had told Dickon that, and I trusted Dickon's memory and Philip's judgement. What had happened to him? A family tragedy, mental breakdown, bankruptcy? There were two ways to find out. I could ask Ronnie Laing himself. Even to me that seemed unnecessarily foolhardy. Or I could ask his wife. I fished out the scrap of paper with her work number on it and dialled.

I'd expected Kay to be hostile, but she was almost embarrassingly eager to see me. 'Come this afternoon,' she said. 'Straight after school. Three o'clock. It's the last day of term, so there'll be no meetings. Everyone will want to be away on time.' The directions she gave were very precise and businesslike, but her voice was shaking.

The school was in Wallsend in a busy street not far from the town centre. Cranes from the shipyard towered above cramped houses. The building was red-brick Victorian and could once have been a workhouse. The kids came out a class at a time with their teachers. I don't know if that was a regular thing, or if it was meant to give the parents a chance to say goodbye before the long holiday. Kay's class was the last into the playground. She held a mucky little boy firmly by the hand and the other children filed out in a crocodile behind her. They were remarkably well behaved and even the parents seemed daunted by her. They collected the kids and kept their distance. But once the yard was empty, the bright professional smile disappeared. She looked ten years older and wretched.

I walked through the gate into the playground and was six years old again, thinking, *Another school. Another routine to understand. More teachers to please.* Then Kay saw me and I turned back into the adult. I was the one with the responsibility to make things right. She hurried over and took my hand impulsively. 'Miss Bartholomew, it was good of you to contact me. Come in.' I wasn't sure the responsibility was something I was up to. She seemed to be expecting too much.

We talked in her classroom, perched on low tables. She hadn't had a chance to clear up after the school day. There were still jam jars with paintbrushes on the bench, sand on the floor, piles of flash cards and library books.

'I'll come in over the weekend to clear up,' she said. 'I don't think I can face it today.' Usually, I could tell, she wouldn't have dreamt of leaving it in a mess.

'I was so sorry,' I said. 'About Thomas.'

'You found him, the police said.'

I nodded, waited for her to lead the conversation. I was feeling my way here. Everything had to be at her pace.

'Was it the first time you'd visited? Or had you managed to see him before?'

'It was my first visit. I never met him.' I was going to add 'alive', but that would have been crass.

'Ah.' She tried to control her disappointment. What had she hoped to get from me? Absolution? *Don't worry. Thomas forgave you for pushing him out of the house. He told me he loved you. He understood.* Would that have helped? Anyway, it wasn't something I was prepared to lie about.

'I wish I'd done things differently,' she said simply.

'You're not guilty. You didn't kill him.'

'But I feel as if I did.' She paused. 'It was my decision to ask him to leave, you know, not Ronnie's.' She seemed to be expecting me to speak. Would it have made her feel better if I'd had a go at her? Is that why she'd asked me there? 'Ronnie doesn't mean to put me under pressure,' she went on. 'But he needs me. More perhaps than Thomas ever did. Thomas never understood that.'

I didn't answer. Of course Thomas wouldn't understand. I couldn't understand. She was his mother. At last she continued. 'It wasn't Ronnie's fault. Honestly.'

'Why does he need you so much?' I'd lost patience. I mean, he was a grown man, wasn't he? Capable of looking after himself.

She took a long time to reply. In the distance there was the hum of a floor polisher. The tap at the sink in the corner was dripping.

'When he was young he saw action overseas. Some of the things he witnessed still give him nightmares.'

Suddenly the stuff Dickon had told me made sense. That was why Philip had been sympathetic to Ronnie. It explained the dens in the woods and the campfires. Boys' games. Even if Ronnie had had a difficult time as a soldier, he'd need to feel proud of some of it. The friendships, perhaps, the skills he'd learned. There'd have to be some good memories or he'd go under altogether. It was something I was starting to realize for myself.

I was about to rattle on about post-traumatic stress. Ask if Ronnie had arranged counselling, tell her that even the army recognizes it as an illness now. I did a special study at college, so I'm pretty clued up. And of course since then I've had personal experience. I knew about flashbacks and panic attacks. I knew exactly what he was going through. I'd always thought we had something in common. *Was it the Falklands?* I was going to say. *The Gulf?* I'd read up on the conflicts, knew more about them than other people my age. I saw Ronnie in a different light. Not just as someone screwed up and desperately shy, but as a bit of a hero.

But before I had a chance to show off she started to speak again. 'It wasn't the British army. That would have been easier. He could have asked for help. He did start the training, but he couldn't finish. Not his fault.'

Was anything his fault? I wanted to ask. But I had the sense not to interrupt.

'So he worked abroad,' she said. 'There's an agency . . .'

Still I didn't get it.

'. . . run by former British officers. They provide assistance in conflicts when the government can't be seen to be involved.'

'He was a mercenary!' That time I couldn't help it. I was shocked. He'd always seemed too gentle for his own good. I'd imagined him bullied by an overcontrolling wife. And I thought I was a good judge of character. I couldn't imagine him peddling violence.

'No.' She sounded shocked too. 'He was an idealist.
He thought he was helping. Anyway, he didn't work
for them for too long. It affected him too deeply.'

Just long enough to get the cash for the garage, I
thought, and wondered what the Methodist Wives
would have made of his past.

'It took some time before he could trust me to talk
about it,' Kay said. 'He's a private man, very reserved.
Perhaps he comes across as unfriendly. I know my
mother and father couldn't warm to him, but their
judgement is suspect at times.'

'Has he ever tried to get professional help?'

She shook her head. 'He's too proud. He says it
wouldn't help anyway, to relive those experiences. He
needs to believe he's in control.'

'And is he?' I asked.

'What do you mean?'

'Does he still have nightmares?'

'Not so often. Not nearly so often.'

'What about the other symptoms? The fits of
anger, the depression, the sleeplessness.'

'Things improved when Thomas left home.' It was
a terrible admission for her to make. 'He provoked
Ronnie. He didn't understand. Ronnie wouldn't let me
explain. As I've told you, he saw the illness as something he had to deal with alone.'

Not really alone, I thought. He drew you into it.
You and Thomas and the kids.

'Getting involved in the campaign with the
Countryside Consortium helped. It was something he
could get passionate about. It stopped him thinking
quite so much about himself. He was good at the

outdoor work. People recognized that and it gave him confidence.'

'Wasn't it awkward for you to think about him and Philip Samson becoming friends?'

'What do you mean? Philip was a lovely man. He was so busy before he was ill, rushing round the globe for the television programmes and new commissions, but he still found time for Ronnie. It was a tragedy when he died. It shook us all.'

She was convincing all right. I thought she'd spent so long blocking out the knowledge that Philip was Thomas's father that she'd almost conned herself. I stared at her. She was still sitting on the little table, but she had her head bowed and her hands clasped like someone praying. Perhaps she was. She didn't look up.

'I know,' I said.

She raised her head. For a moment it seemed she'd forgotten where she was. I wondered if she was remembering Philip as a student, the irresponsible passion of that spring twenty years before. 'I'm sorry?'

'I know that Philip Samson was Thomas's father.'

'Where on earth did you get that idea from?' She looked at me as if I'd made a joke in poor taste. Some instinct of self-preservation stopped me telling her. *From Philip. That's why I came to your house before Thomas's death. Philip wanted to trace him.* Instead I said, 'Isn't it true, then?'

'Of course it's not true. I'd never met Philip before Ronnie started going to the Countryside Consortium meetings, and I never knew him well. Ronnie met him at one of Joanna's social evenings and they seemed to get on. The closest I'd got to him before then was through seeing him on the television.'

I believed her. If it wasn't true, she was way ahead in the Dan Meech school of acting. I was still trying to get my head round the implications of it when she started talking, pouring out a story which had been bottled up all that time, which she'd never told anyone, not Ronnie or her mother or her son.

'I was young,' she said. 'Naïve. I wasn't like the young girls today, who are brought up to see sex wherever they look. If I led him on, I didn't know what I was doing. I've gone over and over it in my head. I *feel* it was my fault but I don't see how it could have been. I was still a child. Not legally perhaps, but in every way it matters. He was old enough to be my father. He was the responsible person.

'I used to baby-sit. Mum and Dad arranged it. *We've fixed you up a little extra job.* Proud as punch, not so much for me, but because they could do a favour for a smart friend. And I enjoyed going there at first. It was a treat to spend time in the big house. There was a freezer with a box of choc-ices and I was allowed to help myself. That shows you how sophisticated I was! I'd put the children to bed, switch on the television and eat ice cream and it was my idea of a good night out. Afterwards I'd get a lift home in the car with the leather seats and the radio. In my memory Frank Sinatra's always on the radio. "Fly Me To The Moon". It can't always have been playing, but that's what I remember. You know the tune?'

I nodded, but she didn't really expect a response. It had taken me a moment to concentrate on what she was saying, but now I was hooked. It's like when you know the end of a story but you don't know how it's going to get there. That's still exciting, isn't it? And there was something mesmerizing about watching this woman who was usually so controlled and self-protective suddenly letting go, just telling it as it came to her, desperate to get it right.

'The policeman, Inspector Farrier, asked me about Thomas's father,' she said, 'and I didn't tell him. I couldn't. Not even when it might have helped him track down the killer. I was too ashamed. Not by what I'd done, but that I could be so stupid. Can you believe it? I was afraid that they'd laugh at me, so I kept quiet.'

She was wearing a calf-length cotton dress with a flower print. It had small covered buttons at the neck and the wrist. She looked very prim and schoolmis-tressy, literally buttoned up. But she was shaking with anger at herself and the man who'd taken advantage of her.

'He had a wife. That made him safe. I thought that and so did my parents. I didn't like the wife as much. She wasn't friendly to me. When he tried to press me with gifts or persuade me to stay a bit longer, she'd say, "I expect Kay would rather go home." Her mouth was pinched with disapproval. I thought it was me she disapproved of, but it wasn't. It was Mr Pool.'

She broke off and stared out of the window. I wondered if speaking his name was a big thing for her, the first confession, but it wasn't that. She hadn't even realized. She was just reliving it in her head.

'It happened one night when Mrs Pool was at her mother's. I think there'd been a row. She'd taken the children with her. I don't think he planned it, he wasn't that devious. I mean, I don't think he even remembered it was Friday and I always baby-sat on Friday night. When I rang the doorbell he seemed surprised to see me. I'd hate to think he'd set it up. He'd been drinking. I don't know if that was the cause of the row with his wife or the result of it. I always hated to see Thomas drunk. Perhaps that was why.

'He asked me in. Usually the children were in their pyjamas ready for bed when I arrived and I took them up and tucked them in and read them stories. They'd be waiting for me in the living room. But I saw from the hall that they weren't there. "Are they in their rooms already?" I asked, and started up the stairs. He followed me. At the top, near the landing, he put his arms around me. I could smell the whisky. He was whispering in my ear. "You're a lovely girl, Kay. You know I think you're a lovely girl." And then he was unbuttoning my blouse.'

She stopped abruptly. Her arms were folded across her chest. Her mouth was a line. Even today she couldn't bring herself to describe the details.

'It was rape,' I said. 'Not your fault.'

'I could have fought. I'm not even sure if I screamed. It was such a shock. I couldn't believe it. And I'd been brought up to be polite. It was like a nightmare I was powerless to stop. I thought the scene would run to its end like bad dreams do, and then I'd wake up. But of course I never did.'

'What happened next?'

'Harry Pool drove me home. As if nothing had happened.'

'He must have realized that Thomas was his son.'

'I suppose so. We never discussed it. They didn't

ask me to baby-sit again. My mother asked if I'd done something to upset them. I couldn't tell my parents what had happened. There was this dreadful embarrassment. Harry was my dad's best friend. Dad admired him. His energy, his enterprise, all the money he made. They wouldn't have believed me and I didn't want to make a fuss. And it never dawned on me until too late that I could actually be pregnant.'

'Why did Thomas start working at Harry Pool's?'

'Harry offered him the job. He made out that he was doing his old mate's grandson a favour. What could I say? Thomas needed work. I didn't like it but there wasn't much I could do.'

'I think Thomas might have found out that Harry was his father. You didn't tell him?'

'No!'

'Does Ronnie know?'

'I never told him,' she said. 'But Ronnie has his own ways of digging out information.'

Chapter Thirty-four

What happened next was farcical. It was like one of those interludes in Shakespeare when the mood suddenly changes. You know, everything's really heavy and people are obsessing about statesmanship or death, and then in the next scene you get a couple of clowns or jolly rustics drinking and joking.

I was thinking through the implications of everything Kay had told me. There was too much to take in all at once. It had never occurred to me that Philip might not be Thomas's father. Why would he lie? Wasn't the deathbed the time for truth? And what would be the point? Had it just been a ruse to get me to accept the money? That seemed too elaborate to make sense, and I had to start all over again.

Perhaps the story hadn't been invented by Philip at all, but by someone else. It had certainly been his signature on the bottom of the typed sheet. I recognized the handwriting from the letter he'd left me in Marrakech. But there could have been a lot of papers which needed his signature before he died. Legal stuff, drawn up by Stuart Howdon. Perhaps by then Philip had been too ill to read through everything properly. He trusted Stuart. He could have told him about our fling in Morocco. But why would Stuart send me on a wild-goose chase to track down Thomas Mariner? The obvious answer was because he wanted Thomas dead. I just couldn't work out why. At that point I gave up and turned my attention to Harry Pool.

So Harry Pool was a bastard who'd assaulted Kay Mariner and got her pregnant. She'd kept the secret for twenty years, demanding nothing of him, trying to pull together a life for herself and her kids. It seemed to me that it had taken more courage than screwed-up Ronnie swanning back from some Third World skirmish with a bag full of money and a few unpleasant dreams. That must sound unsympathetic. Perhaps I should have had more fellow feeling for Ronnie. But his self-obsession irritated me. I was beginning to understand how irritating I must be. Not something it was pleasant to face.

Harry must have worked out that he was Thomas's father. No one had ever suggested that he was thick. And when he heard from his old pal Archie that Thomas was going through a bad time, some vestige of conscience made him offer the boy a job. Or more likely it was that male pride again. He couldn't stand the thought of his son being unemployed. It must have been hard when Thomas left home to live in a hostel with junkies and asylum seekers. Harry wouldn't have liked that.

So Thomas started working at the haulage yard. But Pool couldn't leave it at that. He couldn't resist telling Thomas they were related. He had to poke the bear. And maybe instead of being all grateful, and full of admiration for Harry's money and the flash car and the big house, Thomas got angry on his mother's behalf. Angry and self-righteous. He wrote the letter to Shona Murray, threatening Harry with exposure over whichever racket he was operating – smuggled fuel or smuggled people. Perhaps he even threatened to tell Archie Mariner that his best mate wasn't a good guy after all. Perhaps that was what led to his death, and Philip and Stuart had nothing to do with it.

All this was going round in my head as I drove back to Newbiggin. As I've said, it was pretty heavy. Tragedy not comedy. Not many laughs. Then when I got back to Sea View it was like walking into a madhouse. Ray and all his mates from the folk club were there drinking home-brewed beer out of old cider bottles and bursting into song every five minutes and generally making prats of themselves.

Jess had been looking out for me. 'Lizzie, pet, there you are. You've got ten minutes to change before the mini-bus gets here.'

I must have looked blank.

'The ceilidh, the engagement party. You've not forgotten?'

She looked so disappointed that I lied. 'Of course not. I'd just not realized there'd be a mini-bus.'

She beamed. 'Ray laid it on so we could have a few drinks.'

'Great,' I said. I had to shout. A fat bearded bloke was sitting on the table and playing a penny whistle in my ear. 'Great.'

The lassie who was getting engaged lived on her parents' farm in the hills and the ceilidh was held in a real barn. I mean, there were stalls down one side and bales of hay, and the sweet smell of cows, but it wasn't so mucky that I felt uncomfortable. I'm a town girl at heart. I've always thought the countryside's full of things to catch you out – bulls and electric fences and piles of shit.

The barn was as tall as a church and you could see right up through the rafters to the slate roof. Swallows had nested there. Someone must have been in during the day with a long ladder, because there were bunches of garden flowers tied to the beams and along the wooden railings of the stalls. A low stage built from pallets stood at one end and that's where the musicians played. There was a young woman with long straight hair on the Northumbrian pipes and two old geezers on guitar and accordion, and often one or two of Ray's friends joined in. The guests were of all ages. There were elderly couples in their Sunday best and little kids in party clothes. Not many teenagers. Perhaps they'd slink along later when the pubs closed. A shared supper was being laid out. Women ferried in stuff from their cars in relays – bowls of salad and cold meat covered by cling-film, Tupperware boxes of fancy cakes, flans and quiches, and dishes of fruit.

It all seemed too good to be true. A townie's dream of country living. The community coming together in celebration, the sort of event the incomers from Newcastle in their barn conversions would brag about to their friends over dinner. And perhaps it was too good to be true. I had the same feeling as when I'd looked at Joanna's photos. This was a fiction and we were all colluding in it. People in the country aren't any nicer than everyone else. They don't get on any better. But I'm a cynic and why shouldn't they cover over the cracks to give the young couple a good party? We can tell the story of our lives whichever way we want.

I had a good time. I'd imagined myself sat against the wall cringing with embarrassment, but once I let go of the crap about Thomas Mariner and had a few drinks, I really started to enjoy myself. Ray's friends were nerds, but they were harmless nerds. They asked me to dance and swung me around the floor until I was breathless, but none of them tried anything on. They didn't expect anything more from me. Jess had probably warned them I'd been through a bad time and ordered them to treat me with kid gloves. When I took a break from the dance floor it wasn't because I was being snotty about it, but because I was exhausted. I didn't spend ten miles walking over the hills every weekend in big boots. I didn't have their stamina.

I sat out next to a little elderly man with bright beady eyes and an almost impenetrable accent. They say Ashington people are impossible to understand but I'm used to those. After a while, though, I tuned into his voice and I didn't miss much of what he was saying. It was clear he loved to have an audience, especially an audience of a woman younger than himself. He must have been a real charmer in his day. And it seemed then that there was no escape from Thomas Mariner, because as the old man talked about growing up in the valley, gossip mostly about person- alities, I realized that this was where Stuart Howdon had lived as a boy. The characters I'd been fretting about all day returned to haunt me.

It started off with the old man shouting to a friend, who seemed to be sleeping, 'Did you see in the paper that there's talk of Howdon standing for Parliament?

Someone's got to speak out for the farmers, he says. And what would he know about that?'

The friend stirred but didn't respond, and the old man turned his attention to me. 'He'll stand as an independent, they say. Or representing that Consortium.' He snorted.

'Do you not think much of them, then?' Interested despite myself. I'd have thought he'd be a supporter.

'You're not one of that bunch, are you?' He looked at me warily.

I shook my head. 'What's wrong with them?'

'They're out for themselves.'

'In what way?'

'Money and ambition. What else is there? Howdon getting himself to London and mixing with the folk he's seen on the telly. That's what this is about.'

'The Consortium's got people talking, though.' It seemed strange to be defending them here. I'd have thought it would be the other way about.

'Rallies and marches. What good will that do?'

'They always get a good turn-out.'

'Of course they do. If the squire hires a coach and says take the day off and go to London, you'll go.' He hesitated. 'They've attracted a right bad crowd. And even the decent people seem to lose their reason. They've had a hard time round here and they want someone to kick out at. The Consortium plays on that. It fires them up and lets them loose.'

'How do you know Stuart Howdon?'

'He's a local lad.' The old man fixed me with his tiny birdlike eyes. 'Are you sure you're not one of them?'

317

'Na. Promise. It's not my sort of thing.'

The old man stood up and carefully set down his pint. He wore a shiny old suit and a threadbare shirt. His shoes were so highly polished that they reflected the lamps swung from the rafters. 'Now, young lady, why don't you take my hand. I want these people to see me with the bonniest lass in the room.' He pulled me to my feet and swung me into the dancing.

I'm not sure what time it was when we finished. We'd all drunk too much, but no one was sick and no one started a fight. Perhaps that's what it means to be grown up. Ray and Jess hadn't moved away from each other's side all evening. I'd talked to Ray's friends and found them to be all right. Normal, funny people with a strange taste in music. They had other lives. One was a teacher, I remember, and there was a doctor too.

At last the music stopped and we all went outside. Jess and Ray were snogging somewhere in the shadow. It was a clear night with a full moon, and because there were no streetlights and only a scatter of house lights in the valley, the stars shone really brightly. It had been a good evening, but all at once I felt lonely again. I wanted someone to share the night and the view with. Jess and Ray emerged with bruised lips and starry eyes and I was so jealous of them I wanted to cry. I understood what the old man had been saying when he talked about the Consortium. When you're feeling miserable you want to kick out and the target doesn't matter much. I loved Jess to bits but I couldn't be glad for her. Because I was feeling so miserable I couldn't bear anyone else to be happy. I understood why Stuart Howdon felt bitter and angry, married to someone he couldn't care about. In a mood like that you want to smash someone's face in. You feel like committing murder.

I hadn't even taken my mobile to the party, but when I got in, too wired to sleep, too tactful to sit in the kitchen drinking cocoa with the middle-aged lovebirds, I checked the messages. I don't know what I was expecting. Something from Kay perhaps. I'd given her my number and told her to call if she felt like talking. What I hadn't expected was the child's voice. Dickon. A bit muffled, as if he was talking from a mobile too, or was trying to speak softly so he wouldn't be overheard.

'Lizzie? Are you there, Lizzie? I want to talk to you. Don't phone back here. That wouldn't work. Can you come tomorrow evening? Not to the house. The wood by the old track into the estate. Dusk. I want to show you the badgers.'

I replayed it several times but I couldn't learn any more from it. I couldn't get a clearer idea about whether he was scared or anxious, or just excited about showing me the badgers. I couldn't get excited about them myself. They're big and black, aren't they? Like cows and electric fences, they're best avoided. I blamed myself for not having been in when he phoned. Those thoughts and recriminations kept me awake until dawn.

Chapter Thirty-five

Although by now I should have known my way round Wintrylaw, I stumbled onto the entrance to the wood when I'd almost given up hope of finding it. I was even considering going to the front door and asking for Dickon there. I'd been driving around the lanes, as I had that first time with Ray, and suddenly the approach was familiar: a little humpbacked bridge over a burn, wild overgrown verges, a hawthorn hedge and the wood rising up on one side. Then the stone pillars, covered with lichen and moss so they blended in with the trees, and the grassy track which led through the wood and eventually to the grand house.

I sat in the car, wishing that Dickon had given me a proper time for the meeting. When was dusk, for Christ's sake? I'd stayed in Sea View all day in case he phoned, but there'd been no other messages. For someone who admitted to a hangover and said she felt like death, Jess had been annoyingly happy. She buzzed around the house with a duster, singing and humming. By early evening I'd been glad to get out, though it wasn't dusk, nowhere near.

I'd parked the car in exactly the same place as Ray had dropped me on the day of the funeral. There was a passing place cut out of the verge and I pulled in there so close to the hedge that a passenger would have been trapped. The car was almost hidden by cow parsley and that tall weed with the little pink flower I've always called ragged robin. Philip would have known its proper name. I'd brought a book and started to read, but I must have dozed. When I woke the light was starting to go and I thought it must be almost time.

I walked between the pillars and into the wood. There was a wind, a warm, dry wind, which made the branches creak and the leaves above me murmur. I thought they sounded like a crowd of old ladies gossiping or maybe the sea, and I told myself I'd have to remember that to tell Dickon. Inside the wood it seemed much darker because the canopy blocked out what light was left. That made me jittery. I've never liked the dark and since Nicky took me hostage I can't even sleep without a light. Of course, I hadn't thought to bring a torch, or a flask of coffee, or a rug to sit on. I'd thought Dickon would be there waiting for me and I'd never been in the Girl Guides. I stumbled up the track in the gloom. It forked and I didn't know which way to take. I'd lost all sense of direction. I tried to listen out for cars along the lane, at least to fix that in my mental map, but either there was no traffic or the sound of the wind in the trees hid it. I didn't want to shout out for Dickon. I knew enough to realize that you had to be quiet if you wanted to see animals in the wild, and I didn't want him to be cross with me, or think I wasn't worth bothering with. That was illogical, of course, because my stumbling through the undergrowth would have scared off any animal in the place. It was more about knowing I'd feel really foolish, standing there and yelling, not wanting to make an exhibition of myself.

Then I saw the torch flashing in my direction, a signal. The light was subdued and orange. Dickon must have covered the lens with coloured cellophane as he'd described. It was a relief. I'd been starting to think this was another wild-goose chase. I made my way towards the light. Occasionally the wind blew a gap in the foliage and I had a glimpse of the sky, and brown clouds blowing across a shadowy moon, and the floor of the wood was lit up. Then the gust would drop, so everything seemed darker than ever, and I had to focus hard to see the pinprick of torchlight.

He was crouched on a bank. Earlier in the year it had been covered with bluebells, but now only the fleshy, spear-like leaves were left. I couldn't see them at first, because I was blinded by the orange light which was directed in my face, as if he wanted to be sure it was me and not some stranger. I saw them when I looked down to protect my eyes.

'Lizzie Bartholomew,' he said. It wasn't Dickon. It was an adult voice, gentle, halting. Ronnie Laing.

'Where's Dickon?'

'Joanna wouldn't let him out in the end. He picked up a chill. You know how it is with kids.'

'Tell him I hope he's better soon.' I realized even then that Dickon had been used to set me up.

'Don't you want to see the badgers, Lizzie?' His voice was really something, you know? The slowness which overcame the stutter was seductive, soft.

'No thanks.'

'Sit down, Lizzie.' Still slow, but not an invitation

322

this time. More like an order. Obedience has never been my thing.

'Piss off.'

'Sit down.' He sounded apologetic as he held out the knife, almost as if it was some kind of peace offering. At that moment the wind blew the branch above us, letting in the moonlight, which shone on the blade.

I looked at him. I knew if I ran he'd catch me. He was fitter than I was and he knew the wood. If I caught him off guard, maybe I could get the knife off him. That thought really came into my head. Talk about self-delusion. One term of lessons in women's self-defence and I thought I could take on a mercenary. But I sat. I didn't think I had a choice. And at least at that point I was still thinking.

'Did Howdon set you up to this?' I asked.

He didn't answer. His eyes were fixed on the knife blade. He tilted it, backwards and forwards, so the reflected torchlight moved. He seemed mesmerized, as if this were a strange form of self-hypnosis. I was mesmerized too, but I continued to talk.

'Howdon must be behind all this. He forged the papers for me to sign. But why did he want Thomas dead? Why did he let me think Philip was the boy's natural father?'

I was talking to fight off the panic, the old helplessness which had started to insinuate itself into my brain as soon as I sat down. I was a hostage again, squatting on the floor, held at knifepoint by a lunatic I'd thought I understood, I'd felt some sympathy for. I imagined Jess raising her eyes to the ceiling. *Don't you ever learn, Lizzie Bartholomew? Won't you ever look after yourself?*

Nicky moves me to the floor when they gather outside his door. They talk to him all night. They've cleared the other kids off the corridor and they negotiate with him to open the door, just a crack.

Their voices are soft and reassuring, but I can't take in the words, and I don't think Nicky's listening either. He's still whispering, saying where he's going to cut me, how he's going to hurt me. Then he says, 'They can kill me, but I'll take you with me. Are you ready to die, Miss?' That's when I wet myself.

Occasionally he shouts back to them, but it's never anything that makes sense. It's not like he's having a real conversation with them.

I don't know how long I've been there. It could be days.

Suddenly my eyes are seared by a bright light. Phosphorescent white. Brighter than anything I've ever known. A voice commands, 'Run, Lizzie, run.' But I don't run. My brain's too sluggish. The message gets slowly to my legs and I stagger to my feet. Nicky's responses are quicker. He lifts the knife above his head. I see it through eyes half shut against the light and wait for it to strike.

There's an explosion, so loud I expect the windows to shatter. Framed in the door is a man I don't recognize, a thug in dark clothes and a baseball cap. He holds a gun, which now is pointing to the floor. And when I turn round Nicky is lying in a heap in the corner with blood seeping through his clothes. Then I lose it. I crouch beside the boy and stroke his hair away from his face and say it was all my fault and I never meant him to die.

In the wood I hadn't lost it. I was still in control, still talking. Shaking perhaps, but holding myself together. 'There was something going on within the Countryside Consortium. Was that it? Did Thomas find out?'

My mind was racing. Ronnie must have done the killing. Howdon would be too squeamish, too soft. He'd not want blood on his suit or his hands or his fat belly. Had Ronnie taken money to kill his own stepson? When I'd seen them together in Whitley Bay, was Howdon paying Ronnie to get rid of me? Was this the result? Another nuisance disposed of?

Ronnie looked up suddenly from the knife. His face was underlit by the torch. His eyes were in shadow. The sockets looked hollow. 'Did you sleep with Philip?' he asked.

'What the fuck has that got to do with you?'

'I'd understand if you had.' His voice was a dreamy whisper. It was as if *he'd* had sex with Philip and was running the pictures in his head. 'He was a wonderful man.'

'What would you know about that?' I couldn't just sit there any more, passive. I had to put up a challenge, provoke a response. Perhaps then Ronnie would lose concentration and forget about the knife.

'He was famous, a celebrity, on the television. But he still had time for his friends. He had time for me. I'd have gone under if it hadn't been for him. He believed the best in everyone.'

'Why did he get mixed up in the Consortium?' The more I'd learned about the organization, the more I'd regretted Philip's involvement with it. They were a bunch of self-seeking whingers. Philip hadn't been like that.

'He believed in the dream,' Ronnie said. Then he paused and the voice slowed and softened again, slurring over the start of a stutter. 'At least he believed in Joanna and she believed in the dream.'

'What dream would that be, Ronnie? The country-side for country people? It's a bit fascist that, for me.'

He obviously didn't like the question or the tone. He ignored it.

'What's the plan here, Ronnie? Are we going to sit on our bums all night like a couple of turds, or are you going to let me go back to the car and we'll forget all about it. I know what it's like to get carried away, after all. Is that a deal, eh, Ronnie? One lunatic to another.'

'I can't let you go,' he said. It was as if he was sorry. *Just following orders.* Is that how it had been in his African jungle?

'Howdon need never know. I'll say I ran away.'

'I can't let you go,' he said again.

'Yes, you can, Ronnie.' Her voice was clear and loud. I hadn't heard footsteps, any movement at all to make me aware of her presence. Perhaps she'd been there all the time, listening to our conversation. She came closer and then it was as if she was talking to a child. 'That's quite enough now. Quite enough killing.'

He swung round the torch and we stared at Joanna. She had style. It was as if she'd dressed just for the effect she created in this moment, as if she

326

knew this would be how we'd first see her. She wore boots, tight trousers like jodhpurs and a loose white shirt. Her hair was down and blown by the wind. Lara Croft's mother would look like this. She was unreal.

'You don't understand,' Ronnie said. The stutter had returned.

'No? Let her go. Come to me, Lizzie. Walk away from him. He won't hurt you.'

It was like when they'd shouted at me to run that night at the unit. But this time I did what she said. I stood up and walked towards her, and Ronnie sat where he was, fiddling impotently with his knife.

'Go home,' she said more gently. 'Go home to Kay and the girls. Your car's in the drive.'

And he just got up and scarpered, bounding down the bank and away from us. It was as if we were two performing dogs in a circus and she was the ringmaster standing there with her long boots and her white shirt. All she needed was the whip.

'You can't let him get away. He's a lunatic, a killer.'

'The police will know where to find him,' she said. 'He hasn't got the brains or the guts to run away.' She sounded exhausted. 'Come to the house. I need a drink and so do you.'

Chapter Thirty-six

When did I work it all out? Not in logical steps, and it didn't come in a flash like moonlight breaking through a gap in the trees. It was more like a fairy tale that you hear once when you're a child, then forget about, until you hear a snatch of it again and the whole lot comes back. Perhaps I'd known all along but couldn't face the truth. The implications were too much for me to cope with.

I followed Joanna down the bank towards the house. She was sure-footed but I slithered and tripped, and she stopped every now and again for me to catch her up. She took me in through a back door. It wasn't as if it were the tradesman's entrance and she wanted to put me down; it was the way the family used and she wanted to make me feel included. That's how I saw it, at least. There was a scruffy hall with a narrow staircase ahead of us. I suppose once servants would have used it, but tonight Flora was there, dressed in pink pyjamas, sitting on the top stair and looking down anxiously. She must have been waiting for her mother's return.

'It's all right, darling,' Joanna said with a mixture of exasperation and affection. 'I'm back and I'm fine. You can go to bed now. I'll come up once I've had a drink.'

The pale figure disappeared without a word.

'She's such a worrier.' Joanna was pulling her boots off. She dumped them with a pile of others in a wicker basket next to the back door. There was a row of hooks with waxed jackets and green padded anoraks. 'She misses her father of course. He spoilt her rotten. I should try to make more time for her. Things should be easier now.'

Her feet must have been sweating, because her socks left damp footprints on the stained quarry tiles. I followed them down a long, dimly lit corridor past sacks of potatoes, empty Calor Gas canisters and a couple of ancient hoovers. Then we were in the kitchen and it was another *Swallows and Amazons* moment. It was just the sort of kitchen I'd read about in the musty, rather worthy children's books that got donated to the kids' homes. A scrubbed pine table. A huge bowl of fruit you could help yourself from. An Aga. A wooden frame for drying washing suspended from the ceiling with a rope to lower it. A fat ginger cat in a basket. Paintings which Flora and Dickon must have done years before at playgroup, but which were still stuck to the walls with brittle ancient Sellotape. A rocking chair, with a patchwork cushion, next to the stove. I had time to take in the details before Joanna lit candles and turned off the central light.

'Sit down,' she said. 'Red OK?'

I was going to say I was driving, then I realized I needed a drink as much as she did and I could sort out a taxi. Or stay over. Because it was as if we had that sort of relationship already. Friendship. Lizzie noname Bartholomew could be invited to stay with the famous photographer Joanna Samson in Wintrylaw

329

House. Or could invite herself to stay. *Is it OK if I crash here?* I could say that. It probably doesn't mean anything to you, but it was important. It held out the hope or the promise of security. Like I'd become properly respectable. Real. Not the creation any more of two middle-aged ladies and a collie bitch. I could be a part of a house which had stood for hundreds of years. A part of the family. I could almost believe I was related to Philip and to Dickon.

She got an already opened bottle of red from the larder and poured two goldfish-bowl-sized glasses. We sat on each side of the table.

'So,' she said. 'We have to decide what to do next.'

I didn't answer. I was enjoying the wine. I mean *really* enjoying it, the smell and the taste.

'What should we do?' She was insistent, pulling me back to the problem. I didn't want to think about it. I wanted that moment, with the wine in my nose and on my throat and tongue to last. But she couldn't let it alone. 'I mean, it's up to you, isn't it? You'd be the one to press charges after tonight. You'd be the vital witness.'

'No,' I said. 'I don't grass. Anyway, it's up to you.'

'What do you mean?'

'Ronnie didn't kill Thomas.'

'Not on his own,' she said. 'I accept that. Stuart must have been involved. Stuart was pulling the strings.'

'No.' And in that word I threw it all away – the chance of being a part of this. I turned away the good wine, winter walks along the beach with Dickon, family Sunday lunches at this table, girlie conversations with Joanna on the phone. All that was on offer. I could tell. Why the scruples? It wasn't as if I owed Philip anything, as if Thomas had really been his son. I suppose it was pride. It was a dumb time to discover that I had some pride after all. But Joanna had bought everyone else one way or another. She wasn't going to buy me.

'Stuart didn't invent the commission to track down Thomas Mariner,' I said. 'He believed in Philip's illegitimate son as much as I did. It wasn't Stuart or Philip who invited me to the funeral and offered me money. It was you. You set the whole thing up.'

'Philip would have been glad you were there.' She dipped her mouth towards the wine, and her whole face seemed swallowed up by the enormous glass. 'You had quite an effect on him.'

'He told you?'

'Of course. We shared everything. He talked about leaving you some money in his will but he thought you might be offended. "She's a free spirit. Independent. She'll remember me anyway. And if she doesn't, that's fine. At least the memory won't have been bought."'

'Weren't you jealous?'

'Of course I was bloody jealous. But he was dying. What could I say?'

I remembered how Philip had described Joanna in Marrakech. *She's a saint. She denies me nothing.* At the time I'd thought it a dry, almost ironic comment, but it had been true. Because of his illness she'd felt obliged to fulfil his dreams. He'd been cruel and careless of her feelings. He'd taken advantage of her.

'Tell me what happened.' It might seem ridiculous, but I didn't feel at all scared during this conversation.

331

ANN CLEEVES

Perhaps it was because of where it was taking place. I mean, it wasn't like the Gothic setting of a windy wood in the shattered moonlight. This was safe, domestic.

She got up and fetched another bottle of wine and a corkscrew. 'Are you hungry? I think there's some cheese.'

She wasn't trying to distract me. Even then she felt some obligation as a host. She put a lump of Stilton on a plate and brought out butter and crackers, still in their wrappers.

'I suppose,' she said, 'it was all about money. I hate to admit it, but that was what it came down to.'

'You formed the Countryside Consortium as a money-making venture?'

'No, not at all. Not at first. I mean, I really believed we were in danger of losing a landscape I loved. There'd been so much change, so much red tape, people from the town telling us what to do. I wanted Wintrylaw to stay as it always had been for Flora and Dickon. I wanted to see my grandchildren play where I'd played.' She looked up at me. 'That's not too much to ask, is it?'

I shrugged. She'd been lucky to have it first time round. 'I've never really believed in inherited wealth.'

'Oh, God,' she cried. 'Wealth didn't come into it. It was about survival.'

I thought all that was relative. With her good wine and expensive cheese she seemed to be surviving fine. But this time I didn't say anything. This was her story. Let her tell it her own way.

'People thought we were well off. We had the house and the land. Philip's TV series. My photography. But it was all precarious. We weren't any

332

good at saving. Things like pensions and health insurance seem so tedious, don't they? You really wouldn't want to be seen as the sort of person who bothered about that. Then Philip got ill and the telly dried up. He was always freelance, so there was no sick pay. Nothing. And once he knew he was dying there was so much he wanted to do and see.'

'The Atlas Mountains.'

'Quite. And I couldn't tell him it was impossible.'

No. You were a saint. You denied him nothing.

'So I started taking it from the Consortium. Borrowing it at first. In the beginning I really intended to pay it back. The group had so much money. You wouldn't believe how generous people were. Not only rich people. Cheques came in by every post. And the committee couldn't decide what to spend it on. While they were squabbling among themselves about who deserved it most, it just piled up in the bank. Such a waste . . .'

'It can't have been that easy. There must have been an accounting system.'

'It was a shambles. Really. Everyone was taken by surprise by how quickly the organization grew. There were a few pieces in the Sunday papers and in the glossy country living magazines, and the campaign seemed to capture the public's imagination. None of us were ready for the success. The whole office was run by a couple of middle-aged volunteers and a schoolboy.'

'Marcus Tate?'

'The son of one of our supporters. Because our marketing was very slick, everyone assumed a competent machine to back it up. It wasn't true. The office

looked impressive enough – we were donated some
hardware by a business supporter – but no one there
really understood what was going on.' She held her
glass with both hands. 'We were credited with far
more power than we actually had. Some journalists
thought we were devils, evil landowners who would
deny access to common land to harmless walkers.
Our supporters saw us as the saviours of every rural
tradition – from village schools to the right to hunt. Of
course we were neither. We were a bunch of well-
meaning amateurs.'

Well-meaning?

'Then Thomas Mariner found out that you were
stealing?'

'Thomas Mariner had his own agenda.' Joanna's
voice was frosty. 'He hated Ronnie Laing. He joined
up to make trouble. I didn't discover that until later.'

And he loved Nell Ravendale, I thought. He was
planning a grand gesture to impress her. Nell hated
the Consortium. She was in the camp which saw them
as devils. She'd dragged Dan to the Wintrylaw fund-
raiser to spy out the opposition. That was why she'd
been so circumspect in her description of Ronnie
Laing. Thomas intended to cause as much of a scandal
around Joanna's theft as possible. There'd be no hush-
up, no tactical retirement and discreet repayment
plan. He'd make sure of that. That was why he'd
stirred up Shona Murray's interest. It was part of his
strategy for getting back the love of his life.

'Was Harry Pool one of your supporters?'

'He gave us a big donation early on.'

Perhaps Thomas had known about that. And when
he'd started as a volunteer in the office he'd wondered

where all the money had gone. I cut a sliver of Stilton and perched it on a water biscuit.

'I didn't mean to kill him,' she said, almost to herself. The wind blew a tuneless whistle outside the window. 'Of course not. I thought I'd persuade him. Anyway, he was surprisingly difficult to track down without drawing attention to myself. He stopped coming into the office. No one seemed to know where he was staying. That's where you came in.'

Ronnie knew where Thomas lived, I thought. Marcus had told him. But only just before Thomas died. By then Joanna had woven her intricate fiction to entrap me. Dickon had said she was good at stories.

'If you were so hard up, how could you afford the £10,000 in cash for me?'

'What?' Now the impatience was directed at me. It was as if I were quibbling over a few pence change. I wondered then just how much she had ripped off the Consortium. 'Oh, Stuart saw to all that. He was devoted to Philip. He believed in Thomas as Philip's son and in Philip's request to give you work. He knew *I* didn't have the money. And at that point he was trying to protect me from the knowledge that Philip had a racy past. I'd set it up for Stuart to find the instruction himself, along with a lot of other papers. It wasn't hard to get Philip to sign it.'

'Stuart's devoted to you.' He must have known she was involved. The meeting with Ronnie in Whitley Bay had been to discuss damage limitation. They'd suspected she was a murderer but still they had tried to protect her.

'Yes,' she said. 'I suppose he is.'

'But not so devoted that he'll take the blame for

ANN CLEEVES

two murders. He won't be prepared to sacrifice himself.'

'Not two murders,' she said, offended, as if I'd accused her of being some kind of monster. 'Only one.'

'What happened to Marcus?'

'He was a sweet boy. He had rather a crush. The older woman thing. He never really knew his mother.'

'He came to see you the night he died.'

'Mmm.'

'And?'

'He was getting a bit flaky about the money, a bit anxious that he'd be implicated if the police started sniffing around the office looking at Thomas's things. He didn't believe I could have killed Thomas. Of course not. Like I said he had a bit of a crush. But he might have worked it out eventually.'

'You got him drunk?'

'He got himself drunk.'

'You can't have known he'd drive himself over the bridge.'

She didn't answer but she looked smug. She wanted me to know how clever she was.

'Did you tamper with the car?'

'I followed him down the Spine Road. Got a bit close to him. Got him scared. He lost concentration. She looked up from the empty glass and gave me her seductive, *I'm your best friend in the world* smile. 'I didn't mean to kill him. Of course not. I just wanted to warn him that it wouldn't be a good idea to talk to his father or the police about any financial irregularities. It was an accident. These things happen. Young drivers . . .' She shrugged.

336

'Is that what will happen to me when I leave Wintrylaw tonight? I'm already over the limit. Will I have an accident too?'

'Of course not.' She was hurt that I could contemplate such a thing. She was good. Really, she was *very* good. She paused, then continued, choosing her words carefully, knowing that I'd understand their significance. 'I think we have an understanding. You know I had no option but to kill Thomas. Any good mother would have done the same. Think about it. Philip had just died. I was all that Flora and Dickon had in the world. If Thomas revealed where our money had come from, if I went to prison, there'd be no one to look after them. They'd have had to go into care. Can you imagine what that would have done to them? Just after their father's death?'

Of course I could imagine, and she knew fine well I could. She'd found out all about me. Philip had told her.

'What will happen if you go to the police now? It would be much, much worse.'

Her words were relentless. I felt I'd been beaten to a crumpled heap on the floor and she was kicking me, one blow after another until my mind and my body were numb.

'There'd be publicity. Would foster parents want the children of a murderer in their own homes? The kids' friends would find out. Imagine the taunting and the bullying at school. And then there'd be the prison visits. Flora might be able to cope with that, but I'm not sure about Dickon.'

I knew she was manipulating me. I wasn't even sure she cared that much about what would happen

337

to Flora and Dickon. But she was getting to me and she knew it.

'It's not as if I'm a danger to society,' she went on. 'It's not as if I'd do anything like that again. If you talk to the police, it wouldn't be me you'd be punishing, it would be them.'

'I'd look after them myself.' OK, crazy I know, but she'd driven me to it.

'Come off it!' All the pride and arrogance that she'd hidden under those soft, relentless words suddenly flashed through. 'You're mad. You stabbed someone. You're no better than me. Worse, because there was no reason for it. You could have killed him. Do you think social services would give *any* kid to you?'

I wanted to tell her that there was a reason for it. I'd been taken hostage and seen a boy killed. I wasn't in my right mind. But that would have turned me into a victim again and it was time to let that go.

We stared at each other across the table. The fat candle spluttered then recovered its flame. I got up. She must have thought she'd won, because she didn't try to stop me. I found my way to the big front door and let myself out that way. I wasn't a member of this family and I didn't want to be. I looked up to Dickon's window but the curtains were drawn and it was in darkness.

I drove back carefully, very slowly, aware that I was in no fit state to be on the road. It wasn't just the wine. I knew that if I had any sense I'd stop at the first phone box and call Farrier and tell him everything I knew. But I couldn't do it. I couldn't do it to Dickon. I couldn't put him through everything I'd had to survive. I decided I had to give it a few days. I thought some event, some *deus ex machina* in the shape of Ronnie Laing or Stuart Howdon, might arrange things for me. Ronnie was mad enough to kill her. The kids would still have to go into care, but they could hang on to their picture of their mother. They wouldn't need to know she'd killed a young lad. Or she might suddenly develop a conscience and shop herself. Or kill herself, leaving a note to say she couldn't live without her husband. They'd go for that.

When I got to Sea View, Jess was on her way to bed. She was wrapped up in the dreadful mauve candlewick dressing gown that looks like a toilet mat and has lost all its threads.

'Hello, pet,' she said. 'Did you see the badgers?'

'Na,' I said. 'They weren't playing tonight.'

Chapter Thirty-seven

'You think too much,' Farrier said.

I don't know how he could tell what I was thinking. He came to see me while I was waiting for the
miracle to happen – for Joanna to die or disappear.
He came to tell me she'd been arrested. I hadn't
expected that. Not without my help. It was the pride
again. I'd thought I was the only person capable of
putting her away. While I was waiting, the flashbacks
had returned, more frequently than ever, but somehow I wasn't so troubled by them. I didn't let them
get to me in the same way.

'What's happened to the kids?'

'They're with foster parents in Heaton. A really
nice couple. A big house backing onto the park. I
asked. I thought you'd want to know.'

Heaton. Where Philip had come from. There was
something reassuring about that.

'You don't seem surprised about Joanna,' he said,
probing.

We were on the white bench outside Sea View.
Jess had gone to Asda. Ray had taken her in the van
because she had to do a big shop. She'd arranged a
party, a big do. I thought she and Ray were intending to announce their engagement and I was so

exhausted, so wrung out and emotionally dead, that I didn't care any more. I'd move on, find somewhere to stay. There was always Absalom House.

'No, I'm not surprised.'

'How did you find out?'

I looked up at him. 'Is this you and me talking? Or is it work, official?'

'You and me.'

'Because I won't be a witness.'

'She cut herself that day at Thomas's. There were traces of blood which weren't his. When we arrested her we did a test. The DNA matches. We won't need witnesses like you. Between ourselves, I think there'll be a guilty plea.'

'She told me she killed him,' I said. 'She thought I cared so much about the kids I'd not give her away.'

'You haven't.'

'I was still thinking about it.'

'I know. I can tell.'

We looked out to the bay, to St Bartholomew's at one end, solid, the colour of coal dust, and south to Blyth power station and the wind turbines with their feet in the sea.

'I sent the accountants into the Countryside Consortium,' Farrier said. 'I wasn't sure much would come of it. Routine. There'd been a hint in that letter Thomas had sent to Shona Murray. I wasn't quite straight about that.'

'How had Thomas found out Joanna was on the fiddle?'

'Some of the members were grumbling about where all the money had gone. No one suspected her, mind.'

341

ANN CLEEVES

'Of course not. She's a saint.'

'Thomas had only joined up to make trouble. He saw himself as a spy. An infiltrator. According to Shona. He saw some of the letters of complaint and got into the computer system to find out more. He must have said something to Marcus. That's how Joanna first suspected him.' Farrier didn't look at me at all during this conversation. It was as if he were reporting to a colleague. A superior. 'Then Ronnie Laing talked. His wife brought him in. He was brooding, she said. He had something on his mind. It was making him ill. And then that solicitor made a statement. Rats leaving a sinking ship.'

'It'll have been a shock for Joanna, that. She thought she had them charmed.'

'She thought she had *me* charmed.' Farrier looked up at me then and grinned to show that he was only human and he'd enjoyed the flattery. I bet Joanna took him the back way into the house too. She'll have sat him at the kitchen table, offered him tea or wine.

'But you weren't taken in.' In the distance there was a police siren. You hear them all the time in Newbiggin. Or it could have been a fire engine. It was the summer holidays and bored kids are always setting fires on the mound. 'I didn't realize all that was going on.'

'It was a murder investigation. We don't just sit on our hands.' He smiled to show he wasn't offended that I thought so little of him. He was wearing a sports jacket which had no shape at all, a blue shirt, a shiny tie which looked as if it had been pressed with too hot an iron.

I thought if I cried he'd put his arm around me to comfort me, but I couldn't bring myself to do it. I've told you I've got a thing about older men. This wasn't the time, though. Everything was complicated enough.

'You won't need me to stick around for the court case?'

'Na. Like I said, we've plenty of evidence. You don't need to put yourself through that. Take yourself away.'

So I did. I bought a cheap flight with a charter company to Agadir, then took the bus to Taroudannt and spent the last of Philip's money on a week in the Palais Salaam. There's satellite television in my room, but I don't watch it. I don't want to see any English news.

I still find Morocco stunning. It's something to do with the intense light and the smells. The colours don't explode in my head any more, but I don't mind that. This way is more restful. I can lie by the pool in the Palais Salaam and watch the bulbuls flitting under the tall trees and still think I'm in paradise. If I slide into the water and ease the tension from my muscles, I can almost forget about Dickon.

His paradise has been sold to pay off Joanna's debts. She hadn't stolen nearly enough, it seems. Wintrylaw will be a country club and there's already talk of felling trees where the bluebells grow. A golf course is essential, according to the managing director of the development company. I saw him on *Look North*. He had an expensive toupee and he'd been ripped off by his dentist; his false teeth moved as he spoke. So there'll be no more badger watching or building dens or wading through the surf towards the sun. No more *Swallows and Amazons* for Dickon.

And should I really care? All those kids in the unit, and the kids I worked with in placement, they didn't have the chance of one week of that sort of life. They lived in shitty high-rise blocks and their adventures had to do with keeping out of the way of smackheads and joyriders, so why should I weep for Dickon and not for them?

Tomorrow I'm going home. Jess is getting married and they want me to be bridesmaid. Ray asked me. He blushed and stammered and talked about what an honour it would be. At first I didn't know what he was going on about. I had to say yes. He looked at me with his pleading bloodhound eyes and I couldn't refuse. They're being done in St Bartholomew's. The vicar's agreed, though Ray was married before. It'll be weird, walking up the aisle behind Jess. I've even got a cheesy dress. We bought it from the Hospice Shop in Jesmond for twenty-five quid. As Jess says, you get really good second-hand stuff in Jesmond.

They won't have any more bad boys in Sea View. Ray put his foot down. They're going to take over that bit of the house again, and turn Jessie's rooms in the roof into a self-contained flat. They say they'll need the rent. It's mine if I want it. I expect they're just being kind. Jess won't want to think she's turned me out onto the street. I've told them I'll think about it.